RESURGENCE

A. J. FLOWER

alizé
press

First published in 2016
by Alizé Press

ISBN: 978-0-9954690-0-6

To my mother, Valerie

CONTENTS

RESURGENCE

CHAPTER I

JULY 8 1913

To her horror, the field was empty; she stood frozen, and then checked her watch: five past three. She was late, later than she had ever been, and she knew the consequences; she had to be here at three o' clock precisely, otherwise he wouldn't stay, he couldn't risk it.

'Where is he?' she thought anxiously.

She scoured the landscape and listened intently . . . nothing, just a skylark chirping away.

She looked all around her . . . still nothing.

As if it would make a difference she ran down the embankment into the field, she had to do something. Had her slight lateness cost her the greatest escape? Her heart began to race, fretful at the thought.

Reaching the middle of the open field she stopped, she took a deep breath to calm herself and scoured all four corners carefully, there was nothing. She didn't want to let go; she wanted to know why he wasn't here.

As she stood in silence the importance of the treasured jacket she was wearing with its carefully selected accompaniments suddenly began to ebb. She felt a little silly. 'Damn him', she thought, 'five minutes can't be too late . . . would it have killed him to wait five minutes!'

Defeated, but still not wanting to believe it wasn't going to happen, she impulsively began to retrace her steps back to the embankment.

Then she heard something; she stood quite still and listened.

'There!' She thought, 'that was definitely a distant hum, a traction engine perhaps at work a few fields away? No, maybe a motorcar up at the house . . . no,' she knew no one was expected there until later.

She thought of all the possibilities over and over trying

to keep herself from getting too hopeful again.

It seemed to be coming from the direction she had entered the field; she decided that if she could get back up onto the river embankment, she might be able to hear it better. She ran to the base of the slope, grabbing at the long grass to stay steady and began to pull herself up to the summit.

No sooner had she climbed three feet, there it was, louder than ever; the sound she had been longing to hear.

It came so suddenly and so deafeningly that she fell backwards to the ground and instinctively clamped a hand to an ear. She would have covered both her ears if the sudden blast of air hadn't been blowing her dress up to her head - there were some feminine instincts that were hard to lose.

Overwhelmingly relieved but a little annoyed, as she knew he had done this on purpose, she rolled onto her front and looked back into the field - to see the rear of a two-seat biplane flying away from her.

'You idiot, Jack,' she thought, 'you just wanted to make an entrance.' She didn't really mind, now that he was here; she only wished she could make an entrance like that in front of someone one day.

She watched jealously as the aircraft banked round to the left in the distance and turned to fly back over the field. She waited until it was about sixty yards off, and then waved both her arms. The plane suddenly rolled its wings sharply to the left, then over to the right and back to the left again, as it flew over her head. He had seen her.

She calmly made her way back into the field. The plane circled to the far end, then, very low, it came back towards her and touched down smoothly on the flat ground. She walked over as the plane drew to a standstill, blasting out a wall of wind as it did so. The pilot turned off the engine.

Inside Mary was thrilled he was here - but after that little display - she was determined not let it show too much.

The pilot removed his flying cap and goggles, leapt down from the cockpit and strode towards her, looking pleased with himself.

"You're late," she said to him, trying to sound indignant.

"I wanted to show you my new manoeuvre, didn't I," he grinned, "what did you think?"

"What new manoeuvre? Trying to remove my dress by surprising me over the embankment? Hardly a manoeuvre."

At that, they both laughed.

"Only one of many uses it has, Mary," he went on. "It's called a steep dive - some of the boys call it a 'silent dive', because during it you can't hear the engine and anyone on the ground can't hear you coming either. That is, until you pull out right on top of them."

"How's it done?" she couldn't help asking earnestly, with a little appealing smile; hoping he would agree to teach her.

"I'm very well by the way. . . thank you for asking."

Mary was taken aback for a moment, and her playful expression faded. "I'm sorry."

He grinned at her. "Oh, that's alright . . . at least I know you were impressed."

She looked at him and smiled gratefully, but couldn't help unashamedly staying silent, hoping he would continue to talk about the manoeuvre.

"You want to start off at about a thousand," he explained. "You fully remove the throttle and push the stick sharply from you, which causes you to dive steeply and accelerate rapidly. You have to hold the dive until you're about fifty feet off the ground, then re-engage the throttle fully and pull the stick towards you with all your might. If you've not chickened out and you pull out low enough, the sudden noise to anyone on the ground you've snuck up on is deafening and the down draught of air is immense, enough to lift most people off their feet."

He stretched out his hand, leant on the plane and turned a little serious. "You have to be incredibly careful though," he continued, "controlling the speed as you dive is almost impossible. If you're going too fast when you pull out, the g-forces could cause the plane to disintegrate, or if you pull up too sharply to slow yourself down, you might get pushed into your seat and have trouble breathing, or worse all the fuel will roll to one end of the tank and stall the engine."

"If it's so dangerous," Mary interrupted, "there must be a good reason why you practice it, beyond trying to lift girls' dresses over their heads?"

"Well, yes, a silent dive's great for attacking ground targets or leaving a problem in a hurry. Anyone on your tail, unless they're stupid, will never follow you into a dive that steep - especially when you're in one of these ladies as it dives so fast. That one was the best I've managed so far, but I still bottled it a few seconds before I should have - didn't get anywhere near close enough to the ground, and your dress was nowhere near high enough - "

He grinned as she slapped him on the arm.

"Well just for that you've got to show me," she countered.

"Not a chance! Anyway it's not like clipping the tops off trees or skimming a lake, it'll scare the wits out of you!"

"Were you scared?"

He looked at the return of her cheeky smile and knew from experience nothing short of taking her for another lesson was going to satisfy her; his reply was to throw a pair of flying goggles and a cap into her hands.

"I want to take off this time," she said as they made their way up to the plane.

"I haven't left much room," he replied doubtfully. "Are you sure you're ready for such a short take off? I'd only just manage it myself."

"I'll just do what I usually do, except quicker," she said flippantly.

He looked at her with an expression of concerned resignation as they climbed into the cockpits. Mary went in the rear; in this type of two-seat aircraft the passenger sat in the front and the pilot in the rear so that in the absence of a passenger, the plane remained balanced.

She secured herself comfortably in the cockpit and looked along the nose of the plane, which was pointing up to the sky. It was a beautiful day, just a few clouds, and she couldn't wait to be among them.

This was it; she was here, where she had been longing to be for weeks. If her parents had known what she was about to do they would have locked her away for good.

Jack took position at the front of the aircraft with his hand on the propeller ready to start it. Mary knew the procedure backwards from the dozens of lessons she'd had and the hundreds of daydreams at the silent breakfast table.

She turned the engine master switch on, setting the throttle to the 1000-RPM position and moving the props full forward. Then she engaged the engine starter.

"Contact!" she shouted joyfully.

At her command, Jack pulled the propeller to the ground with his full body weight and instinctively stepped back. The engine was already nicely warmed up and the propeller spun instantly into an invisible whirlpool of air, raising a terrific rhythmic buzzing sound and sending a gush of wind back at Mary's face.

The plane was not the only thing that was buzzing; Mary's heart pounded fresh blood around her body so excitedly the color of her cheeks changed in half a breath, she was alive again - living the moment she longed for every week.

Jack leaped into the front cockpit, turned to her and gave her the thumbs up. This was the signal; that it was all hers and it was time to begin. She gently nudged the throttle forward, the buzz of the engine became higher in pitch and the wind over her face gushed in response.

Slowly the aircraft rolled forward. She had done this before, but never with so little space so she pushed the engine hard; it responded and they picked up speed. She pushed the throttle as far as she dared, looking at the oncoming hills rising rapidly in front of them and then back at the speedometer. Forty-five - fifty - fifty-five miles per hour, she would need at least eighty to get off the ground. They were almost at the hill when they reached seventy, the tail end of the aircraft lifted from the ground and they were running level.

She adjusted the stick accordingly and soon the wheels were rising slowly off the turf. Instincts Mary was born with, not that she fully realised it yet, took over; fiercely but confidently she pulled the stick towards her and the plane leapt up.

There was a sudden sharp jerk as the tail end of the plane skimmed the ground and ripped some daisies from their roots. As they cleared the hill, she lowered the nose slightly so as not to lose too much speed.

She was away.

Once she was level she began to gain height slowly and, confident in the simple manoeuvre she was now undertaking, she looked at Jack. He turned and bowed his head slightly in approval.

He should have been impressed, but sadly he wasn't. He had never taken her skills with an aircraft seriously, no matter what ability she demonstrated; for the simple fact that she was a woman. He sat back and sighed a little at their lack of interaction before starting the lesson. This was what he dwelt on most after seeing her, his lack of progress at getting her more interested in him. He was happy to humour her fascination with flying, but never looked upon her abilities as anything more than the natural result of his training. Her talent and ability was all around him but he didn't see it. He thought of her, right now up in the sky, as a wealthy girl being indulged, nothing more. This mingled with the on-going hope that, given she was a particularly stunning girl, his attentions to her would lead to things other than just flying lessons.

They had met two years earlier at a fund-raising fête on the estate where Mary lived; he had tried to impress her with tales of his abilities, but it was his descriptions of flying that mesmerised her. They talked for hours, but not on the usual topics of two young people walking in public. Where she should have been strolling next to him minding her poise and gestures, she was instead gesticulating wildly out of intense interest, miming the details of flying an aircraft as he was describing them to her, fascinated and determined to understand.

It looked, at a distance, as though they were arguing. Twice her mother intervened, both to see if the young officer was all right and not to let Mary wander too far un-chaperoned.

Mary could not get enough information; what a world, truly of your very own, and what an experience! If she could learn to fly, she felt she would fly away and keep flying, going wherever she pleased.

She begged to see where he worked, to see the planes, but it was made quite clear that no civilians were allowed near the field. However, certain it would impress her enough to take more of an interest in him, he promised to fly over her family estate the very next day.

A promise he kept.

Up and down the river he flew as she embraced the sight with awe. She ran and ran along the line he was flying, reaching out with her arms, trying to get closer, which led her to the top of the river embankment overlooking the flat field. Anxious to 'embrace' the results of his efforts and seeing the field she was in was flat enough, Jack landed and let her sit in the cockpit to see how it worked.

To his great disappointment, she showed very little interest in him, except when it came for him to leave.

Noticing the second cockpit she asked innocently, "can

it take passengers?"

A quick and forbidden trip up the following week led to another and then another where, flying straight and level, he allowed her to take control of the plane using the training instruments in the second cockpit.

With Jack nervously waiting to regain control of the plane the moment anything went wrong, Mary flew in a straight line for the first time. She marvelled at how this machine embraced and responded to her touch - as if its wings were her very own outstretched arms matching the oncoming rush of air to lift them higher and higher. She was dancing solo amongst the clouds, with an impenetrable self-contained euphoria, while the world she felt so alienated from all her life, could only look on jealously. She felt she had truly found her vocation; it was as if everything else she had done was just leading up to this, and she wanted to learn how to make this flying machine do everything it possibly could.

After almost two years of lessons, Jack shouldn't have been worried about her short take off.

Before gaining more height after just missing the hill, she eased the plane over towards the direction of her family estate. She knew she was supposed to head west, away from the direction of the aerodrome, in case any other aircraft should see them. Jack's superiors naturally believed his story of wanting as many flying hours as possible, but if they had known the truth the consequences for him would have been dire. The Flying Corps was still a very young service; there hadn't been aircraft for Jack's superiors to impress young girls with in their youth, so they wouldn't have understood - it certainly wasn't like teaching a girl to ride a camel.

Mary looked down over the estate. She saw an army of servants out on the terraces preparing furniture for the evening's entertainment, gardeners at work towards the driveway and for a moment maybe even a glimpse of her mother, standing staunchly at one of the back entrances.

She was looking out into the garden, wondering where her daughter was no doubt. Blessedly unaware that every time one of those noisy, death trap flying machines flew over and scared everyone, it was her daughter. Mary just loved that thought.

Having taken care of this little obligation to herself, she turned the plane west. Jack looked on as she smoothly took the aircraft down to the river and began to follow it at low altitude.

They had danced up and under the clouds many times but recently he had been teaching her the rudiments of low-level flying. Like everything else, she soon took to it. She loved the way that closer to the ground, you could really feel how fast the machine could go as the treetops flickered under them in a blur.

Jack looked round at her again, he thought she was incredibly beautiful, and each kind word and cheeky smile she gave him meant a great deal. But still it never lead to anything. He was once again reminded that when they were up in the air that was it, no chance of small talk up here - certainly it was far too noisy and to distract the pilot was not a good idea. But more than that, he could feel how he would lose her once they were airborne. In recent lessons he had simply peeked round and watched her rather than the flying, he could tell he didn't exist to her and she was somewhere else completely.

He didn't know much about why she loved it so much; most women thought these were amusing contraptions or 'ghastly noisy machines' up close. It was the one thing that kept him intrigued about her, rather than purely infatuated. Every time he looked at her up there he saw there was something going on inside her when she was flying, and it didn't seem to involve him or any other living being.

He turned away again; he knew she wasn't being deliberately selfish, it just happened to her.

As a railway bridge came up they suddenly turned right, away from the river. Excitedly the plane rose and began to surf the trees along the embankment, he could feel she had seen something.

Further over to the right was a distant train travelling at high speed away from them. Mary dipped the nose, rolled elegantly towards the railway track and gave chase. As the dark red carriages drew nearer he felt her gain a little height, and then a little more as though she was gauging something. He looked ahead and saw there was a long line of thick white smoke flowing from the locomotive; he knew her well enough now to guess what was coming next.

As they approached the trail of smoke, just at its end, Mary made the final adjustments and decreased their speed as much as she dared. They began to touch its surface, but just on the very tip of the trailing edge. The wheels of the aircraft nudging it gently and straight ahead it looked like they were ploughing through snow, or the clouds even. 'Maybe that's what she wanted,' he thought, she had done the same to the tops of rolling, cottony clouds.

'How daft,' - but he never felt unsafe when she did this, not that it dawned on him why. The skill involved to achieve such pleasure-seeking effects was far from inconsiderable.

Having cleared the train, they began to climb higher towards the ocean blue sky, and soon they were once again flying straight and level.

After an hour or so, they were back at the field. Mary came in low over the hedgerow, still a little fast so she disengaged the throttle and tilted the nose up slightly. The plane responded and began to slow quickly. The air could now be heard whistling all around them as a quietness emerged, the drone from the engine subsiding. The front wheels clipped the grass; Mary responded to the plane's message of a shudder and with a minute bump brought the great machine back down to earth.

With a quick swoop, they came to a standstill. A final

flutter, and the engine stopped.

For a moment they both sat there; the stillness after a long flight was always irresistible and it took a moment to realise what had just happened. Mary leapt from the cockpit to the ground and pulled off her hat and goggles. The brightness that had been restored to her eyes tingled, and then faded just an octave as she noticed she was back in the real world once more. There, stretched out before her was the direction back to her parent's house, and she would now be being missed.

Jack walked up and she flung her arms around him gratefully.

"Thank you, that was wonderful," she panted, beaming from ear to ear. Imagining pilots shook hands after a lesson, she always offered him hers and he took it dutifully, like the young gentleman he was.

She could feel he appreciated the hug but the situation always seemed to require more, even though they both had to get moving and had places to be.

She asked a little more desperately than after previous lessons, "Please can I see you again in a week?"

She knew deep down he only really came to see her, but she didn't return his affections. It wasn't that she didn't think it was possible, but she never thought about it until it was time to say goodbye. Until then it was always about getting up into the sky. It was as if she never could quite get around to it, and they never had the time afterwards.

"Of course," he said warmly. "As long as I get to see you. Maybe we could meet a little earlier next week, perhaps half past two? It'd be nice to see more of you."

Mary agreed as she backed away and began her quick trot in the direction of the estate.

She didn't look back. It was getting more awkward to leave him with nothing else and expect him to keep coming back to give her lessons. She didn't mean to be callous but without him the flying was all over.

She was glad to have promised something to make him

11

happy, but he was too much of a young gentleman to take advantage of the situation anyway. That was the problem, she sometimes felt, with most young men who crossed her path; they were neither interesting nor bold enough to hold her attention for very long. Jack was interesting enough, but he had too many social graces instilled in him and he lacked the courage to risk what they already had to make the first move in any meaningful way.

Quickly but with unenthused urgency, she retraced her steps back to a little cottage at the edge of her parents estate. Dusk was in its early stages. The sky was still its rich summer blue, but it was now dimmer, the shadows on the ground had all merged into one and everything felt just that little bit darker, as it does at the end of long summer days before the sun begins to go down properly.

The estate cottage doors were never locked; making her way in she ran as light footedly as she could in her riding boots upstairs to one of the bedrooms.

It was completely empty except for one piece of furniture - an old wardrobe that she had never known be used. Opening it she took off the jacket she was wearing and paused for just a moment to gaze at the only garment other than her riding boots she enjoyed wearing. It was a dark green, double breasted man's tunic. With green epaulettes and faded gold buttons, it had obviously belonged to someone in the army. Though a modern tunic, it showed faded signs of wear.

She had found it at the stables of a family friend, plugging a gap in the wall of a barn. Knowing instantly it would be useful to her, she immediately hid it in her saddlebags and smuggled it to this lonely location on the edge of her parents' estate; since then, it had become the dress code of her escapes. When she wore it, she felt ready for anything.

She had the pick, four times a year, of any clothing she liked from any of the finest fashion houses of London or Paris, as long as it was what her parents thought appropriate for their daughter. However, this was the only garment she would have paid money for. Pushing the hanger into its rough sturdy sleeves she put it away for the next time.

The whole ensemble she was wearing was carefully planned to accommodate this tunic.

The faded pink dress she wore was the thinnest and simplest dress she had from the house wardrobe that was decided for her. Ending as it did just below her knees she had long outgrown its length but had insisted on keeping it for sentimental reasons, much to the bemusement of her maid who was oblivious to the real reason for keeping it.

With the jacket buttoned up over it the whole thing was a little tight, but she didn't mind; it was the closest thing to functionality she could muster in her life. It was even more durable and sturdy than her riding clothes, built especially to take the elements; perfect for what she had been doing that afternoon - and not just up in the plane. To get to her rendezvous unobserved she had to walk the length of the outermost stretch of her family's great estate, the furthest route from the house. Buttoned up nice and tight with no frills, no long dresses down to her toes, shawls or ornate sleeves to have to watch all the time slowing her down, she could run easily in her tunic if she thought she was going to be spotted by someone.

She emerged from the cottage; once again back in her simple dark pink dress, she checked her watch and felt she still had some time before she would be seriously missed.

She walked with a lack of care and purpose that would have been considered unseemly in the house she lived - but out here she was her own woman, she relaxed her shoulders and breathed out refreshed with euphoria after her flying. She walked a little through some nearby trees, a favourite spot of hers, this far out was not only safer from disturbances, but it was an area of her families extensive gardens that no guest would ever have the time to travel to, no matter how long they were staying. Therefore it was not as cultivated as the rest of the grounds, not quite as tamed by the family's army of gardeners; there were loosely assembled log piles to encourage wildlife to make homes and patches of grass were left to allow forbidden but beautiful bunches of wildflowers to grow. It felt untouched by her parents' hands; it felt like somewhere else, and Mary loved that.

She walked into a clearing and the sunlight shone on her back; she stopped and closed her eyes. The sun's warmth was like two large loving hands placed on the back of her shoulders, her heart now picking up a beat again, she leaned back ever so slightly to let the sun reach further down the back of her dress and the heat ran along her spine as if the hands were stroking her slowly.

She bit her bottom lip, smiled and opened her eyes, breathing out slowly to half-heartedly calm her rapid heartbeat. She looked around to make absolutely sure no one was watching - although it was a pulse quickening thought to imagine that someone might be.

Still biting her bottom lip she raised her hands to her shoulders and pulled off the straps of her dress, they were too tight to slip down so she raised her arms and pushed the dress straps down to her hips, taking the rest of the dress with them.

She then gripped the base of her white petticoat underdress and lifted it clean off over her head, letting the sun touch the whole of her back. She dropped to the ground where she was standing and lay there topless, with her long shapely golden back to the heat.

Bathing in the sun was the furthest thing from an acceptable pastime expected of a nineteen year old, unattached girl around the family estate; that was one of the other reasons why it suited her.

Nothing that was actually expected of her ever did. Even on a sprawling six hundred acre estate with countless tightly packed trees, pristine hedges, walls, statues and tall flower beds it was no small task to find ample privacy to get away with it just long enough to enjoy it, before being disturbed and chastised.

It was a very simple pleasure, but to her it was a valued indulgence; being able to get away with it long enough for her mind to be able to switch off and achieve some kind of peace, meant a great deal to her.

This moment was exactly as she liked it; warm and still. After the flying had blown away her worries it was easier to lie here and just allow the tick-tock of bleak day to day thoughts and anxieties, the kind of things that keep you awake just as you get into bed, to subside. Her mind was clear and quiet.

Mary knew all the peaceful places on this estate; she had been born here, in the same monstrous four-story eighteenth century residence she still lived in, with her parents and four younger sisters.

She was the result of a very suitable union between her father, Lord Robert Dane and her mother Elizabeth, the only daughter of another big-nosed ennobled family, ostensibly of distant Irish descent.

Her father was the latest in an abundant line of extremely wealthy, traditional and very English landed gentlemen who ran the family's extensive estate and interests in the city. It was a story so conventional, so unsurprisingly English to Mary, that it fatigued her greatly on rare occasions when some sheltered individual would press her for her parents' background.

This long line of gentlemen had lived in and run this thriving rural estate, with its many traditional enterprises such as farming, breeding and forestry; the profits all going to the upkeep of the home and the family. To an onlooker, it might have appeared to be a paradise of chocolate-box England and a testament to the privileges of birth and breeding, but to Mary it had never appeared as such.

Mary's escapes had developed her into a very different person from the rest of her family, and not just on the inside.

Mary's mother was about five foot six, thin and dainty in a cultured elegant sort of a way with thick curly black hair, hazel eyes and dark thin eyebrows. All of this blended together beautifully and Mary's younger siblings had followed suit. Her father, though now quite grey, was as a young man, everything good breeding and an expensive education demanded. All that was now left of that image was the faded remnant in his shoulders of the build he had sported in his youth as a champion rower.

Since her twelfth birthday, however, Mary had found herself developing along altogether different lines - and curves. Entirely of her body's own free will it seemed, she had grown to almost six foot and had a voluminous, long and curly head of golden blonde hair, blue eyes and the fulsome, properly grown feminine build you would more likely see below the neck of a strapping Norwegian beauty than an English lady. Facets of her lifestyle that she had led differently to her siblings had also aided in the development of this physique.

It had all started when she was six and her father had some labourers working by the river, which straddled one edge of her family's estate. They were tasked to build a new rowing boat for the gamekeeper, to her father's strict specifications.

From the day they appeased her interest by letting her chop up some tiny glorified shavings under the guise of helping and her maid was forced to sit and wait for her to finish for hours, Mary was captivated. From then on, she was there every day for weeks, in any weather.

She craved the peace she experienced in loosing herself to the craft of something practical. Using her hands to create something and getting better at it; she learnt she needed the release of energy it gave her and she became terribly angry one day when she was told it was no longer allowed because the weather was too bad.

This was a very important day for her. That day, shortly after her seventh birthday, she learnt how to sneak away, and she found doing so made the time spent away feel even more prized.

She would feign sickness, sneak out of a lounge window and spend blissful days in the drizzle, with craftsmen oblivious to her flight; unobserved, unsupervised, unbound for the very first time.

The whole pattern of her life then began to change; she simply existed from one opportunity to escape to the next. To go to a world that was entirely her own, to do something that she enjoyed, and to come home feeling fulfilled, was an intoxicating sensation to her and she couldn't understand why whenever she was caught she was so cruelly punished.

When the boat was completed, she felt her life was over. Since that day she never stopped searching for a reason to sneak away to live in a way that was hers. Like the boat she found other short-term solutions; less satisfying, but they had their moments.

She would learn to ride the family's horses; work hard to get better at it and cross her parents again when she would ruin her clothes and miss meals by riding them at all hours in any weather. She did this because she knew she could be alone, and away from the tedium of life at home. She knew her sisters would not ride in the cold, biting February rain; she could have the thrill of escape and lose herself again.

These activities had led her to lead a marginally more athletic life than the rest of her family, which had added to her unique physicality. Her mother always claimed at parties that she was a throw back to her distant Irish genes, her mother's grandfather's family had all been blonde and impressive to look at.

By now, at nineteen, any man no matter how cold his blood would have taken great pleasure in seeing her indulging herself in the secluded bathing she loved so much. Her figure was full and striking. Long golden legs led up to a healthy pair of hips. As she lay there on her front the sun seemed to delight in caressing her long curving back and her breasts, from which she wished to be disassociated throughout her life, had to be allowed a little extra room to enable her to lay on the ground with the placing of her right arm under her head. She was a prize any man could happily spend a lifetime fighting for.

To make her heart leap, she suddenly rolled over onto her back without checking to see if anyone had appeared and flung her arms out to embrace the sun's heat into her chest. She imagined the masculine hands running down her front creating this heat; she often wondered if that's what it felt like, to have someone who loves you put their hands on you.

She never knew why she hadn't pursued this feeling with Jack, the thought crept into her mind again as she opened her eyes once more - for some reason, she just didn't believe he could make her feel like this.

She suddenly heard a very familiar little ringing sound; it was her little watch, the alarm she had set was ringing, letting her know it was time to leave her world and return to someone else's.

Managing to force herself to her feet she picked up her white cotton underdress and put it back on over her head, tucked it in, then pulled up the shoulder straps of her faded pink dress from around her waist and placed them back where they should be.

Slowly, now with her head down as the sun rapidly disappeared, she began the walk of shame, because her emergent surroundings were telling her to be ashamed of what she had just done. As the gorgeous clusters of wildflowers disappeared and the statues, water features and cruelly restrained flowerbeds became more numerous, signifying she was approaching the house, there came the numbing apprehension.

A huge stone terrace overlooked the garden at the rear of the manor. On it were a dozen household staff busily preparing tables, glassware and decorative flower arrangements. A few gardeners were hand clipping grass strands at the lawn edges that had dared to grow separately from their neighbors.

Standing on the terrace, flanked by the butler and a footman and sternly regarding her with a sharp penetrating stare, was her mother.

WALK OF SHAME

The muster of gardeners and servants stopped what they were doing and froze; they stared at Mary as if they were spellbound by her sudden appearance. This was a bad sign; there had obviously been a great deal of concern as to her whereabouts, a full-scale search looked as if it had been imminent.

Mary's chest became tight with anxiety, but she was determined not to let them see. Pretending to be oblivious, she continued to walk calmly towards the house without looking at anyone.

Upon seeing her approach, Mary's mother stood at the edge of the terrace and looked down on her contemptuously. Mary climbed the steps as if she were a criminal approaching the judge for sentencing.

The only reason she was barely allowed to leave the house unaccompanied in the first place was because she was supposed to be simply 'taking the air' in the garden. Even in the family's own garden this had to be undertaken in a blanket of ceremony, usually requiring an hour and a half of dressing, followed by a very public and almost ritualistic walking in one full circle, admiring the flowerbeds and commenting on the inconsistencies of the prevailing season.

To get outside without the company of her sisters was no mean feat. Mary had to feign ill temperament toward them each time she wanted this precious privacy. They would never understand, let alone keep her secret.

Taking the air in the garden without her sisters seemed, to her mother, selfish and wasteful. If her mother had found out that she'd been using that time to bathe in the sun with her body half exposed, she would never have been allowed to show an inch of flesh to the open air ever again. It was probably not possible to surmise what her mother and father's reaction would have been, emotional or physical, upon discovering just how much air their daughter was taking every Tuesday.

Young women of Mary's age were normally, for the most part, destined for indoor occupations and have little time allotted to them for 'taking air'; what time they did have was seemingly forever encroached upon by the ceremony of dressing. Always dressing; for everything from breakfast to simply 'being seen' in your own house in the afternoon - it was all her sisters seemed to do.

Her mother was flanked by two footmen, and the families old bulldog of a butler loomed in the background. Her mother usually had no intention of extracting answers from her on the spot as to why she was late and so improperly dressed.

They had had it all out before - but always in private.

Today, however, was different.

Mary made to walk around her mother, not even making eye contact. The blockade of servants moved to cut her off as if she were under arrest.

Her mother, in a vain attempt not to let her anger show through too much in front of the servants, barked at her in a half-hushed tone: "Where have you been?"

Mary kept on walking as her mother marched up to her side.

As Mary passed her the nearest footman, a tall visceral man, grabbed Mary's left arm with a cold hand and held her in place.

Mary jerked to a halt in surprise; this had never happened before. He gripped her tight and it began to hurt. Mary was taken aback and gave him a confused scowl; she tried to shake herself loose but he increased his grip further. She began to lose control of her breathing as her head ran to keep up with what was happening.

Her mother caught up with her and Mary looked at her in hurt confusion.

"Mother, he's hurting me, tell him to let go."

For a servant to do this was unthinkable. Mary expected her mother to tell the footman to collect his coat and leave immediately, but she didn't. This was planned.

Her mother stood in front of her.

"Well then, you can look at me while I'm talking to you!" she barked. "Where have you been?"

"I told you," Mary pleaded, "I was walking. Tell him to let go of my arm mother, he's really hurting me!"

Her mother showed no compassion. This was new low. Mary looked around at the staff working in the garden, watching her from the corner of their eyes; taking thinly veiled pleasure in seeing this privileged, disobedient girl getting what she needed.

Mary felt a few tears suddenly well up in panic at this very public humiliation. She looked at her mother for some help, but none came. She had seen her mother this angry before, but never in front of the staff. Usually, great pains were taken to dish out punishment in private.

"You told no one you were leaving the house. You were gone for four hours!" Her mother then moved close to Mary's face so she could whisper the next few words; "you were told how important tonight was to us."

Mary squirmed under the pressure of the footman's grip, as her mother bitterly uttered words that were meant to make Mary feel guilty. "You know your father is in ill health - have you any idea what you're doing to him? When he heard you'd disappeared off again, today of all days he . . . he had to be sedated this morning!"

"Sedated!" Mary suddenly shouted defiantly, "I don't think a case of Cockburn 58 counts as a medical sedative!"

Her mother hadn't anticipated this and she seethed through a desperate whisper; "How dare you! Don't you ever take responsibility for what your actions do to other people?"

"How can you say that standing there having them do this to me mother?"

With that, Mary wrenched herself away from the footman. His grip held firm but before he could pull her back towards him, Mary raised her right leg, swivelled on the left and rammed the heel of her heavy riding boot as hard as she could into his ankle.

The footman lunged forward in pain, gawping with his eyes growing as large as duck eggs. His grip weakened and Mary took advantage of this; she put her knee hard into his chest and he flew backwards, stumbling and landing on a table a maid had been working to set.

The maid screamed and two boot boys grabbed Mary on either arm.

Her mother retreated, her face aghast with horror at this display. She wailed as she stumbled back into the house; "Get her to her room, get her up there, you have two hours, you'll be ready and down here for seven!"

Mary didn't know why tonight was so important or what kind of threshold it was she had just crossed to warrant this treatment.

Her mother secretly knew that these spats of independence were going to stop. From the approaching evening on, events were going to overtake her daughter. Whether she liked it or not, Mary was going to have too much to think about to have time to 'take air' for the rest of her life.

This was why Mary thought of all her time spent away from this house and her family as an escape.

From as early as she could remember, her needs, worries and fears had always been for her to deal with alone. Her younger siblings, who followed her in quick succession, each garnered her parents' attention over her. She only had a blurry taste of memories of what it was like to be actually parented. She had been expected to learn the fine arts of fairness, sharing and proper behaviour, before she was old enough to understand them even as ideas, and long before her siblings were expected to.

Her mother, without knowing it, had to move on to

parenting her sisters before Mary could be connected with in the same way. As a result she was just punished, harshly, every time she didn't want to share her favourite breakfast, a toy, or a gift, or if she became angry and resentful for any reason. Unfortunately, nobody considered for a moment, that this might be because she didn't understand.

She knew now, more or less, because she had taught herself by watching others and listening to her instincts. Being left to teach herself how to grow up, how to deal with her emotions and to solve her own problems, had taught her self-reliance - a dangerously inappropriate trait for a woman of her background.

Back when she was six, and had just started to sneak away to build her boat, when she had been caught the third time after her location was reported to her mother by a gardener, her parents were furious.

She was dragged away, humiliated, from the boat builders by her father and taken to his study, where he lost control. He shouted and shook her by the shoulders so hard it hurt. He made her cry with pain. Her tears didn't seem at all precious to him; she thought they were supposed to be and seeing that he didn't care shocked and hurt her. She could never hug her father again after that.

The next day was spent alone, at a desk facing a wall, with a maid watching her.

She couldn't understand why doing something that made her happy, that didn't hurt anyone, was so wrong.

This experience didn't dissuade her from continuing to try; it couldn't. The longing to be away - even if it defied her parents' wishes - was overpowering.

Suffocating with all the manhandling bodies around her, Mary was led into the house. The great lounge she walked through was garlanded with fresh flowers. Maids in white aprons and young male servants in tailcoats buttoned up over their grey and navy striped waistcoats were bustling in and out of the cavernous dining room, where stiffly starched linens and monogrammed family silverware was being painstakingly set.

Tonight was obviously a significant occasion indeed.

In her short life she had seen so many of these events. Endless parades, parties, gatherings, dinners and soirees; they had all seemed so important at the time, but now no one could even remember what they were for. So why should anyone care so much every time?

That's why it never stuck in her head when she was told about them; why should it matter to all these people? Why shave years off your life expectancy by allowing your nervous system to be tested for weeks on end by problems with menus, floral arrangements, seating plans and a shortage of fish knives?

She often thought; 'To a woman like my grandmother, at the end of her life, what did all those parties, graces and obligations matter if she didn't enjoy them - so . . . why should they be any more important now?'

She couldn't understand it.

Up two flights of great oak stairs was the landing on which her bedroom was located. Outside, her lady's maid, Ruth, a girl the same age as Mary but used to doing her mother's bidding, waited dutifully.

Mary was deposited at the door like a prisoner arriving at a cell.

"Miss," Ruth spoke quietly, her head down in embarrassment at seeing her lady manhandled in such a manner. "Everything for you this evening is ready."

"I'll wash first - then you can come and help," Mary replied reluctantly.

"Yes miss." Ruth curtsied gently and stepped aside.

Upon entering her room, Mary closed the door firmly behind her and breathed a momentary sigh.

As her guard went down, a few tears came.

The sneaking off was always the best part; coming back after it was all over was always terrifying, and the final approach to the house was always the worst moment - but it had never been as bad as that.

'And why should it be anyway!' Mary always screamed out in her mind. 'What's so bad about the way I want to live - the things I want to do - they make me happy!'

She felt her arm; it was sore where the footman had gripped her. She couldn't believe her mother could stand by and watch someone hurt her like that. She had loved her mother; or at least, the idea of what a mother was supposed to be; but the reality had sadly changed over time. These weren't the actions of a caring mother.

She looked desperately around her room for some solace; it was a large perfectly square affair, with faded lilac fabric covered walls, matching curtains and a huge iron bedstead. Windows overlooked the garden and one wall housed a mighty mirrored mahogany wardrobe.

The room was littered with all the accoutrements one would expect of a young lady of Mary's class. Another young woman would have been proud of such an extravaganza but to Mary it was more of an extension of her parents' wishes than anything else. Everything in the room had been chosen for her; she could have had more of a say - the trouble was she didn't particularly want any of it. Nonetheless, it was what a girl of her upbringing would be expected to own, so it was bought for her.

About the only possessions that she actually used amongst the bazaar of furnishings in this room was a book placed beside her bed and another small collection of books tucked away in a drawer, that no one else knew about.

Reading in private was an activity usually only reserved for her father in his study. For Mary, to have one book from the household library in her room to read before bed was quite permissible. Anything more and it would require dressing for and doing in the library at the appropriate time in the day, with a sister or three.

For Mary, a book before bed had for a long time been a form of escape, though in recent years, it had lost its edge. As her mind and body grew, she began to yearn to experience the things she read about in real life; she found the amazing places books took her to, too intangible now, and her imagination had become over strained.

This little collection was of seven books, all of them by numerous travel writers, who wrote in immersive detail about the places they had visited. One of them was a woman, whose work had given Mary many ideas.

She loved reading the author's experiences of the curios and eccentricities of other cultures. Moreover, she adored the idea of having the freedom to see and experience all these amazing places; the people, the foods and especially the feelings these places seemed to conjure up in others, to inspire them to write so lyrically about them.

In a cunning attempt to get her to read in the company of her family more often, she had previously been gifted a book entitled *Hints to Lady Travellers: At Home and Abroad.* Mary couldn't wait to get between its pages, but when the first chapter offered practical advice on how to travel with one's own portable bath, she soon went off it.

She moved to a dresser and plucked from her dress strap the only possession in the world she really treasured, which she took everywhere - her sterling silver pocket watch, the only vaguely feminine object that mattered to her; it had been a gift from her grandmother.

She adored her grandmother, who had been widowed many years earlier and for a while became the family matriarch. Mary had never known her when she had been married to her grandfather. She got the impression from her parents that when her grandfather died, her grandmother came out of her prescribed shell and took on a new confidence, which somehow seemed an embarrassment to them.

She was the only member of her family whom Mary would say had a personality and wasn't just another walking duty receptacle. She would and could say anything to anyone; Mary loved her for it and owed the vaguely interesting passing of many formal dining occasions to her grandmother.

On one occasion at a very large formal dinner one guest was an elderly widow of a comparable age to her grandmother.

It appeared she and her grandmother had known each other for a very long time. Sat next to each other at dinner, they gossiped and reminisced together about the past, a conversation that certain other guests appeared reluctant to listen to; so much so that everyone else attempted to drown them out with louder, drier and even less interesting talk than usual.

At one point, an associate of Mary's father held up the serving of the meat course, a shoulder of lamb, by exclaiming indignantly at length of some recent business affairs in which he felt he had been mistreated. He was gesticulating so wildly, that the servant couldn't put the meat on his plate.

Eventually Mary's grandmother leaned slowly forward, eyeing the man beadily and spoke over him - "Will you let the man serve the lamb shoulder, or does he first have to remove the chip from yours?"

Everybody stifled a smile, except Mary's parents who glared at her with poisonous intensity.

Eventually these two old friends decided the conversation around the rest of the table was boring them and they left before the full meal was served. As they left, Mary's grandmother declared jovially, "Come upstairs Caroline dear, I have about ten days worth of gin hidden away and it needs putting to good use." As they tottered out, the assembled dinner guests remained seated, awkwardly, with their heads down.

Mary watched, envious and delighted as the two intertwined souls walked away supporting each other; holding hands while steadying their stroll with a walking stick in the other hand. Mary could feel an ancient bond between these two women and would love to have known what forged it.

After a few such incidents, something changed. Her grandmother was spotted around the great house less and less. When she did appear she would be put away at the back of every room and when Mary wanted to run to see her, she would feel the sudden grip of her mother's hand on her shoulder, preventing her.

Mary would then sit and perform whatever dull obligation was scheduled; a lunch with guests perhaps, a musical recital by one of her sisters. Occasionally, she would look over to her grandmother. Frail, thinning and hunched over, she would always appear in a high-necked black silk gown that ebbed away from her neck in placid folds; sitting still, lonely and isolated with her maid standing guard over her. Eventually she was permanently shut away in her apartments, in the upper reaches of the house.

Whenever Mary or anyone else asked after her, her mother would say that she was sick, but no doctors came to the house, just solicitors. The servants guarded the apartments like a prison.

It was on her fourteenth birthday that Mary last saw her grandmother; by now Mary was ready for her mother's hand and darted over to the dark corner in which her grandmother was placed before she could be stopped. She hugged and kissed her, and her grandmother held her tight, tenderly, something Mary had never felt from anyone else.

They were allowed to talk for a little while. Mary didn't think she looked sick at all, but she didn't look well in other ways. She beamed at Mary tearfully. Though the skin around her eyes was heavenly pale and ancient like a decayed Greek statue, the glistening jewels that were her sapphire blue eyes, that looked just like Mary's, still twinkled at the sight of her first granddaughter.

Mary desperately wanted to know what was wrong with her, why she had been shut away for so long. Her grandmother checked to see who was listening, took

Mary's hand, held it tight and whispered, "It doesn't do to be yourself, even in your own home my darling."

She then gestured to her maid and had a little black pouch put into her hand. She gave it to Mary.

Inside was a watch. It was white faced with gold hands and a gilded gold leaf pattern around the inside of the dial. A short silver chain ran up to a silver bow-tie shape, hidden behind which a small clip for fastening to clothes. Mary thought it was beautiful; she hugged and kissed her grandmother gratefully.

Her grandmother then showed her how to work the little alarm bell it had built into it.

"I haven't used it since I was a little girl, not much older than you," she said, sounding like she was thinking back fondly. "I wish . . . I hadn't stopped using it."

Mary detected very potent regret in her grandmother's voice that she wasn't used to hearing. "What did you use it for, grandmamma?"

Her grandmother beamed at her again, put her cold hand on Mary's cheek and said warmly with a little laugh, "I know, my darling, that you will find that out for yourself soon enough. I've seen the way you ride those horses."

Her grandmother died a few weeks later; Mary never really got over the loss. After she died, she was never talked about, and it was as if she had never existed. Mary couldn't understand why, but she had her watch and would sometimes take it out just to look at it, as if she sometimes needed proof that her grandmother had once lived.

It didn't take long for Mary to start using it as her grandmother once had, though it was a while before Mary herself made the connection.

It had been Mary's tool of escape ever since it was given to her. Using its small alarm bell, if Mary knew she had two hours before search parties would be despatched for her because it was time to dress for dinner, she could set the watch to ring in two hours and escape from the house. Then, she could lose herself to whatever she wanted with her mind free, knowing her little watch would keep her safe, as if her grandmother was still watching over her somehow.

Mary held it up to the light before putting it down, as she had done many time before, to look at what parts of the innards could be seen through a gap in the face where the hands were fixed. The curious thing about the watch that always puzzled Mary was that it never needed winding; there wasn't even a dial around the rim to do so.

The cogs and instruments she could see fascinated her, they were all made of a rich green metal, just like a dark emerald. She didn't know if the strange material somehow kept the watch ticking and she didn't want to risk breaking it by trying to open the case.

She put it down on the dresser, as she always did after wondering about its secrets and thinking of her grandmother.

Mary suddenly froze . . . She had seen what was hanging on her wardrobe.

Her heart sank into her stomach at the sight of six feet of silver silk gauze with intricate woven patterns in gold. It was straight style with a high waist. Short sleeves with a tie effect, a stomacher panel of gold net sewn with glass beads, silver cord and real pearls. Epaulettes of fine crepe, cross-over effects on a front bodice with a paste metal buckle. Tight fastenings at the back partly concealed by a panel of gold net, all on top of a dark blue nylon underskirt.

This was her debutante dress; they were usually white but this was the fourth year running, so some colour was allowed to establish that she wasn't wearing the same dress every year.

At the same time once a year, young women of high standing families at court, who had reached marrying age, were paraded in front of the Queen who would announce the commencement of the debutante season; then they would all retire for a huge ball in which these young ladies were introduced to suitable bachelors. In hundreds of huge ennobled houses across the country, wealthy aristocratic families would then follow suit.

She stepped over to it, lost in its gaudy, layered depths of pearls and gold. She felt an ache at the back of her head, a kind of longing ache - for just one more day without this - just another day.

This was the reason tonight was so important; all the guests, all the food and all the expense. Tonight, in this gilded straight jacket, she would be paraded in front of a suitable bachelor, no doubt already picked by her father as she couldn't be trusted any more.

Wealthy enough to keep this great house afloat; he would propose, and that would be that. Once she had produced an heir she would simply become his commodity, to be kept forever in his great house, just like her mother and her grandmother. Naturally a myriad of activities were available to her, but she didn't want to run a household. She didn't want to live out the existence everyone had prescribed for her.

Since she had turned sixteen, three times her family had put her through this ritual and three times she had seen off the clean, perpendicular young man that had come to admire her as though she were a lot at an auction. This was quite an achievement, as on these occasions she had hardly been permitted to say a single word; her parents usually did all the talking for her.

It had been easy in the beginning. The first had been the eldest son of someone who owned lots of transatlantic liners, a distant relation to some old American who was apparently the richest man on earth. He soon went off her when he discovered she could shoot better than him. Quite the humiliation - her parents were horrified. After that she was sat down for a very long lesson on how a prospective wife should be humble, caring and always selfless.

With the last one, her parents were on their guard; at

last year's ball they had got to the ritual of sitting both her and him down in the drawing room together, closely accompanied by her father. The young gentleman had suggested he talk to her father later that evening and then they should walk out together the following day. She knew what that meant; she declined his offer there and then. Her father almost spat his moustache off his face.

She could say no again, of course she could - but it wasn't ever that simple. There was too much at stake for all around her, and the consequences, that would affect so many people, were all on her shoulders.

Her parents laboured for months to persuade the families of these young bucks that it was a good idea for their son to meet their daughter. They had a name, and these families had money, it's not a new tale; it was going on all over. The wealth was no longer in the hands of the great English aristocratic families, but their names were still ancient, famous and their estates still expensive to upkeep. The money was with new industrial families, heirs to railway, steel and shipping fortunes; money that the old families needed to keep their houses, to live as they had always done. In return the new wealth jumped leap years up the social ladder.

Her parents needed her to give up whatever ideas of a life of her own she had, and become the quiet, dutiful and sedentary wife. That was the whole reason she was born. They needed her to do this, badly. The family money was running out, though it was almost a state secret; in addition, alcoholism had killed her grandfather and her father had the same problem, exacerbated by the state of the family finances.

The pressure to accept her fate came not only from above, but also from below. Her sisters had no life of their own; that is, until she married. With Mary married to a rich and influential man, they could accompany her to all of his social engagements where she would introduce them to society, where they would make friends and find a husband, and build their own futures - unburdened by the duty to keep their family afloat, a worry which sat firmly on the shoulder of their eldest sister. Until then, they were trapped - like Mary.

The strain of what was expected of her was overwhelming. Mary sometimes actually envied people who could be content with dressing and deciding on menus every day, just because they appeared to have that serenity in life she so badly craved. She longed for that feeling, but it was in short supply.

She could have had the pick of any dress, diamond, rich husband or soft furnishing in the world, but all she wanted was five more minutes alone, with her mind at peace, doing something she enjoyed.

Mary jumped as her bedroom door closed behind her. She turned to see her mother standing looking at her. She had been enjoying watching Mary stare at the dress for some time.

Mary turned away; she felt her mother move slowly up behind her, until she could feel her breath on the back of her neck.

"That's it now; you are never to leave the house unaccompanied again, I forbid it . . . Mary, do you understand me?"

Her mother made to grab Mary's sore arm to turn her around. As she was pulled to face her, Mary grabbed her mother's right arm and gave it a gentle squeeze.

Her mother flinched in severe pain and moved her hand to her arm, as the sudden agony shot up her side.

"Did he do that?" Mary asked knowingly. "Did he do to you what the footman just did to me . . . ? How was it - did it make you cry too?"

Her mother breathed in deeply to calm herself.

"That's enough," she said as she exhaled. "Perhaps if you had stayed in the house today like you were asked, he wouldn't have - "

"Don't you put that on me mother!" Mary's argued

firmly. "Don't put your cowardice on me, I didn't make you marry him, but don't you see you're just - "

A flash of hurtful anger shot across her mother's eyes, and she gripped Mary by her collar and pushed here against the wardrobe.

"Don't you dare call me a coward," she spluttered, losing her composure, "don't you dare!"

Her hands were shaking and her eyes were glazed with tears. She fought to regain her poise and let go of Mary.

Mary didn't say anything, she just looked at her mother and watched her turn and move to the window.

There was a very uncomfortable silence; her mother began to breathe deeply again to calm herself. When she spoke again, it was slow, and from the window looking out over the estate.

"You think you are so tremendously brave and courageous for defying our wishes and disappearing all the time." She suddenly turned with a look of insolence. "Well . . . a brave woman, would have stayed today - a woman of true and real strength, character and a sense duty would have stayed and not run away. So . . . which one of us is actually the coward!"

Mary didn't have anything to say; her mother began to move closer to her again as she spoke with increasing spite.

"All you do is run away from your responsibilities - have you any idea what it takes to stay? To live, every day, as the moral foundation of a family like this and of our home, to give your life to ensuring the prosperity and proper conduct of your children, servants and an entire county of tenants!"

"I don't want it," Mary interrupted bluntly, not looking at her.

Her mother stopped dead in her tracks. "I beg your pardon," she said slowly.

"I don't want it!"

There was a long silence before Mary's mother could

speak again.

"And you . . . actually find your current - feckless and wasteful existence - appealing in some way?"

Mary moved slowly to her, drawing strength from the truth in her own feelings and calmly replied, "As a matter of fact, mother, yes I do." She raised up both her arms, outstretched as if gesturing to their entire world.

"Take all these elaborate layers of lies off me," she struck the gaudy dress with one hand, "all of it; and I'll be standing here, completely naked, with everything I need in the world; a healthy body, air to breathe and a pair of hands I can do anything with."

Her mother stared at her, up and down, with profound confusion.

"I love waking up in the morning," Mary continued. "Imagining all the things I could do with them, all the work I could do, the skills I could master, the things I could achieve and the places those things could take me to, the things I could see! And not knowing where those places are yet is the best part!"

Mary moved closer to her mother. "I fool you, I sneak away and I go and find them. The things I can do with these hands mother!"

She held her hands in front of her, looked down at them as if they were precious infants and then looked back at her mother.

"You wouldn't believe . . . you couldn't begin to believe. And you will never know the satisfaction - the serenity that comes from that - if you were capable of feeling what I can feel, if you were to know what I have experienced; you'd be on your knees, begging him for a divorce!"

Mary's mother's temples turned red, her mouth began to quiver in rage and her eyes welled up again. She slapped her daughter hard across the face.

"You unimaginably shameful creature!" she hissed at Mary.

As her mother breathed out heavily again, her confusion turned to a mocking smile.

"So, you don't want it, well then . . . you will have nothing, you will represent nothing, and you will be - nothing. You know what your father will do if you don't take part in the season this time."

"I understand from Lady Rothermeare; I would be packed off to Europe with an allowance and a companion."

"Unlike Lady Rothermeare's daughter, you would actually enjoy that wouldn't you - well . . . pity. In some ways, disgrace is the only vocation you're capable of rising to; if you were a man, there might still have been a use for you." Mary's mother stopped seething through a whisper and continued in a loud official tone, "you're not going anywhere; you will marry the gentleman who is coming to see you this evening, or it will be your sister who takes the estate and you will become my companion; solitary and forever at my beck and call for the rest of your life."

Her mother marched to the door and then turned for one last blow:

"Either way, that's about all you will ever know."

The servants were summoned in and her mother retired to prepare for the guests. Mary stood, looking at nothing; she was turned to face the mirror and it began.

First came the underdress, then the petticoat and the bodice. Ruth knew Mary didn't like it too tight, but it was impossible to avoid. She likened it to getting lots of strings of sausages, hanging them up in a bunch and then cupping both hands around them and squeezing them until they burst. That's what she felt like.

On top of that came the dress itself, then the jewellery, then the gloves, then the headdress, and then finally the Ostrich feathers.

She desperately entertained foolish, childish thoughts of some last minute escape: but of course, there wasn't one. 'Even if I could somehow get out of the house and away from the servants, where would I go?' She kept sobbing to herself. She had no money of her own so what could she do? She could shoot, ride, fly, row - but it was all useless to her.

Another woman might have been savouring this as one of the most precious memories of her life, to Mary it was a death ritual, and her maid knew it. Once she was complete, Ruth stood behind her looking into the mirror Mary was gazing at.

Ruth would have loved and felt privileged to have shared this special close moment with someone to whom it mattered. Instead, it simply felt like she had just worked painstakingly to dress a stone statue.

"Will that be all, miss?"

Mary didn't answer; she just stood and looked with dead eyes at the monstrosity she had become. Ruth withdrew to the door.

Mary could hear the clock strike seven, and automatically she moved with a condemned rigidity towards the door.

Left at the landing, she slowly began to descend the staircase, with Ruth and two other female servants watching her dress carefully.

Each step she took, Mary became tenser; her rigid spine seemed to quiver as if her body was getting ready to experience deep pain. She wanted so desperately to cry, but something stopped her - probably some residue of the graces her parents had tried to instil in her for the kind of moment this was supposed to be.

The glow of the lights and the hum of the assembled crowd that shone up through the centre of the stairwell from the rooms below were not the least bit convivial to her. It was like a stairwell into a snake pit, the conversational masses of snakes hissing as their prey was lowered to them.

Every step was perfect, she moved just as a lady should, but her face stared straight ahead, her expression -

blank.

Halfway down she came face to face with a window. It was criss-crossed with decorative iron strips, through one of the patterns she caught a brief glimpse of a setting sky, perhaps even the corner of a cloud between the trees outside the window.

She remembered a beautiful drawing in one of her travel journals of something called the Bridge of Sighs in a place built on water, called Venice. While beautiful it was apparently where prisoners who had received a life penalty were led, across the bridge and then down into a dungeon where they were imprisoned for life. The tiny stone windows in the bridge, not even big enough to fit your hand into; affording a miniscule glimpse of the beautiful outside world you were being taken away from, all the carefree people going about their business below you, oblivious to your situation; it would be a last cruel taste of the world they were about to leave before they left it.

In some way, she now felt she knew what that sensation was like.

As the quick view of a cloud she had probably touched that very day disappeared, she turned on the last landing and began her final descent to the ground floor.

The house was already half filled with guests. The rear terrace was bustling with black and white jacketed men inter-dispersed with faded-colour females.

Her mother was in the grand entrance hallway greeting the guests.

Her sisters were there to greet Mary in the drawing room and they began to chatter and fuss over her.

"You've never looked more radiant - "

"I want one just like it!"

"They'll never buy one that's not white again, you know that."

Mary didn't say anything. She barely heard them; their empty words drifted through her like white noise.

Dinner would be a while yet so she followed her sisters

out onto the terrace. It was a brilliant night, warm, the sky packed full of stars and not a breath of wind.

Guests were enjoying drinks and hors d'oeuvres across the breadth of the rear of the house. All gazes that came up from conversation were directed towards Mary - she was the reason they were all here. Her name, one of the biggest yet unattached and the man she was destined to meet, an international celebrity as far as wealth was concerned.

She found herself at the terrace balcony, staring down at the garden, oblivious to everything around her.

She suddenly felt a presence at the back of her; a dinner jacketed arm appeared from behind, holding a glass of champagne.

"You look like you need a few of these, better get started," said a male voice she didn't recognise.

Mary didn't turn to see who it was; she dismissed it, shaking her head slightly and continuing to stare out at the garden.

The arm holding the champagne was firmly still for a moment, and then it withdrew.

"You're the boss," the voice said. "Well, never forget; you die if you worry, you die if you don't."

Mary didn't take any notice, at first. The party chatter always washed over her, but slowly the words this stranger spoke seemed to speak to her. She realised she actually quite liked what he had said and turned to see who it was; she was disappointed to find no one there - whoever it was had moved on.

She suddenly noticed her mother standing near her. The whole atmosphere at the back of the house changed - something was about to happen. Her sisters were arranged near her on the terrace; the younger two were beaming, but the eldest knew what was at stake and glared at Mary.

Up the Terrace steps from the garden Mary had climbed a few hours before, came her father, with yet another upright, dutifully poised young man at his side.

They were both smiling; they had obviously already had the conversation. That was it, her father's mind was made up, there was nothing now to stop this man proposing without any further ritual and her parents would do anything to speed along the moment.

If she avoided becoming engaged now, next year she would be twenty, her reputation for failing to find a husband secure, her eligibility for marriage tarnished, her usefulness as a person, diminished.

As they approached, her youngest sister giggled naively and the stolen gazes from the masses increased in their regularity. Her father went through the motions of an introduction; the young man became rigid in bearing and brought his hand lightly and slickly forward, ready for her to accept it.

She didn't hear what her father said; she didn't catch who he was. He looked exactly like the others. The condescending smiles beamed at her from all directions, her mother and father on one side, him in front, and her sisters on the other. What a beautiful moment the world was telling her this should be, how happy she should be and how guilty she should feel for having any other feelings.

Behind the charming facade, her father's eyes suddenly took upon a cold stare; he moved closer and leaned in to the young man's ear. Purposefully loud enough so Mary could hear but not anyone else, he spoke to the young man quietly but firmly.

"As I said, her behaviour in past courtships has been somewhat . . . irregular. But I understand that will not be a problem for you?"

"No sir, not in the slightest," the young man replied, still holding Mary's gaze with a smile.

"Remember," her father went on, "you don't take a hand to her until you've given her your last name, then, it's no longer any of my concern."

The young man's smile turned wry. "I understand

perfectly, sir. I hope, for her sake, your daughter does," he said, still with his hand held out.

Mary became numbed with shock; unbelievably her hand still automatically raised itself to be taken by his.

Everything seemed to slow down; she thought she heard a ringing in her ears. The numbness inside her seemed to take over her entire body.

Her father's voice came through this slow high-pitched whine: "Perhaps you'd like to withdraw to the drawing room after dinner." Those words overwhelmed her, her spine began to quiver again as if some horrendous pressure was enacting upon it. Her heart began to pound, she wasn't breathing - her breath was being held in by something.

Years of emotion, years of pressure, years of moments where she wanted to scream out to the world, anger at herself for being so naïve about what they had done to her grandmother, all these feelings now seemed to rampage into one. Her chest began to hurt as her body cried out for air.

It appeared as if in slow motion: this young man's wry face started to turn from her father back to her, then she watched as his brow fell, his smile began to dissipate and slowly his face turned to confusion, then a little distasteful concern.

She felt something tickle her chin, then her chest. She looked down; there was blood on her bodice - it was dripping from her face. Instinctively she raised her now shivering hand to her mouth. Her nose was gushing blood; she began to feel dizzy, she couldn't stop shaking.

It was probably only a few seconds, but it seemed like an eternity. Everyone glared at her, her father frowned in confusion, and her mother gawped. The young man stared at her in embarrassed amazement.

She fell forward, but came to rest on his arm. Gripping desperately at his sleeves she pulled herself up, there in front of her were the steps, down into the garden, her beloved garden.

She lunged for them; her first step was shaky, but then some strength came back to her lower body and she began to run frantically.

She got down two steps without a problem, but her clothes were not built for movement; she tripped on the dress and fell. Her left arm was twisted and her temple hit the stone steps with a ping. There was an agonised gasp from the crowd.

As she came to rest at the bottom she looked up, a crowd of shocked onlookers hastily gathered at the top - she only caught their silhouettes. Her father pushed his way to the front of the crowd and began to hurriedly stride down the steps towards her, his fists clenched.

She didn't hesitate. She gripped the muddy ground savagely and crawled like an animal for the first few moments, built up momentum and came to her feet. She stepped on her dress again, but instead of falling it ripped and then ripped again, until her feet had some room.

She pummelled for the darkness, darting round every tree, their branches and leaves feeling like wasp stings as they struck her face. Her shoes came off and she fell again; she raised herself on her right arm and carried on running. She began breathing again; whining in desperate pain every time she exhaled. To see her anyone would have thought she was running from her death - maybe she was. Tears began to stream down her face.

It was like a nightmare, frantically running into a black night, not daring for a moment to stop and look back at what was chasing her, for fear it might catch up.

She only stopped running when she came again to the river at the far side of the estate. She collapsed at the bank. Turned, panting, her teeth clenched, blood and tears dripped from her face.

Looking back she immediately expected to see her father, but there was no one.

She lay panting, her gaze fixed upon the distant trees,

expecting any moment an army of concerned men to emerge and drag her back before she could catch her breath.

Then she saw the jetty; the family's little rowing boat she had helped to build, sat perfectly still on the flat calm water. Again she crawled, and then got to her feet. She collapsed into the boat, pulled off its mooring rope and pushed the jetty away with all the strength she had left.

Slowly, the soft current took up the boat's movement and the bank ebbed away.

Steadily, the sight of the garden became silhouetted against the moonlight. She had difficulty letting go of her panic at first; but began to take some comfort in the distance slowly being put between her and the bank.

Once it disappeared, she knew any pursuers wouldn't be able to see her in the dark anymore and she collapsed onto her back in the bottom of the boat, her body strained and exhausted.

She lay there for some time, trying to stop the pain in her chest, eventually feeling her hard heartbeat slowly relax itself, helped by the sound of the calm water trickling by. As her breath returned to her, the ringing in her ears slowly subsided.

She closed her eyes; for a while she thought she might be dying, as it was everything she had been told it should be in church. It had become so peaceful, and slowly her body seemed to come to rest.

She was alone again. As she opened her eyes one last time, she saw the stars. They seemed brighter than normal.

There was the faint wisp of a cloud directly above her. 'That's where I'm going,' she thought. 'That's where you go when you die.'

A smile may have crossed her lips as her eyes closed again, and she drifted peacefully away.

CHAPTER III

SILENT DIVE

When she opened her eyes again, Mary was confused to see the limp branch of a willow tree playfully tickling her nose; not quite what she thought being dead ought to be like.

Coming round, she discovered she was still lying on her back in the boat. While the blood from her nose was now dry, her arm was cut open above the elbow and her left temple was very tender. The boat had got caught up in a willow tree; god knows where she was or how long she had been unconscious.

Realising she was still very much alive, and the boat was going nowhere, she clamoured slowly over the side onto the embankment. Emerging from the tree onto the open bank, she surveyed her surroundings.

The river curved to the right and off to where the flat horizon met the stars. The night was still completely clear, not a wisp of haze to be seen. It was tranquil and calm, and as her eyes became more accustomed to the dark, she saw the outline of some buildings about a mile distant from where she stood.

Using her right arm to steady her, she sat down. She ripped off the last torn shard hanging from the bottom of her dress, exposing most of her bare legs, and used it to dab up some of the blood from her arm. It stung like nothing she had ever felt. She remembered a method of stopping a cut bleeding she had read about in one of her more exotic travel journals and even in the dark she managed to wrap the wound up.

In spite of what had just happened, she felt strangely calm; it was like a great peace had come over the world in the wake of her ordeal, but that was sadly not to last. Her mind was now clearing; she was alone and could think. She felt her head throb with pain. She rubbed her upper lip, and found the grainy remnants of dried blood in her hand.

'How could they do this to me?' she suddenly thought, 'what kind of parents do this to their daughter?'

Standing there, looking down at the powdery dried blood in her hand, she suddenly felt very self-aware. 'Look what they have made me, how much of my blood do I have to shed before they've had enough.'

Still, she knew this breakdown was not enough to escape them or reform their ideals. Her family had seen, in all its horrid realism, her desperation to be free from what they were trying to do to her. They had drawn blood from her without even touching her; they had seen her crawl, weeping in desperation through mud and blood like some deranged animal.

She thought of her grandmother; the bruises she had on her body in her last months - they had done this before.

God know what they'd do with her now; they would probably think she was ill, or mad. She looked at herself and as she looked down, more tears began to drip into her shaking hands and mingle with the blood.

An agonising stream of panicked thoughts and feelings began to overwhelm her. 'How could they have brought me to this? Or did I bring myself to this . . . no, there was nothing else I could do, there really wasn't'.

She looked around at the empty landscape.

'I can't go back now, but where could I go?' She could have kicked herself for asking that question; she already knew the answer, and she had known it for a long time - nowhere.

There was a sudden shot of pain from her arm, she clenched it but that only made it bleed through the dressing. Looking again towards the silhouette of buildings away to the left, she decided that at least she was alive, and she needed a doctor. Pushing herself to her feet once more, she plodded down the embankment towards the buildings.

They were actually a lot closer than they appeared at

first, only a few field lengths away. They were a funny shape, not like houses; it looked a little like a farm so she kept a look out for animals.

As she came within a few hundred yards, she saw the flicker of light in some of the closest buildings, which were one story and very long.

'Good' she thought, 'someone obviously lives here.'

She then began to imagine - what a state she would look, walking into the light of a room filled with perfect strangers. She came very close to the building until she could almost hear murmurings from inside; but she found tears welling up in her eyes again, at the thought of throwing her battered, torn and dirty body into someone else's home, and for what - to be taken back to her parents?

She fell down again, and began to sob desperately.

She looked back in the direction she had come, as if she was looking towards her parents' house and for the first time ever, instead of feeling frustration or guilt, she felt nothing but a cold hatred. The fantasy of what her parents had been, or should have been, was now gone completely.

She saw no future at all; her idea of what the world held for her was now a complete blank.

'So,' she thought, 'why not spoil their lives as totally as they have mine?' She thought of marching back to the house and smashing up the place - blurting out all the nasty family secrets her parents wanted to keep under wraps to the entire assembled party.

Then, it dawned on her that she had just had that opportunity, and hadn't taken it. She knew scandal was the nightmare of her parents, but it meant nothing to her - 'who'd believe me after tonight anyway?' she thought.

Her tears began to subside as she remembered the serene bliss she had felt when she was in the boat, drifting away peacefully. She let her mind rest on those thoughts for a while, and she embraced the sensation; how it had been as if she had found a warm blanket to wrap around herself and keep her from all the horror in the world - because she thought she was dying.

It all became clear again and as it did so some strength began to return, the same strength that had tore her away from the house.

She had wanted to die; she knew all hope of a future was now gone.

She thought that whatever awaited her in death, how wonderful it would be to face it as the person she really was, the person she was when she snuck away: a human being of courage, passion and a spirit that didn't belong here.

Turning again to the direction of the river, she thought of the water. 'After all, swimming underwater is such a pleasure,' she thought, 'everything would be so tranquil and quiet; it would just be a simple case of not bothering to come up for air.'

She calmly got to her feet again and smiling with the comfort of knowing she had a way out, she began to walk back to the river.

She had only walked a few paces when she was suddenly struck bluntly in the head; she fell again.

Gripping her forehead in pain, she looked up.

Had her father found her and struck her to subdue her?

No, there was no one there, just a large flat object sticking out of the darkness above her. As she stood up, she wondered how she hadn't seen it until it was right on top of her. She had been staring at the light from the windows and her eyes needed some time to adjust to the black of the night around her again.

As she became able to see more, she realised there were two of these objects suspended in mid air in front of her and she began to see along them. In some way, they appeared to be familiar - she was sure she had seen them before.

As the sight became clearer, she saw what it was.

Healthy warmth suddenly shot up from her cold damp chest. She froze in disbelief and then she smiled. It was her aeroplane!

Blinking her eyes to make sure it wasn't an illusion, she staggered round it, inspecting it all over, reaching out and touching it as if it were the face of an old friend.

As she walked round, she noticed there was another one parked just next to it. Looking further down the field into the dark, it soon became apparent there were many more all lined up together, the moonlight picking out the edges of their wings. It was a beautiful sight.

It didn't take any thought at all; Mary knew what she was going to do straight away. This was a much more suitable way to go than the river, it was almost as if it were an act of kindness from someone watching over her.

She knew it would have to be quick; the hut wasn't far away and as soon as the engine started up it would attract immediate attention. Reaching into the cockpit, she couldn't see a thing, but knew by heart where everything was. She turned on the fuel flow; starter and ignition then stumbled to the propeller. Reaching high, she stole herself for the biggest effort of her life; she knew she would only get a few attempts to start the engine before the noise attracted attention. With a little jump off the ground, she pulled the blade towards her with her full body weight.

Either the engine was still warm or she must have summoned more strength than she realised, because as soon as she fell to the ground a huge gust of wind blew her back as the familiar rhythmic growl of the engine washed over her. Though she couldn't see it she knew, inches away, there was that invisible whirlpool of propellers spinning.

She didn't waste a second; elated, she flung herself at the cockpit. Despite the adrenaline, her arm was giving her extreme pain now; she grabbed the stick with one hand and nudging the throttle with her now almost limp arm, the plane bounced forward instantly.

She couldn't really tell if there was any pursuit from the huts as she pulled away. Looking ahead it was impossible to say how much open space she had to take off, but by now she didn't care.

She didn't look back; she had decided on her fate and it brought her peace like she had never found in life.

As the plane began to leave the ground, she knew she had walked on the earth for the last time, but she was leaving the way she had always wanted to live and now that was all she needed to be happy. It didn't matter if her future could now be measured in minutes - for the first time in her life - she had a future; one that she liked and no one could take it away from her now.

There must have been trees very close in front of the plane, because as she rose sharply, the stars and the horizon became visible all of a sudden. As she climbed higher she knew she was heading west in the direction of the estate, as hanging low, just above the horizon, was a soothing dim red glow where the sun had gone hours earlier. She used the line of the horizon picked out by this glare to keep the plane level. Then came another gift: she saw the moonlight picking out a shimmering silver and blue squiggle - it was the river. She levelled off at a few hundred feet and began to follow it.

She had no way of knowing how far she had travelled to reach the aerodrome, nor any idea what time it was; her dearly loved watch was hidden under her dress but it was too black to see it.

Suddenly, she was amazed to see a familiar pattern of lights about a mile over from the river. It was the estate. It shone out from the trees like an angry forest fire.

Maintaining height, she flew parallel to it for a few minutes and then, once she had passed its far side, began to turn back. She knew what she was going to do; she began to fly over, still at a fair height.

She only had the lights to go from, but she knew she was drawing over the house. As she did so, with her one working hand, she mercilessly rammed the stick forward. The plane understood and it dived nose first; sharply to begin with, then as it reached 90 degrees and was facing straight towards the ground it became reluctant for a moment as the wings fought the increasing airspeed, but then it settled solemnly into place.

She threw back the throttle and the engine noise died away, and so began her silent dive.

It was a new experience, even for her. She couldn't hear the engine at all, as the speed increased uncontrollably; the whistle of the wind over the plane drew to a sharp and constant gushing sound. She didn't flinch; she was relaxed and stared carelessly straight ahead.

Her aim was perfect; as the lights of the estate below got closer, more detail emerged. She was diving straight down on the terrace - it's far west side - the exact spot where she had fought her way down the steps to the garden.

The light picked out little black specks as the plane ploughed through the gushing air towards the ground. The specks started to move; it appeared there were still large numbers of people out on the terrace. The party obviously hadn't stopped in her absence.

She didn't intend them any harm, not physically anyway. She wanted them to watch.

The ground was now hurtling towards her; the plane began to shake in a way she hadn't felt before. The noise of the air gushing past her was now almost as loud as the engine had been. She smiled through clenched teeth as it became difficult to keep her eyes open; the rush of air was so powerful her eyelids could barely hold up against it.

She wasn't worried, why should she be, she knew what she was doing - a little more than she realised.

As the ground became so close that she could make out each step from the terrace to the garden, she wrenched the stick back towards her and flung the throttle full forward. The noise from the engine roaring into action was deafening. As the plane instantly responded, it was as if her stomach was climbing out of her mouth; she had never felt forces like it.

The plane violently drew level with the ground; the surge of air as it passed over the terrace was hurricane force, the ground under her seemed to explode, and there was a tremendous smash of things hitting the plane that had been scooped into the air. Something warm and soft struck her cheek and then fell onto her lap. She only caught a glimpse of the house as it passed by her right hand side, and for a moment she thought there was water running down it; she quickly realised it was glass as every single window in the building blew out.

Tearing over the other end of the terrace, her attention had been distracted momentarily by the activity below and she only then became aware of the trees heading straight for her. That was it; she made no attempt to avoid them. She knew she couldn't anyway, she was going too fast; in the instant she had left, she breathed a relaxed sigh.

Taking her hand off the stick she reached down to find out what had fallen into the cockpit. Raising it up so she could see it, she laughed out loud; not a polite conversational laugh, her real laugh from deep within her - it was a toupee.

Those who were there had never seen a plane crash before - not many people had. The trees lit up in a ball of fire and splintering wood. Some guests heard strange swooping sounds in the sky above; it was parts of the propeller that had sheared off as the plane struck the trees - still spinning, flying over their heads.

CHAPTER IV

WATERLOO

When you go to bed, lying down in a dark bedroom, you close your eyes. As they are adjusting to seeing nothing, flowing and ebbing coloured patterns stream across the blackness as your vision begins to cool down, and tries to get used to not seeing light anymore.

It was rather like that, with one or two differences. Mary was not staring at black, but at perfect white - gleaming and bright.

On it went, and on. She had no body, no arms, no legs, no beating heart, no breathing chest, nothing. There was just one colour all around her; just like when you're in bed, lying perfectly still as the waking world drifts away - and you have no body anymore, just a colour.

As this went on, the serene whiteness began to appear to have depth, rather than appear purely as a solid wall of colour. Darker tones emerged here and there from time to time, as if it was made up of thick liquid. Whenever it did this, she felt something. It wasn't easy to describe, but it was a bit like when someone asks you a difficult question while you're very tired; your head throbs just for a moment as you strive for an answer. It was a bit like that, slightly painful each time.

She began to learn that when they appeared, she could keep the dark shades around for longer if she wanted, but in order to do so she had to concentrate hard on them. This was very painful, so she couldn't keep one around for very long. As it happened more frequently, however, she began to get better at it.

Each time they appeared she would try to make them stay a little longer, and each time she did they got more colourful - they even started to take on shapes. For a moment she thought she saw a window in one, but it wasn't like any window she had ever seen; it had panes of glass that seemed to stretch forever in every direction. It had no edge she could see but each time the window appeared amongst the colours, it got bigger and bigger, as if she was seeing more of it each time.

Then, something changed.

They were the most painful colours she had ever tried to keep around, but she couldn't help herself from trying harder, despite the pain, as they yielded much more interesting shapes. While they took form, she realised that amongst them was a face. It was the face of her mother, looking blankly at her. The windows were still there, but behind the image of her mother. It became so painful to concentrate on her that Mary exhausted herself and the image vanished.

Mary couldn't think about anything, it was just not possible; there was only the colours and nothing more.

Mary saw the colours many times, but only the window continued to appear in them, until once again, a large grouping of shades came along. They were painful from the outset. With all her might she tried to look at them, and they took form slowly; as they did, she saw her mother once again. She was still looking straight at her.

It lasted a lot longer this time, and the colours seemed to bring sounds with them. Murmurings at first; her mother's mouth wasn't moving - she just kept on staring. The murmurings got louder and suddenly her mother spoke. It was only softly, but from watching her lips, Mary could tell what she was saying.

Her voice was calm and measured. "You'll get what you need . . . you'll get what you need."

The colours didn't come after that; they never came again, but at least there was no pain either.

Once, Mary was dwelling on this and, deciding there was no need to watch for colours anymore, she closed her eyes.

There was black; for the first time, it was all black.

Slowly, she began to find herself able to think more and more.

'How did I do that?' she asked herself.

'I have eyes I can close?'

For a long time she considered opening them, but she couldn't remember how she had closed them in the first place. She thought long and hard about what it had felt like; there were moments she felt she came close to recollecting, and then the thought ebbed away again. Eventually she remembered that she had just thought about it, and then done it, so that's what she did. She thought about opening her eyes - and she did.

They opened.

There was a brilliant bright white light, but it wasn't like the one before; it was harsh and it hurt. It hurt so badly that it was almost audible inside her head, as the light seemed to penetrate right through her eyes into the back of her skull. She was sure someone was shining a huge bright light at her, but she couldn't see anyone.

The bright light then became divided up with dark lines. As they became clearer she could see it was the windows again, but this time it was becoming very well defined, sharper and richer than ever. The harsh light began to subside, and with it, a noise she didn't even know was there.

She moved her head - she suddenly comprehended that she had a head! - and she saw the end of the window in the form of a wall stretching down in front of her. Then it hit the floor. She realised she was in a large white room, lying on her back in a bed and the windows were actually in the ceiling - the whole room had a decorative glass ceiling.

It hurt but she slowly turned her head sideways; next to her was a bed, which was empty - but beyond that was another bed with someone lying in it. Standing over them were two figures dressed in white; one was a man wearing a stethoscope, the other a young woman dressed a little like a maid, except with a navy blue dress under her white apron.

She was in hospital.

As the feeling came back to her body, she had once again expected to wake up dead, but she wasn't. She was in hospital; she had survived.

As she surveyed her new situation, it became apparent there were several other women dotted around the room. It was a pale white room, with a long dark-wood table running almost the entire length of its centre separating the two rows of beds. On the table were placed various flowers in glass pots, bowls of fruit and a whole array of little silver tools and neatly folded white cloths - even some decorative silver vases towards one end.

She tried to sit up. Her arm didn't hurt anymore, but it was bandaged up tight. Suddenly her forehead itched; she reached up to scratched it and found it too was bandaged.

A nurse ran past the end of her bed, glancing back at her as she ran. Mary's movement had been noticed. She pulled her pillows to the upright position and sat up as best she could.

It was a nice quiet place; everyone was talking so softly. The beds either side of her were empty, but beyond the one on her right some well-dressed individuals, probably family, sat talking quietly with another young patient. All around were little pale-faced nurses going about their business dutifully. They were very impressive young women, rather unadorned Mary thought but very smart and energetic; all with little watches, of similar design to Mary's, attached to their aprons, which they checked habitually.

The nurse that had ran past her returned, bringing with her an older, sterner little woman whose uniform was a little more impressive than the rest of the nurses. She glared at Mary unsympathetically, strode over and placed her fingers above and below Mary's eyes and, with a little more force than was necessary, peeled open her eyelids whilst inspecting each pupil. Turning back to the young nurse, standing considerately behind her, she said in a demanding drone, "Well she's more awake now than she's ever been - inform the doctor."

"Yes matron," was the response. The young nurse softly curtsied and trotted lightly away.

A cheerless, greying doctor with a slight hunch and big fish lips returned with the nurse.

He repeated the matron's actions but would not take his eyes away; he kept staring at Mary intensely.

There was a pause. Without moving any muscle on his face except his mouth, he spoke to her in an attention-seizing schoolmaster's voice.

"Can you tell me your full name?"

Mary tried to answer, but her mouth and throat were bone dry and no words came - she coughed and spluttered. The doctor hurriedly handed her a glass of water and she took a sip. It hurt to swallow but the gulp of water felt like it was wetting a desert, and after a few more sips, she found she could just about speak and be heard.

"Mary Elizabeth Dane."

"And do you remember how you got here?" he went on.

"No."

His brow furrowed a little more. "Do you remember what caused your injuries, Miss Dane?"

"Yes," she coughed. "A . . . plane crash."

The doctor sat up. He seemed to relax a little and took away his fixed gaze. "When you were found, Miss Dane, you were suffering from a bad head injury; you were unconscious with deep cuts and a sprained right arm. You had lost a lot of blood but, remarkably, nothing more serious than that physically. Due to the nature of your - diagnosis - you were brought here. This is the Royal Waterloo Hospital for Children and Women in London."

His tone changed and became a little darker. "You are not to leave this room unescorted. Under no circumstances are you to try to leave this hospital, do you understand? Your family has been informed of your recovery and will be here in due course."

Mary just nodded and she was left alone again. She had no idea of what to make of all this. She remembered everything, but her thoughts went no further than the room she lay in. Though in a strange place and in a situation she knew nothing about, she wasn't remotely anxious. She simply lay there, watching the nurses at work. It was as if a great and lifelong ache had been lifted from her.

Two long slow days went by, in a routine of simple meals and escorted walks up and down the long hospital ward. She longed to go outside and breathe in some fresh air, but was constantly told she wasn't allowed to leave the building, even under escort.

The inside of the hospital was a tranquil enough place but the longer nothing happened, the more her thoughts became troubled.

The calm serenity from which she had woken began to be replaced by the troubling question of what was going to happen now; it ran around in her head over and over with nowhere to go, and only generated more questions.

Why hadn't her family come to see her? She didn't expect them to be happy but at least their daughter was alive. But what were they going to do? It was the same damned situation all over again; the trouble was, as she lamented over and over, she had desperately wanted to die - that was the intention. In those short seconds as she flew over her parents' house, she knew she was committing suicide. Why not - with no future, why be alive?

These thoughts began to upset her with wearisome persistence. She began to feel robbed again. Death was what she wanted, and to die the way she wanted to live: it was perfect. Why was she still here? What was the only route out now? She looked up at the windows on the high ceiling; to jump off the roof? She fought off this thought the moment it appeared. Maybe there was still hope, maybe her parents had actually realised what they had been doing to her all these years, perhaps they could accept the person they now knew she was, and try and help her.

She was taking some comfort in these thoughts on the afternoon of her fourth day awake in the hospital, when a visitor she recognised arrived. She wasn't sure at first but when his black top hat was removed to reveal a perfectly spherical, mole-like head with it's combed over thinning greasy hair sat on arched shoulders, she was certain. He was having his cane, hat and coat taken away by a nurse; he very graciously thanked the young woman. He ran his hands over his head to flatten down what hair he had left and then rubbed them both together to warm them; holding them close to his chest as he did so, like a greedy shopkeeper spying an opportunity to fleece a vulnerable customer.

Without looking directly at her, he waddled over to Mary.

Everything about him was mole-like. Thick round glasses sat on the end of a fat little speckled nose and covered dark spindly eyes. He was a man who obviously enjoyed meals with too many courses. While he was in his late fifties, heavily brace up trousers rose over his portly stomach to a height much more indicative of a very elderly man.

There was already a little wooden chair next to Mary's bed, but he pulled up another. Sitting on it, he brought a dark leather document case up from his side and rested it on the other chair.

He still didn't look at her. He pulled out a few documents; carefully laying them on top of his case, he took a moment to study each of them one by one.

Mary began to feel uncomfortable; his breathing was slow, heavy and unnervingly audible as he calmly studied the pages. He was seemingly unaware of the intimidating atmosphere he was creating by not acknowledging her.

Very suddenly, he looked up at her.

"Good afternoon Miss Dane. We have never actually met but I believe you know who I am." His voice was deep and calm.

"You're my father's private solicitor, Mr Keynes. I remember your visits to the house when my uncle was having some trouble with his health, and you dealt with my grandmother later in her life . . . I believe."

He looked away; down at the pages in his hand, then back to her as he continued to speak. "Yes . . . that's quite correct." He softly cleared his throat with a gentle cough. "What I have to say is quite straightforward, so I won't strain you by staying very long."

Mary interrupted with a question, the earnestness of which surprised even her: "Are my mother and father here?"

He shuffled some papers and stared straight back at her, his eyes masked by the thickness of the lenses in his glasses.

"No," he said quickly, before continuing. "Now that your injuries have healed, they will not be coming here to see you. I have been sent instead to discuss your future."

Mary was confused.

"My future? I wasn't aware that I had one?"

"Of course you do, you're going to be fine - don't be so dramatic my girl," he said, almost soothingly. "After a great deal of deliberation, discussion and some persuading on my part, your parents have decided upon a course of action which - I think - leaves all parties concerned with the best possible outcome."

Mary began to lose track of the intent behind what he was saying. He was a consummate professional, that's why her father employed him.

"You have been charged, Miss Dane and found guilty of seventeen rather serious criminal charges. Luckily for you, your father was able to negate a few of the civil matters through close connections your family has both at home and here in London. Unfortunately, his influence does not extend into the armed forces, who are maintaining certain charges against you."

He looked purposefully at Mary and then back at his papers. "Enough evidence has been amassed," he went on, "to ensure that you are sentenced to a number of years of incarceration in a women's prison. However, in view of your actions immediately preceding and during your theft and subsequent destruction of army property - in addition to the apparent attempt on the lives of a number of people on the night in question - it has been the judgement of the leading practitioners who have examined you that you were not in full command of your faculties. Therefore, it could be argued a prison sentence would be . . . somewhat unsuitable."

What had transpired in the days since she had crashed her plane was now becoming all too clear. Of course this wasn't planned, how could it have been; she hadn't expected to be alive to answer for her actions. Now here she was being held up as a criminal - seemingly a murderer, if she understood some of what he had just said. She knew she hadn't intended to kill any of those people, but what else did it look like?

As she sat there and watched him, gently turning over a few of his papers, she didn't know what to say. This man, the police, the courts; they weren't going to understand what had led her to these actions. She was being made to feel shame, and it was working; guilt began to creep in as he continued his pronouncement.

"In view of this, your family feels compelled to accept my recommendation. You see Miss Dane, even if there were no charges being maintained against you, it is simply not safe to allow you to go home. What you displayed were not the actions of a rational young woman who is in full command of herself. So, everyone understands the help you need, to . . . to live as you should, that you cannot return to the way you were."

This was astonishing; she couldn't believe it. He

actually almost sounded like someone who understood. There was something she still didn't like about what he was saying; it was not quite clear yet where she would be going if not back to her parents' house.

'Where else is there?' she thought; but these issues seemed like trifles. Finally, it appeared, someone realised that she needed help.

He briskly placed his documents back in his case, but he didn't lock up the fastenings just yet. He turned to her again. The soothing nature in which he continued to speak didn't quite seem to match the rest of him; and the way he looked at her, in another situation, might have appeared patronising.

"Now that you are fit to travel," he went on, "tomorrow you will leave this hospital; under escort you will board a train at Kings Cross and journey up to Colchester, where you will take up residence at a medical facility at Severalls. It's brand new and very modern. They only opened it a couple of years ago.

"You will not be allowed to leave but - well, don't let that trouble you, you won't need to. It will be just like a new home," he said, cheerfully insincere. "It's a very special hospital you understand - they look after people who have problems and injuries you can't see with your eyes. It has a special name, they call it an asylum."

He paused. Mary stared at him, confused. She stammered a few bewildered questions.

"An asylum . . . I won't be allowed to leave? Did my parents really . . . how long will I have to stay there?"

"Yes, your parents understand you see. As for how long you have to stay there - well, it doesn't really matter does it? Once you get there you'll realise that you don't really need to leave. It's a remarkable place, they have everything and they practice the - the treatments they perform - well, it's the best in the Empire, maybe even in the world."

His soothing tone definitely didn't match what he was

saying; he was indeed a consummate professional.

"They can do wonderful things, Miss Dane."

That night, she used up all the tears she had left.

CHAPTER V

LUNCH

Early the following morning, the young nurses of the Royal Waterloo Hospital found a breathing corpse lying in Mary's bed. A reasonable breakfast of toasted bread and lumpy porridge was left uneaten. She had been told she would be met and escorted from the hospital at two thirty that afternoon, so she had to be washed and ready to leave by lunch time at the latest.

Hours passed, and by half past eleven she still hadn't moved a muscle; she just lay on her back, her heavily bloodshot eyes staring straight up at the windows in the ceiling, contemplating nothing at all.

Determined that she would be washed and ready whether she liked it or not, the Matron rounded up four nurses to pull her to her feet and drag her in her dank nightgown to the washroom.

She sat there, naked, limp as a dead fish; her lovely vivacious body now pale and taking on a drawn shape with the lack of life and proper nourishment. Her neck seemed to have no strength left in it; her head just hung off her shoulders. Vacant eyes faced the floor as the nurses bathed and scrubbed her clinically. She was certainly taking on the appearance of someone who looked like they belonged in an asylum.

Put in a plain black dress with a matching prickly scarf round her neck, she was lifted and laid onto her bed to await her escort. The last two nurses who placed her back on the mattress couldn't help but stand and look at her for one more moment before they turned away.

It was her eyes they couldn't stop looking at; they were so hauntingly lifeless. She was still breathing, but might as well have been a dead body. They didn't understand, how could they - they were just doing their job. Little wonder, they thought, that she was being taken to where they knew she was going.

There was nothing going through her mind anymore. While physically recovered, her bandages removed, there was no strength left in her body to twitch so much as a toe. Though conscious, all she could see were the windows again.

All the sounds in the room didn't register. Her head was void of thoughts. If anyone in the hospital had known her before all this, to see her now would have been like looking at a magnificent and beautiful clockwork toy, its mechanism completely unwound, broken, conspicuous by its unnerving stillness and silence.

Twelve thirty came and went without incident. Some visitors attended nearby beds, then departed with a few patients to a lounge further down the ward, leaving Mary almost alone save for a few passing nurses.

In her life Mary had met, over the years, one or two people whose voices she thought could cut through a glacier of ice. Not because they were especially loud; they just pierced through absolutely anything and made her pay instant attention.

Out of nowhere, one such voice now managed to penetrate even Mary's catatonic mind and shoot straight into her.

"Miss Mary Dane?"

The voice was female and Scottish, a rolling Falkirk accent. Something about it made Mary want to stand to attention; it acted almost like a cold shower on a woolly mind. For the first time that day she moved using her own strength and her eyes rolled sideways; the raw bloodshot whites felt sore, as they were moistened by the inside of her eyes for the first time in hours.

The imprint of the windows, etched into her vision, faded away into the background again - leaving only the image of one of the most impressive women Mary had ever seen in her life.

Standing right next to her bed, towering at a good six foot, was a proud, broad shouldered lady. Probably pushing sixty, her silver hair was fastened up tight behind her head and the remnant of the brunette it had once been stitched amongst it.

She gazed down at Mary sternly. She was wearing an extremely well kept and very smart medical uniform; a crisply pressed battleship grey dress down to her ankles, and over her shoulders a smooth crimson red cape attached to a white collar, fastened up over her neck with a single brass button. Streaming down from the back of her head was a white drape; Mary had only ever seen such a headdress once before, on a statue in church.

Mary didn't answer, but it didn't matter - somehow it seemed her visitor knew she had the right woman. The broad mouth that sat perched above her expansive, mole dotted, double chin moved again.

"I've come te take ye te lunch, get yerself on yer feet and we'll be on our way."

There was a long pause as Mary just looked at her blankly. This woman's voice had kick-started a cog turning inside Mary's head again, but it was going to take more than that to bring her back.

Mary felt she knew perfectly well where this woman had come to take her. While she was aware everyone around her thought she was insane, the self courage that had got her into this situation was one of the few things that had not completely deserted her, giving her the strength to respond she quietly replied.

"Don't lie to me."

The visitor didn't seem to like this.

"I know where you're taking me," Mary went on, slowly. "You might think I'm mad but I'm not a bloody fool, so please do not treat me as one."

Her little indignant retort over, the visitor's expression didn't change, but the conviction in the way she spoke certainly rose to a new level.

"I've never told a word of a lie in my life missy," she replied, "an am certainly no star-tin now. I'm not from where you think I am, an you're not due to be picked up by them for another two hours. I said I'm here te take ye oot te lunch and that's what am goin te doo."

There was something about the principle in this woman's voice that drew Mary up from her bed; stiffly she sat up but her neck hurt to move, so she wearily turned her whole upper body to face the visitor. Mary had never met anyone like this; she could feel herself being carried along by the commanding nature of the woman's voice, but nonetheless, she was still suspicious - who wouldn't be.

Mary stood and, hunched over with exhaustion, followed her.

As they left the room and began to march down a corridor, all sorts of thoughts raced through Mary's now rapidly awakening mind.

'Maybe this is what they do, send this majestic beast of a woman to trick you into thinking you're being taken for lunch so you'll not put up a fight.' She could have believed that very easily, and was entertaining the idea, but there was something about the way this woman had looked her in the eye and told her that she wasn't lying.

Mary wanted to believe her, but after the last few days, how could she trust anyone, and even if she was lying what could she do about it anyway?

They moved rapidly to a huge dark-red carpeted entrance foyer, with clerks scribbling behind imposing desks and nurses pacing through from all directions. Huge oak stairwells stretched from the floor up into the building; people were streaming in and out and the cool rush of the drizzly London streets breezed in with a chill through the huge open doors.

A porter was standing dutifully at the run up to the exit, holding a beige mackintosh raincoat.

"Get this on yer missy," said the visitor. "It's been raining all mornin and the air's damp."

Mary fed her arms into the coat and it was gently placed on her shoulders. As she looked around, what she saw was disarmingly commonplace; smartly dressed pedestrians routinely going about their daily business. No one was paying any attention to her and there was no fuss whatsoever. For days her every move had been monitored and she had been warned repeatedly not to even leave her bed un-escorted.

Even though she was with this unknown matriarch, she somehow didn't feel as watched anymore.

Now coated up, she turned to her visitor and asked cautiously, "After lunch, will you be bringing me back here to be taken away again?"

Not even looking at her, but concentrating on receiving her gloves from a waiting porter, her visitor replied cryptically, "That'll all depend, on whether ye enjoy yer lunch or not."

On that, she strode out with Mary as quick at her heels as she could be. She hadn't been outside in days; the fresh crisp air was like a refreshing piece of cold fruit on a hot summer's day. Pausing before the first step down to the street, she inhaled deeply.

Looking down at the street, she spotted, parked neatly and half up on the pavement, a shining black Rolls Royce limousine. She had seen motorcars before, but this was the largest and smartest she had ever come across. Standing to attention just to the left of the handle of the rear door was a fit young man in a green military uniform and a brass-badged cap. He was obviously waiting for someone extremely important.

As they approached the last two steps, walking side by side, Mary prepared to take the lead from her visitor. To her amazement this impressive lady kept marching straight ahead toward the waiting car, making no effort to turn left or right down the pavement.

'This thing can't be for us,' Mary thought.

The visitor led Mary straight up to the rear door; the

waiting soldier saluted, and swiftly opened the door for her. "In ye get missy!" came the order.

Mary didn't know what to think. She didn't necessarily dislike this unexpected treatment but couldn't have been more bewildered. She obeyed, albeit cautiously. Slowly putting her head through the open car door; she saw it was completely empty, and climbed in. Settling into the plush black leather seats, her visitor clambered in beside her. The door slammed and the young soldier plonked himself onto the front seat. He started the engine and they immediately sped away from the hospital entrance out onto the rain glistened London streets towards Waterloo Bridge.

The rain had fallen heavily overnight whilst the capitol was asleep. Though looking freshly washed there was an earthy smell to London on wet summer mornings, which always felt on the verge of becoming offensive; especially where gutters hadn't properly drained, causing manure that hadn't yet been scraped from the roads to become soggy and spray up all over the place if the drivers of swift moving motorcars didn't see the smatterings approaching.

This particular driver seemed adept at evading the unpleasantness at speed.

"There's been an accident on Westminster Bridge ma'am," he called out in his wide, south London accent. "We'll have to go the long way."

Mary didn't know why, but she suddenly felt very important. The car picked up speed, and while her travelling companion couldn't have been calmer, there was a definite sense of urgency in the driving that fed Mary's suspicions.

There weren't many motorcars in London, or anywhere for that matter. As they sped along, the masses of cyclists and horse drawn carriages all seemed to make way. Even trams slowed down to allow this car to pass safely.

She began to relax a little more as the car turned east, and moved parallel to the direction of Kings Cross station, making no attempt to turn towards it.

Mary had seen pictures of the state visits of European dignitaries and royals to Britain, always arriving in London in a cavalcade of motorcars; she thought she was a bit silly for thinking of it right at this moment, but that's honestly what this reminded her of. Her situation now actually began to thrill her a little, as she was raced at great speed through the stately streets of the capitol.

She had, of course, been to London many times before, but always to take part in the predictable itinerary her family had prepared; which usually involved copious amounts of shopping and never going anywhere until the men did. Even then, it was only to the same few select private houses and huge hotels. She had never been allowed out on her own to see so much of London at once.

They came to Piccadilly Circus; a place she had heard of but never actually seen. Huge attractively lit lettering adorned the faces of the buildings that flew by as the car sped through the black and white clothed masses, who leapt aside like a monstrous flock of startled penguins to let them pass. There were too many of the gaudy illuminated signs to read, but the biggest one she caught read: *'Bovril and Schweppes Lime Juice.'* She had absolutely no idea what either of those things were.

As the car turned and slowed, then slid down a side street, Mary caught a glimpse of a pretty young girl taking an extremely smartly dressed old man up some stairs to one of the houses. 'Obviously her father,' she thought.

Through Haymarket streams of women dressed in ankle length plaid skirts and matching jackets were promenading with unnatural gaiety. The dominant feature of this neighbourhood appeared to be hats; huge sophisticated hats of every eclectic style imaginable; Mary spotted straw hats, church hats and veiled hats amongst them. Some appeared to be so expansive that they took up more room on the pavement than the person wearing them.

As they cornered towards Westminster, the car braked suddenly to avoid hitting a woman guiding a bicycle with one arm and rearranging her enormous hat with the other.

Mary, drained of thought, struggled not to let this new situation simply wash over her like she was a dumb spectator to its theatrics, and tried to summon the strength to consider what this was all about.

Minutes ago she had been a condemned woman; now she was here.

She suddenly regarded her travelling companion more closely. She wore the uniform of a matron, but Mary had never seen one with a crimson shoulder cape before. Then as she looked closer, on this magnificent lady's left breast was a row of three medal ribbons.

'Has this woman fought in a war of some kind?' she wondered.

"Where are we going?" Mary tried to ask as politely as possible, in the hopes of continuing to get honest answers.

"Ye'll see soon enough, we're almost there."

The towering Palace of Westminster soon eased into view; Mary had never been this close to it. Big Ben soared, almost protectively, overhead, partially lit against a grey drizzly sky.

Hastily, they turned sharply away past a small park and on down a main road bordered by large houses. The driver slowed, and made to turn left into a side street. It looked like another upmarket residential area at first, but as the car turned in, Mary saw a throng of smartly uniformed policemen backing out of the way to let them to go through.

She felt she should recognise this scene. As they drove on past the policemen standing firmly at attention, Mary looked up to see if she could spot a street name. She found it instantly; it was Downing Street.

She was dumbfounded. She looked immediately to her companion, confused but expectant. The great lady turned and looked at her, but there was a little knowing kindness in those stern eyes now, and a half smile at one end of the broad mouth.

The car pulled up outside number 12. A policeman flung open Mary's door, stood back and saluted. Mary thought she should salute back as she climbed out of the car, but she didn't quite know how.

"This way missy," called her companion. They strode slowly up to the gleaming black door of number 12 Downing Street. "Now don't you be worried about a thing missy," was the advice, a little more nurturing now than stern. "They don't stand on ceremony here quite as much as they do over there at number ten. Just feel welcomed, go where you're asked and enjoy your lunch."

"Wh - why am I here?" Mary stammered.

"I told ye, te have lunch." The huge door opened and her companion put her arm round Mary and guided her in. "It will all be explained to yer in here."

The door closed behind them and they were in a charming black and white entrance foyer. Mary had her coat taken from her and she was politely invited by an old white-gloved butler to "step this way".

Down clean and smartly carpeted corridors, she came to a large office, done out with beautifully soothing duck-egg white furnishings, enclosed by wood panelled walls.

A large desk sat at the opposite end of the room, in front of a window. Mary was led to a set of mahogany chairs and seated in front of a round table, decorated in the middle with bottle green floral patterns. Arranged on the table was a selection of finger sandwiches, two pots of tea, scones, jam, clotted cream, some mouth watering looking pastries and sugared fruits.

"Now, ye make yourself comfortable there, I'll be just over here, am sure yer host will be along shortly."

With that, her companion strode to a far corner of the room and made herself comfortable in a big armchair by a side window that overlooked a garden.

As the door closed the room fell perfectly silent, with

the exception of a huge old grandfather clock that slowly ticked away in the background.

Mary didn't know what to do; taking in her surroundings, it was clear this was the office of someone of high import. The door promptly opened again, the white gloved doorman strode in.

"Excuse me ma'am," he said, "but your host has been unavoidably detained. He sends his sincerest regrets and insist you start lunch without him. He will be along presently."

"Nee mind missy," announced her companion as she rose from her chair. "Let's get some o this down ye, here - " she said, handing Mary a plate, " - after that hospital I expect you're ready for something a wee bit more spiriting. Don't worry about politeness; if your host says to eat, you eat. Make sure ye get some o' that ham in those sandwiches, it's fresh off the bone - rebuild yer strength."

Mary didn't realise how hungry she was until she tucked into her first sandwich. Extravagant fine foods had never held much interest for her - she had been exposed to the finest French cuisine from the hands of her family's chef since she was a baby - this dainty but generous affair, however, was extremely welcome after the last week. The lovely warm fruit-filled scones went down a treat; the clotted cream was thicker than she was used to, but it was incredibly smooth. She said so to her companion and was told, "That's the real stuff missy, made in Kelso up in the borders, none o' that Devon nonsense."

Happily nourished and by now very much aware that these people were not yet taking her to an asylum, Mary began to ponder her curious new situation with interest. She had been told if she enjoyed her lunch she would not be taken back to the hospital - and she had very much enjoyed her lovely little lunch - but what now?

She trusted in her companion's word that she would know soon enough. And she did. Loud footsteps began to approach the office door and her companion requested her to stand.

No sooner had she got to her feet, Mary saw the door fly open at the hands of the butler and in strode a tall thin elegant man; perhaps in his forties, with a big forehead, a parrot like nose and a thin mouth. A natural, relaxed and friendly expression lay across his face and the eyes were filled with a casual interest and intellect.

"Miss Mary Dane I presume?" he said courteously.

"Yes?" she replied, as friendly as possible.

"Please accept my apologies for missing lunch," he went on. "An occupational hazard in my profession. How do you do." He took her hand. "My name is Sir Edward Grey, I'm His Majesty's Secretary of State for Foreign Affairs, I'm sure you've never heard of me."

A little smile put Mary at ease following the grandiose introduction.

"How do you do," she replied quietly.

Gesturing to the desk, he invited her to sit. He strode intently to the chair on the other side; once seated he opened a neatly placed dark brown file that had been arranged for him on the desk. Carefully, he took out a series of crisp, freshly printed papers and spilt them in to two piles.

He then thumbed through a couple of drawers looking for a pen.

"You'll have to forgive me," he said offhandedly. "This isn't actually my office - its owner very kindly loans it to me from time to time. The fewer people know you're here the better, you see."

Pulling out a black fountain pen and two tiny pots of ink, one black, one red, he sat facing Mary, now giving her his full attention.

"Miss Dane, thank you very much indeed for coming to see me; I hope the journey over was pleasant?"

Mary didn't know what to say; she was confused, exhausted and overwhelmed - and the fear of the impending situation still loomed over her.

"I imagine you're a little mystified," he continued. "I apologise for the secrecy under which you have been brought here but it was absolutely necessary. Now let me see - " he studied the paper in his hand. "To come straight to the point, I am in possession of the full facts of your situation. I understand you're headed for the hospital at Severalls?"

"Yes," was all Mary could muster.

"My sympathies. There will be almost certainly no return from there." He looked at her forlornly. "You know that don't you."

It wasn't a question; he could tell she knew what Severalls was.

Mary nodded. Her eyes strained as if about to produce tears, but there weren't any; she had long exhausted them. Her situation, however, was still no less overwhelming to her.

Grey could see it in her, so he got straight to what he wanted to say. "I have here a list of the charges brought against you, Miss Dane."

To baffle Mary even further his next words were spoken as if he were quietly impressed. "It's most extensive: theft and destruction of military equipment, dangerous flying, twelve thousand pounds worth of property destruction, twenty five counts of injuries to innocent bystanders that range from broken limbs, a couple of concussions and . . . even one man who appears to be filing a claim for damages after receiving a scratched cornea, inflicted by a flying strawberry flavoured French macaroon purchased from Angelina, Paris."

Grey looked up at her, still strangely relaxed and unperturbed by what he was reading. "My wife would very much like to know how your mother gets fresh macaroons from Paris to your home in time for them to still be edible?"

Mary had no idea where this was going, or how he could be so relaxed, even faintly amused by her criminal record. She simply thought hard and answered him as best she could. "My mother's aunt visits Paris frequently, she buys them on the morning of her last day and returns to London on the Pullman Boat Train Express. It's almost twice as fast as most other trains and it's easier to avoid your hand luggage being inspected by customs. When she gets to Victoria she travels straight to my parents' estate by motorcar and they are usually served the following evening."

"I see, well . . . thank you for that but I don't think I'll tell my wife after all, I don't want her paying outrageous sums for a Pullman just to get fresh macaroons from Angelina's." He smiled, Mary felt a little more relaxed, and couldn't help but be slightly amused by the way he was talking; her crimes seemed like a welcome dose of diverting trivia to him.

"Miss Dane, I wonder if you wouldn't mind telling me - have you given much thought to your future?"

"I don't have one, do I sir," she replied coldly.

"We'll, I'm hoping you'll let me be the judge of that," he said confidently. Then raising his voice to an official tone, he went on, "Miss Dane, I have a high ranking member of His Majesty's armed forces who is prepared to swear in a court of law that your actions on the night of Monday the eighth were the accidental result of a mechanical fault during a night time training exercise. That you were in no way malicious, were and are according to army doctors completely sane, and in perfect psychological health."

Mary was by now exhaustingly weary of false hope; but this was the Foreign Secretary and she could tell he was deadly serious.

"Sir," she uttered. "I don't know what you mean, why are you telling me this? You're not joking are you, you're not . . . this isn't some cruel game my parents are . . . "

She raised her hand to her mouth, despite the lack of tears she had to stop herself from crying out loudly. Her companion appeared at her side with a hand on her shoulder and a silk handkerchief to comfort her.

"No Mary, I am most certainly not. This said officer was present at your parents' engagement that evening, as a chaperone for a young lady, and he didn't see a mad woman trying to kill her family, he saw someone pull off an extremely difficult and until now experimental manoeuvre with flawless perfection, from high altitude, at night, and immediately wanted to know who that person was."

He leaned forward. "Mary . . . I can't imagine what drove you to do such a thing, but no one has ever flown an aircraft like that before - it's just a pity those trees were in the way - you obviously knew what you were doing, didn't you?" She nodded and he continued. "I also have a report here regarding an investigation into His Majesty's Royal Aircraft Factory, where you took the aircraft from. One Lieutenant Jack Raynham has come forward and put us in the full picture regarding your clandestine lessons with him over the past two years."

"It wasn't his fault, sir, I - "

"Please don't trouble yourself," he calmly interrupted with a raised hand. "There will be no repercussions; he's actually been given a position as a senior instructor."

There was a long silent pause as Mary struggled to wake up out of herself and desperately tried to take in what he was saying.

"Sir . . . why would you . . . anyone do this for me?" Mary spoke softly, trying to control her whirling emotions. " - and even if I don't go to the hospital, where else do I have - a woman my age, I . . . my parents, I can't go back to them - I can't!"

"They don't know anything about this arrangement Mary," he interjected firmly, "and won't unless you want them to. As for the hospital . . . well, I'm willing to do this for you, if you would kindly consent to doing something for me."

"What can I do?" She half wailed.

"I'd like you to accept my next proposition."

"Wh - what's that?" She asked cautiously.

"I'd like to offer you a job," he said very sincerely.

There was a long silence. Mary didn't know how to react.

"What do you . . . as what, sir?" She spluttered.

He spoke to her with the utmost candour. "Mary, as a pilot in His Majesty's Royal Flying Corps."

Her shattered nerves and spent mind left her only a blank expression with which to receive this statement. A brief inane gawp passed her lips, then back to blank and confused.

"A pilot . . . how?"

"Your instructor has provided us with a complete and detailed overview of what training you have received: it adds up to just over two hundred flying hours. Mary, the standard requirement for a new pilot is currently twenty-four. That makes you one of the most experienced flyers in the Empire right now. I can count on one hand those with a similar level of experience, much less who can get an aircraft to perform high risk manoeuvres at night, and regardless of your motives - we currently have a dire need of people with these skills."

She desperately wanted to believe him, but she knew it could never be true, she kept looking for clues that this was some sort of trick. "But sir - women aren't allowed to serve in the army."

His next response was a little slower; he was choosing his words very carefully.

"We . . . currently have an operational squadron, under secondment to a new government department. It is a highly secret affair and operates outside of the Flying Corps current order of battle. It doesn't appear in any newspapers or books . . . or anything in fact. It operates in secret you understand, no one, with the exception of a few good men, me, yourself and Matron Wallace here knows it exists.

"That being the case, if you agree, you will have to sign the official secrets act and I'm afraid you won't be able to tell anyone about your new occupation. But, this secrecy does afford us the luxury of being able to be a little more . . . irregular in how we operate. Only the very best in their particular fields get picked to join this squadron; it doesn't matter if they're male, female or where they come from, as long as we know we can trust them. There are already several women working for the Flying Corps as part of this detachment, though you'll be the first female pilot. You'll be employed with a temporary commissioned rank, but with full pay. After a certain probationary period with the squadron, if you are indeed deemed fit by the CO, you will be granted a full commission and permanent employment."

Though drained and bewildered, a little part of Mary began to glow again - he was perfectly serious. She didn't have the strength to cartwheel around the room. She barely had it within herself to smile; but she did, and in her response, though still laden with disbelief, she had never uttered more sincere words in her life.

"Yes . . . sir, I would like that very much."

He beamed gratifyingly. "I'm glad Miss Dane. I have a few documents I will need you to sign, which I will push through to the relevant authorities straight away. After which Matron Wallace will travel with you to Victoria, you will get a train south to an aerodrome - I'm afraid I can't say where - you'll be issued with your uniform, equipment and be allocated an aircraft. All being well we should be able to get you flown out to your squadron tomorrow, if the weather holds. Once there you will have to pass an army medical of course, but your recent activities will be taken into account."

"That quickly?" Mary asked, rushing to keep up.

"Yes, if we can't get you to the squadron tomorrow it may be some time before we get another opportunity you see . . . you'll understand why when you get there. I'm afraid I have told you as much as I can about where you're going, but you will be well taken care of. The Matron here will have a little more for you over the next day or so. Before I wish you good luck, I suppose I should ask if you have any further questions for me - if I can answer them of course?"

She thought she ought to, but couldn't think of a thing. An hour earlier her mind and body had let go, she was willing to slip away into oblivion, she had been beaten. Now it was like waking up from the longest un-restful sleep of her life. Her thoughts couldn't process quickly enough; she kept asking herself if she was dreaming. She had never known such luck; that such good fortune existed in the world.

Suddenly her thoughts turned to the people, who, if they were present, would have put an end to this whole thing before it started, and would never have allowed her to make such a decision for herself.

"You mentioned sir, that my family would know nothing of this?"

"No, as far as they are concerned you're where they sent you, up in Colchester. Should they make any enquiries they will be told your condition is stable but that you are not well enough to receive visitors. Your father's influence does not extend into my portion of the world. If you wish, they can be told more elaborate cover stories but never the actual truth - but I should imagine that's not something that troubles you just now," he finished slowly.

She shook her head.

Grey turned to three freshly prepared documents on his desk; one by one he laid them in front of her and invited her to sign at the bottom. Two were full of tiny, vigorously typed Windsor-serif letters that she could barely read. The last one was a little more interesting.

"That one is for you to take away with you, Miss Dane . . . or perhaps I should now call you Pilot Officer Dane," he said. She picked it up; it was firm and made that delightful crisp brittle sound a stiff, brand new sheet of paper makes when it is held.

At the top was printed a jet-black crest of the British crown. At the bottom were a number of extremely elaborate signatures and small type. But in the middle lay big printed words that, much to the delight of Matron Wallace, Mary couldn't help illicitly reading over and over again on the long journey south from London.

This is to certify that Acting Pilot Officer
Mary Elizabeth Dane
Two Squadron
Has graduated at the Central Flying School, and is a qualified
flyer in the Royal Flying Corps.

CHAPTER VI

NAVIGATOR

It was barely an airfield at all. Somewhere in the flat, plain countryside south of London, Mary had been shown into a small square room, with a narrow mirrored wardrobe, a little table and a canvass bed, all inside a long wooden hut. While she had been both bemused and excited when her head hit the pillow, she found herself waking from one of the most restful night's sleep she had had in months.

Sitting up expectantly, she peeked out the window next to her bed. A fresh morning was brewing outside. There were a few other huts off to the right, a lone windsock in the distance and parked up across a flat stretch of lawn from the window she was looking out of, were two aeroplanes - one of which was going to be hers; she felt an upbeat tingle in her stomach at this thought.

Her body would still take some time to recover from the last few days, but her limbs were on the mend and colour was returning to her cheeks. The wounds on the inside would take a lot longer however - not that she fully understood it yet.

She still couldn't believe her new situation was real, and maybe she wouldn't until she was up there, flying for a living. Nevertheless, here she was.

There was a knock at the door; in strode Matron Wallace with a breakfast tray.

"Mornin Pilot Officer. Now I don't want ye te think ye'll be gettin' this treatment every mornin'. Usually ye go doon te the mess for breakfast with everyone else but, given the ordeal o' the last few days, yer commandin' officer thought ye might like breakfast in bed te celebrate yer new job."

"Thank you," Mary replied as she sat up straight. "I

can't say I have ever eaten in my bed before."

The tray was laid in front of her, on which was a pot of tea, a glass of fresh orange juice, then a round white plate with a large, toasted, heavily buttered muffin in the middle, over which cascaded a hillock of scrambled eggs, looking like they were topped off with a little pinch of salt.

"It's your CO's favourite breakfast; he says to give you that and ye'll be ready for anything today. Incidentally, breakfast in bed is something he swears by as a reward. He's a stickler for regulations otherwise but if ye've done something te impress him, and that's no' as easy as most people think, ye may find yerself woken like this."

The Matron placed a small silver tin on the bedside table next to Mary before continuing. "Now, you fly out this morning at half past ten, that gives ye an hour an' a half to get ready. Yer uniform for today is in the wardrobe, the rest has been sent on ahead. There's a wee ditty bag in the drawer to put yer wash items and effects in." She gestured to the small silver tin. "There's a small bath through there for ye te wash. Be ready for ten and I'll come and fetch ye."

"Thank you." Mary thought she ought to salute; she tried but the Matron was obviously not impressed.

"Aye well, we'll work on that, but ye don't need te salute in bed."

"I'll remember that."

"See that ye do."

Half heartedly hiding a little grin, the Matron left Mary to her breakfast. And what an experience it was, her first breakfast in bed. The tea was strong and revitalising, the orange juice, freshly pressed. The trio of muffin, salty butter and eggs was a match made in heaven. She felt almost mischievous eating in bed; it felt like such a wonderful, delicious indulgence. She saw the logic straight away.

Her attention fell on the little silver tin next to her bed; 'effects', the Matron had called it. The tin itself had no markings and a simple pull-off lid. Opening it, Mary found it full of white, torn loincloth. Scooping it up, she found it was heavy. Obviously there was something wrapped up to keep it safe.

Unravelling it carefully, having no idea what it was, her heart skipped and she let in a little gasp as she saw what was inside; it was her beloved little watch. Still without a scratch and showing nine fifteen. She pressed it to her bosom; being reunited with a lifelong friend was a comfort in these strange new surroundings.

There wasn't much hot water for a bath, but she didn't mind, though the cold made her arm ache a little. The cut was fully healed and it didn't hurt to move but there were obviously a few deeper wounds that still needed some time to mend.

Drying off, she buttoned up over her chest a white cotton shirt. It was a man's shirt, with no obvious alterations made for her. Her breasts sat underneath, pushing the shirt out and making it look a little small on her. 'No matter,' she thought, 'the uniform will press it all down. 'Of course! I should have a uniform, shouldn't I?'

She slowly opened the wardrobe door; it reminded her straight away of the feeling she got when she used to retrieve her old tunic from the wardrobe in the estate cottage. Except this time, an array of brand new garments greeted her and she needed no imagination to embellish them.

First to catch her eye, stowed at the bottom, was a brand new pair of shiny brown brogue officers boots. They were the most well made and sturdy boots she had ever seen; they would have been a prized possession back when she rode horses.

A pair of smooth dark-beige trousers and braces was next. Then to her delight, the centrepiece, hanging in the middle, was a flawless military green RFC officer's tunic; with a rank pip on each shoulder, the letters Royal Flying Corps embroidered at the top of one arm and a gleaming set of gold pilots wings stitched to the left breast. Jack had occasionally worn one like it and was the kind she had admired most. It was streamlined, compact and easy to move in. She had been told it was nicknamed the 'maternity jacket', as it lacked external buttons that could catch on the wires or structure of an aircraft.

She took great care and delight in putting on the whole ensemble. The little wardrobe mirror proudly displayed to her what she had become. It was a new experience for her; she had never been one for admiring her own appearance, not surprising given she had rarely owned anything she was happy to wear.

She beamed with joy, and then laughed out loud, but had to try and control herself as it made her chest hurt. She knew it was such a silly thought, that's why it made her laugh - but she couldn't help thinking that the figure that greeted her in the mirror was somewhat heroic looking.

She was there for some time; giggles aside, she had never felt more proud of herself in her life.

Her long blonde curls still draped over her shoulders. Panicking all of a sudden, she realised she had nothing to tie her hair back with; then she remembered the loincloth used to wrap her watch. She opened the tin, unravelled it again and tore away a strip. It was primitive but did the job.

Securing her hair back as best she could, she looked about as smart as anyone in the service. Knowing she had to be on her way, she couldn't resist one more little gaze in the mirror.

'If my family could see me now,' she thought. Another little giggle made its way up to her chest. 'What would they think?

She was enjoying laughing so much. She was feeling things again, except now there was no guilt in the pleasure she was taking; no one around her telling here it was wrong, or making her feel selfish, or ashamed.

Fear, however, was still in plentiful supply. As she

thought of the coming days, she knew she still had a lot to prove; anxious thoughts like, 'What if I'm no good, what if I make a mistake, what will others actually think of a female pilot?' ran through her mind.

It was all too good to be true; she was terrified of ruining it all and losing what she had been given by doing something wrong. This morning's salute was a petty affair, but it started to worry her that she had made a bad impression.

Putting what she had in her ditty bag and throwing it over her shoulder, she put on her green peaked officers cap and was let out of her room when the Matron returned.

"This way, Pilot Officer," the Matron said proudly.

They left through a door in the side of the hut. A fresh morning enveloped them. It was dead quiet, except for a few birds. The occasional ping from the distant windsock tapping against the metal pole on which it hung was the only sign there was even a breath of wind. The sun was casting a nourishing warm glow on the moist, trim grass, just like it did every fresh summer's morning; but Mary had never noticed it before. Her mind seemed clearer now than it ever had been in her life.

As she walked, her future resting simply in the skill of her own two hands, her clothes smart and undemanding with everything she had in the world in a small bag over her shoulder - she felt as free as a bird.

"We'll there ye go, number eight, that's yours." The Matron pointed to the closest aircraft.

Regarding it as though it were some holy altar, Mary approached it slowly and with great reverence. She ran her hands along the front and paused to take in the whole profile as she got to the two cockpits. It was similar to the one she had learned to fly in, except much newer and she could have sworn it was slimmer somehow.

It was mostly the trademark dark army green but didn't have any of the usual markings on it. The chrome exhausts were hardly blackened and the seats and controls were all gleaming. Leaning into the cockpit, running her hand over the switches and smooth freshly cast brass dials, excited her sense of touch.

Standing there in her uniform, like Jack had done, she felt she now matched her surroundings, instead of feeling like a guest in the presence of this machine. If only he could see her now, they would have to salute each other - 'Ah the salute!' she thought.

Before she met anyone else, she wanted the Matron to show her how to salute properly - she didn't want to repeat this morning's embarrassment. The Matron had exactly the same idea, and walking to meet her with some urgency she said quietly, "The field CO is coming over. He'll want te brief ye a little before you leave, when he walks up salute him."

"How?"

"Nothing te it, just stand upright, imagine yer drawing the handle of a tea pot in the air with yer right hand, and the handle joins yer hat at yer forheed."

"What's a forheed?"

"This bit here," said the Matron, urgently pointing to the right side of her forehead. "Hold it there, count to two and then put it straight back down to your side - here we go, c'mon now."

Mary bounded dutifully back to the other side of the plane. There was indeed a grey haired, pencil thin officer with a cane striding over. She stood nervously to attention.

"Good morning Matron," he said softly, "and good morning to our new officer."

Mary drew the handle of a tea pot in the air, it reached her head, then as she began to count to two, to her amazement, he did exactly the same; two came and they put their hands back to their sides at the same time.

He quickly studied her appearance, noting things as he went, right down to her boots, then looking back up to her eyes.

"Good," he said, seemingly satisfied. "How do you do." He put out his hand, and Mary shook it firmly.

The officer strode casually towards the plane. "I take it you haven't found your steed wanting?"

Mary watched him as he gestured to the plane while strolling away; suddenly the Matron's shoulder was in her back urging her to follow him.

"Yes sir, quite - " Mary answered, " - quite beautiful."

He turned and paused a moment at her choice of words but then, still agreeable, he continued. "Yes she certainly is, not long out of the works, but she has had some running in. Tell me, what did you train in?"

"I believe it was called a B.E.2, sir."

"Ahh," he replied knowingly, "quite the stalwart. This is an R.E.1, stands for Reconnaissance Experimental. Officially there are only two in the world but . . . well your squadron is as unofficial at its gets. You'll find this steed a little firmer in almost every way I'm sure." He winked at her; Mary just looked a little disturbed. "Now, your navigator will be along shortly, once airborne he'll give you everything you need to get where you're going." He gazed up at the sky. "Fine day for it, should have no problems. Ah here he is now, well good luck and very good to have met you."

They saluted once again and he strode away; back in the direction he came from, was another figure.

A young officer this time; Mary didn't feel he was much older than her. Tall and well proportioned, with a straight, clean face bearing a light frown and evidence of blonde hair peeking out from under his cap. He was carrying a dark document satchel case and wore a light brown greatcoat over his uniform, hiding his rank.

He saluted Mary as he strode by and spoke briskly, "your navigator, ready when you are." His voice was even and deep. It had a peculiar air of authority about it and there was a hint of a regional accent behind his smooth English, but Mary couldn't quite place it.

He threw the satchel into the passenger cockpit and climbed in without another word.

Mary turned to Matron Wallace. "The CO of the base I just spoke to, what was all that about firmness?"

"These public school types are all the same missy," she replied knowingly, "especially when they get to that age - bodies knackered so the mind gets too willin'."

Mary laughed and smiled affectionately at her.

"Nae time fer long goodbyes now missy, off ye go."

Mary didn't know quite how to thank the lady who had very quickly become something of a guardian to her over the last day or two; plucking her from the hospital and being at her side throughout the tumultuous events of the last few days.

The Matron understood and dutifully saluted her one more time. Mary returned it perfectly. Her navigator had put on his flying cap and gloves; climbed back to the ground and was making his way to the front of the plane ready to pull the propeller.

Climbing into the cockpit, Mary was back where she had longed to be so many times. Now, she could fly as much as she wanted, and she was being paid for it. If she had been a younger woman, more like her sisters, she might have let out a squeal of joy at this moment. Instead, she restrained herself to shouting -"contact!"

With a few tugs the engine was purring, it was a little smoother than she was used to, the plane was obviously almost factory fresh. Her navigator expertly leapt back into the cockpit, and gave her the thumbs up.

Easing the plane forward, she guided it towards the vast, open field straddled by the windsock. The only obstacle was a long hedgerow about two miles distant - plenty of room.

It was no challenge at all for her to get airborne. The figure of Matron Wallace became a tiny white dot, easing away behind them.

Mary could only assume they were somewhere in Kent.

The landscape was flat, simple and green, inter-dispersed with bright yellow fields of rapeseed. She didn't have much time to enjoy the view; as she gained height her navigator turned and shouted over the engine, "climb to fifteen hundred and steer due south towards those hills!" She nodded and began to do as he said.

Fifteen hundred feet found them almost skimming the cloud layer. The sky was full of thick white cumulous clouds dotted all over, some with flat bases and high tops towering into the sky. Mary longed to get on top of one and start surfing it but thought better.

Very quickly she became aware they were headed straight for the coast, as the horizon turned deep blue. It appeared the hills up ahead were not actually hills, just the land rising to the tip of huge cliffs. As they passed over them, leaving nothing out in front but the open ocean, Mary waited for an instruction from her navigator, but none came. She had expected to be asked to follow the coast east or west, but no. On they flew, out onto the ocean.

Not knowing what to think, Mary remembered Grey mentioning the squadron she was to join had been seconded to a 'new government department.'

'Perhaps a part of the Royal Navy?' she thought, 'we can't land on a ship . . . can we?' She didn't even know if such a thing was possible. 'What kind of ship could an aircraft land on anyway?'

Looking down, there wasn't a ship on the water to be seen in any direction. Her navigator seemed completely unperturbed by this. Mary sat up a little, trying to see if he was reading a map, but he wasn't. He had typed documents in his hand, which he was reading and skimming with a red pen, making notes in the margins and then filing them away again. Occasionally he checked a little gold pocket watch he kept tucked away inside his coat; as he did so, he looked up at the clouds each time.

The fourth time he did this she took the opportunity to

tap him on the back. He turned, still maintaining his seemingly permanent slight frown.

"Is this where we're supposed to be?" she shouted.

"Almost!" he replied confidently. "Just keep holding this bearing." He turned away, and settled into reading again.

She looked round. The coast was almost out of sight; it must have been a good eight miles back. Looking ahead there was still nothing to be seen but open ocean. They couldn't be flying towards another landmass; there wasn't enough fuel to reach one they couldn't already see.

Mary, now a little concerned, scoured the horizon ahead - still no ships.

Her navigator's attention suddenly shifted and now became intently fixed on the clouds around them; he inspected each one in all directions with a squint. His concentration then became held by a cloud formation about three miles off their port side. He stared at it for a few moments, and then turned back to her.

"You see those towers!" he bellowed.

"Yes!"

"Steer straight for them!"

Baffled, Mary obeyed and headed straight for the large mass of soaring white clouds above and away from them. It was a mountainous cumulous formation, probably the remnant of one of the storms that had drenched London the previous day.

Slowly, they got closer; there was by now a clear blue sky above the plane leaving this giant cloud formation they were approaching in full view. Her navigator's demeanour seemed relaxed again; he became more preoccupied with the time and gathering his travelling items together than with navigating.

The cloud suddenly looked a little less white than it did before; it began to get quite dark at the bottom as if it were spontaneously turning into a fierce storm cloud. To her astonishment, Mary quickly realised it wasn't the cloud changing colour, but something darker than it was slowly coming down from inside the cloud itself.

Whatever it was, it was huge; it struck her as if it was somehow the ground itself coming out of the cloud.

As it hit the sunlight, it became lighter in colour, almost a metallic grey. It looked flat at first but then Mary saw curved edges and it began to take on a long oval shape. As they got closer, she could actually see that along the bottom half, running almost its entire length, were dozens of little windows.

Fins then appeared at one end, three at first, one pointing down and two jutting out either side. By the time the huge flying object had fully emerged from the clouds, Mary realised it was some kind of colossal balloon. It vaguely resembled something she had seen in drawings being built in Germany by a man called Zeppelin; long and thin with fins at one end.

But this one was monstrous, much sleeker and appeared to be made out of metal.

They were obviously approaching the back end of whatever this thing was, as Mary was able to make out a rudder like object in between all the fins. To her bemusement there was a long rope running from the top fin to the bottom fin, flying from which was the white pendant of a Royal Navy warship.

Mary couldn't believe something this big could fly; it was easily over a thousand feet in length at least.

Closer and closer they flew and she didn't take her eyes off it for one moment. More and more detail emerged. There were indeed many windows along the bottom of it, and a cluster of them towards the front. Halfway up its side, again running along almost its entire length was a row of what looked like huge window hatches, they reminded her of gun ports on old sailing ships - 'but they couldn't be gun ports,' she thought. ' . . . Could they?'

This immense machine was obviously being manoeuvred intelligently. Once it was clear of the cloud it levelled off and maintained its height; easing gracefully to starboard, the aft end then began to be presented to Mary's plane. They were getting very close to it now; as they did, an opening appeared at the back of the great ship.

The section that was opening down appeared to be a huge hatch door. Once it had lowered to ninety degrees it stopped, as if it were a landing platform leading into the bowels of the ship.

The navigator turned and pointed to it. "That's where we're landing, rise level, then drop airspeed down to a minimum. When you make contact, just think of it as the start of a runway."

Mary gawped at the hole in the back of the ship with its little platform leading in, or at least it seemed little from a distance. "These can't do this!" she exclaimed.

"They can," came the confident reply. "The question is, can you!"

The navigator held her eye sternly for a moment, then turned and relaxed back into his seat.

Mary had never even believed something like this was possible, but she had no choice. She drew up to the height of the platform as best she could. The great ship was obviously moving forward as Mary knew her plane was travelling at considerable speed, but the rear of the ship was only coming up slowly.

Suddenly a shadow was cast over them as the little aeroplane began to fly under the huge tail fin of this behemoth. Ahead, Mary could see the opening stretched right into the ship; she saw two lines of lights on the floor stretching inwards. As she edged closer the ride suddenly became very bumpy. There wasn't much clearance in the hatch for the wings either side of the plane - Mary knew if she got this wrong there would be a very messy crash.

The landing platform was a mere hundred feet away now. Mary kept making little adjustments to keep the plane lined up with the opening, but the more time she had to think about it, the more nervous and indecisive she became. Lots of little adjustments kept throwing them off the precise course needed to land safely on this ledge.

The navigator knew this. He sat up and turned round again. "Today if you please Pilot Officer - I don't intend to miss lunch through your dawdling. It's really easy, just point the plane at the hole and floor it!"

On that Mary rammed the throttle as far as it would go; the plane shot forward and hit the platform with a tyre screeching thud.

In they went, dead straight, the roof washed over them. They were still travelling at full throttle and as the daylight quickly vanished, Mary suddenly saw the inside.

It opened up into a huge hangar like room; there were groups of people all around. Right in front of them was a line of about a dozen aircraft and they were charging straight for them. For a second, Mary held her breath; she knew they would never stop in time to avoid smashing into them. As this thought flashed into her mind, she felt herself being thrown forward as something seemed to grab her plane and force it to a standstill.

As they came to rest, she saw what looked like large rubber bands around the wheels; it was some kind of braking mechanism. Not understanding how it had worked, but glad it did, Mary surveyed her surroundings.

It was beautiful. A large silver-walled hangar, filled with people; some in overalls, some in flying gear, some in smart RFC tunics - all staring straight at her. A stern looking young officer with short dark hair, matching goatee beard around his mouth and black spectacles walked towards the plane. Looking at Mary like she was a bit stupid, he gently rose is right hand made a lowering gesture as if to say turn something down.

The navigator turned to her. "You can switch the engine off now!"

Realising she still had the plane at full throttle creating a deafening roar, she quickly pulled it back and switched the engine off.

With a juddering cough, silence returned to the hangar and the assembled crowd resumed work. Mary and her navigator removed their flying caps and crept down.

There was a metallic clunk as her boots hit the floor. Given that they were up in the air the room was remarkably still.

The stern looking officer walked up to Mary's navigator and saluted. "Welcome back sir, profitable meeting in London I trust?"

"Yes, quite satisfactory thank you Mr Walker," he replied. "Send word to all the senior officers and request the pleasure of their attendance in the ward room in one hour."

"Will we need a head start sir?"

"Yes we will, swing her around on a heading of due south west, and proceed at full speed, I'll have the precise course for you shortly."

"Very good sir."

"By the way Walker this is our new pilot - Dane, isn't it?"

As he gestured to Mary he removed his great coat to reveal his sharp RFC tunic underneath. Below the flying wings was a single blue and red medal ribbon bar of the Distinguished Service Order and Mary was taken quite aback to see a crown and a pip on either shoulder, indicating the rank of Lieutenant Colonel. "I'm Colonel Gresham, your CO."

"How do you do, sir." They shook hands.

"Forgive me," she went on," I didn't realise you were-"

He shook his head. "You needed a navigator and I needed a lift." He turned back to Walker. "Have the Chief show our new pilot to her quarters."

"Yes sir. Chief! Over here please!"

As Walker shouted and gestured to a figure over by the line of parked aircraft, Gresham strode away whilst handing his coat and gloves to a waiting orderly. Mary watched him leave. She hadn't known he was her

Commanding Officer; she began to play the whole flight back in her mind, thinking of things she might have done wrong.

A figure strode up to Mary's side.

Walker made another introduction. "Pilot Officer Dane, this is Chief Petty Officer Blackwell."

Mary turned and to her surprise found a young woman in oily overalls standing before her; a little younger than Mary, shorter and stocky with a head of long, straight dark gingerbread coloured hair tied in a curly bun behind her head.

"How you doing," she exclaimed warmly. Mary took the oily hand that was presented to her and embraced the hearty handshake this casually-spoken little lady gave her.

"The Colonel would like you both in the ward room for a briefing in one hour," Walker interjected. "Chief, show Pilot Officer Dane to her room and give her a quick orientation, she'll have to pick up the rest in her own time."

With that, Walker marched away. Mary looked at the Chief, but didn't quite know what to say.

"I erm . . . was expecting to arrive at an airfield."

"Yes, they don't tell anyone who is assigned to this squadron exactly where it's based until they get here. Well, welcome aboard His Majesty's Airship Resurgence. The twelve planes you see here in the hangar make up the squadron you're assigned to and the squadron goes where the ship goes."

"Resurgence?" Mary said mystified.

"Plenty of time for that shortly - let me get you settled in first. Follow me."

The Chief walked relaxed, with her hands in each front pocked of her overall jacket, and Mary followed her around the left hand side of the line of parked aircraft, up a long ramp of steps to a raised balcony along one wall that overlooked the hangar.

All around was a buzz of activity, new tyres for the

aircraft being wheeled past by tough young men in white shirts and brown braced trousers. Lots of hard at work bodies working with screwdrivers, spanners and wrenches on all manner of machinery.

As they proceeded through a door at the back of the balcony they came to a long corridor with handrails along each wall. Like the hangar and the outside of the ship, the colour scheme was varying shades of silver. It was a noisy corridor with the thumping of some kind of machinery behind the walls but a little further along it began to quieten off.

As they came to a busy intersection they turned left, a little further along they came right, and Mary was met by an awe inspiring sight. The corridor they walked along further towards the front of the airship was flanked on the left hand side by huge windows held in steel frames, affording a view of the tops of the clouds for miles in all directions. Mary had flown now for some time, but to have a view like this - whilst wearing no goggles and not having hundred mile an hour winds in your face - was a whole new experience.

The Chief strode up beside her and took a little look herself. Mary realised she had stopped walking and was staring. "Sorry I . . . I just think it's-"

"Beautiful isn't it? Wait until you've seen a sunset from this height. Come on, time for that later."

Taking a few last looks as they walked the length of the corridor, they eventually moved further inside the ship again, down another passageway along which were a series of evenly spaced doors. Entering one, Mary was met with a good sized square room, two small windows on the opposite wall, a bunk bed to the left, two steel wardrobes, a writing desk and a full length mirror.

"This is our room," the Chief announced.

"Our room?"

"Yes you'll be sharing it with me. You can have top bunk, I prefer to sleep on the bottom believe it or not."

Mary strode tentatively in as the Chief continued the tour.

"We share the desk and wardrobe," the Chief went on routinely. "All your spare uniforms are in there. The washroom is three doors down on the right, this corridor of dorms is for females only, there are nine of us aboard so competition for the washroom's not as bad as the men have got it across the way. Mess hall is about five minutes further towards the bow, keep left and you can't miss it. There's also a café to starboard for off duty evenings. Breakfast's in the mess hall at six, lunch at twelve thirty and both do evening meals from seven. Be sure to get to either on time for dinner this evening - some of the gunners are expert fisherman, yesterday we were flying over central Ireland, there was low overcast so the skipper took us down to almost ground level over a loch and the guys caught buckets of fresh brown trout - so there'll be a few specials on the menu."

Mary stood in the middle of the room, struggling to take in a single word of this barrage of practical domestic information that seemed oddly out of place in such spellbinding surroundings.

She glared at the Chief and at the room all around her. It was too much to take in. After everything she had been through in the last twenty-four hours, she felt she needed another week in a hospital bed to get over what was happening.

The Chief had definitely done this before, she gave Mary a knowing look as their eyes met and she took her little bag from her. Placing it on the top bunk, she took Mary's hand and guided her to sit on the end of the bottom bed. She then pulled a chair out from the writing desk, sat opposite Mary and leaned forward.

"Ok," she began slowly, "what's your first name?"

"Mary."

"Hello Mary. Mine's Ginny - it's short for Virginia because I hate the name Virginia. We can use first names in here but its sirs, ranks and surnames out there. Got it?"

" . . .Yes," replied Mary cautiously.

"Right, this is what they call a quick orientation." Ginny took in a little breath as though preparing to deliver a monologue. "The Resurgence is the name of the ship you are on. It's a new kind of flying machine called an airship. It was built by the Royal Navy and the Air Force and is top secret and very, very experimental. We officially have two roles; one is as a warship and mobile plane carrier put in the sky and the other is a - a bit more complicated."

Mary nodded quickly, bemused and wide-eyed as if to say 'I can imagine.'

"We carry twelve planes including yours," Ginny continued, "there's just over three hundred crew on board; most of them are gunners and stokers. There are thirty odd engineers who work for me, twelve pilots including yourself, a number of cooks and stewards, a few able seamen and quartermasters, and eight bridge officers including the CO and Captain Walker whom you've already met. Walker's second down from the CO. While jointly crewed and operated by the RFC and Royal Navy, most of the work we do is actually for a new government department called the Secret Intelligence Agency. This ship's pretty fast and can fly anywhere in the world so we're often tasked to respond clandestinely to . . . problems, which is one of the reasons for the intense secrecy, and the amount of trouble we get into."

"Trouble . . . what kind of trouble?" Mary asked.

"Well you'll find out about that soon enough I'm sure . . . it's not a good idea to get into the habit of talking about our missions too much, even up here most of our work is done on a need to know basis, in case we're captured. This whole thing has to stay a secret."

Ginny paused before continuing, Mary could only keep staring whilst breathing in through her mouth.

"But, in the hope that I can get to know a little more about you," Ginny smiled, "what I can tell you about me is that, the reason this giant hunk of metal can stay in the air is down to a very volatile and very experimental form of refined hydrogen that fills up most of the ship above the gun deck. My father is the man who invented it and I . . . well, I always preferred his company to my mother's. He died last year, and so I'm now the only one who knows how to keep this thing in the air."

"I see, that's . . ." Mary didn't know what to say. "This," she spluttered, "this is all so . . . incredible . . . what about the other people here, I mean - where do they come from?"

"Oh they have their own stories to tell, not that they can tell you much more than I have about myself. We're all a bit . . . irregular, you see".

Ginny stood up from her chair and sat down with a bounce on the mattress next to Mary.

Looking down at Mary's body all of a sudden, Ginny said with a glowing half-hidden smile, "what about you? You don't look much like other girls who are as well spoken."

Ginny, now very close, leaned back on her left arm to turn her body to face Mary. "Do you have any Viking blood in you?" she asked, still smiling, now a little cheekily.

This was closer body contact than Mary was used to from strangers. Confused but not exactly uncomfortable, she replied, "Irish, I'm told . . . I've erm . . . never seen a bed like this before. It's very nice of you to let me have the top one, why do you prefer the bottom?"

"I don't like heights."

CHAPTER VII

RESURGENCE

After a very quick unpack, Mary was given a whistle-stop tour of her new home. It continued to be conducted with a swiftness that made it feel bizarrely routine. Mary wondered what kind of people could consider this world in the sky a normal workplace.

It was huge and while she got the basics, she knew she would need at least a week to get to know her way around.

There were three decks - not including the gun deck, which lay on top of everything; this was where she was taken first. Huge guns sat in long lines either side of the cavernous space that ran almost the full length of the ship, all perched in front of closed gun-ports.

"She's armed with thirty eleven-inch naval guns, fifteen on either side and a few four-inch forward and aft," Ginny explained.

It was astounding to think all this could be kept up in the air. The gun deck was eerily quiet. "When the main guns are fired," Ginny described, "the noise on this deck is deafening and the entire ship lunges sideways with the recoil. The first thing the chefs do when they hear the action stations alarm is to strap their cooking pots to the stoves."

Below the gun deck and aft was the main hangar she had arrived in earlier, followed by a large engine room that contained four large engines with a smaller one in between.

"What powers this ship to make it move?" Mary asked upon seeing the huge piston rods pounding up and down in the four main engines. "Steam," was Ginny's surprising response, "there's a boiler room directly below us, about fifty stokers at a time working constant shifts to keep us moving. The big four engines are for speed, the middle one is a turbine for cruising. The steam also feeds four electric generators and we have reserve batteries topped up from dynamos fitted to small blades in the fins - so we get a continual supply of juice for most of the time. Amongst the rest of the electrics they power small air-props along the outer hull for manoeuvring."

"Steam? . . . but I didn't see any smoke coming from the outside when I flew in?"

"That's because all the exhaust steam gets fed into a condenser," Ginny said, pointing to pipes on the roof, "it gets gradually turned back to water and deposited in the ships water ballast tanks for stability. Nothing's wasted up here. The gasses from the fires are about the only thing that gets exhausted but they're colourless because of the coal we use."

Various holds came next on this deck and something called a 'magazine'. Amidships were mostly crew quarters, dining and recreation facilities. A large basic mess room was straddled by a separate long formal dining room - that Ginny had never known be used; a lounge, squash court, small library and smoking room. This last room was a particular curiosity; it was wood panelled, with huge bottle-green leather armchairs and dark Moorish rugs strewn across the grey floor.

There was something strange about the floor in this room; Mary enquired as to what it was made from.

"Lead, the floor, ceiling and walls behind the panelling are all lead, it's the same in the boiler room," Ginny explained. "Smoking's not a good idea aboard an airship filled with three hundred and fifty cubic metres of highly flammable gas, but we can spend weeks in the air, so recreational rooms like this are greatly appreciated. Do you smoke?"

"No, I . . . I've never had the opportunity."

"Skipper ordered some - appropriated from a steamer out in the West Indies - blow you sideways when mixed with cognac."

"West Indies?"

"Oh yes, you'd be surprised the places we get to."

Next came the sick bay; a neat collection of four rooms with starched linen beds and an office where Mary was introduced to the ship's doctor, Dr Kilgallen. A balding, rather frustrated looking man with a long white coat that covered a sharp, dark navy pinstripe suit and matching tie, done up in a very tight full Windsor knot that Mary felt made it look as if his permanently furrowed brow and judgemental expression were being caused partially by strangulation.

Formally and briskly, he shook hands with Mary without saying a word.

When leaving Mary quietly asked if there was something she had done to upset the doctor. Ginny smiled and replied, "No he's just always like that - it's because he's the only person aboard over thirty-five."

Forward and on the starboard side was the café, available to crew who were off duty during the evening. Like the smoking room, it was decorated completely differently to the grey and chrome functionality of the rest of the ship.

Ginny said its on-board nickname was the Café de Paris as it captured the style and atmosphere of a sidewalk café in Paris - and it had a five course set menu to match. The seating area was walled on one side with a row of large windows looking out at the sky, making the whole room feel like a long charming sun-lit veranda. The other walls were tastefully decorated in French trelliswork, with ivy and other creeping plants here and there.

Mary got the impression it was a popular spot for off duty crew and, picking up one of the hand written beige menus from a table, she could certainly see why; it included oysters, salmon, roast duckling, sirloin of beef, pâté de campagne, peaches in Chartreuse jelly and chocolate and vanilla éclairs.

Further forward were the senior officer's quarters, the wardroom, and a wireless room in which the great ship could keep in contact with the rest of the world via its two Marconi wireless operators. Further ahead lay a chart room and finally, at the very front of the ship, the bridge. A very long silver stairwell leading up to a room with a lit ceiling was Mary's first glimpse of this nerve centre. Upon ascending it, there lay in front of her a glass-encased space that felt like the beating heart of a huge metropolis.

Some cities of the world are popularly known as twenty-four hour cities. This is because no matter what the ungodly hour of the night, there is always a buzz, always a feeling of something happening.

If ever a single room could possibly capture and embody that curious character trait within its walls, it was the bridge of the Resurgence.

All the walls were made up of huge windows looking out onto the sky. The room started off square, an area that contained two large oak tables, on which were sprawled colourful maps strewn with pencil lines, crosses and symbols. Walking further onto the bridge, this square area opened out into a huge circle, and steps on either far side led down a few feet to a lower section.

Down the steps; this first lower area was much shorter in length and only went for a few paces. In the centre stood a huge oak ship's wheel, fixed to a solid column of brass instruments. It was being gently caressed and nudged by a placid looking fellow, who divided his attention between the windows ahead, and a compass fixed to the top of a brass column.

Captain Walker was found to be standing charge on this level, issuing instructions to numerous junior officers around him and oblivious to Mary and Ginny. After they had spoken to him, each junior officer seemed to criss-cross the bridge like bees pollinating a garden, taking care of this and that with a quiet diligence.

Another set of steps led further down to the third and final level, at the front of the bridge. This was where the curve of the room created a large semi-circular space.

Positioned around the windows that made up the walls were men with binoculars, scouring the skyline ahead and to either side. In the centre, neatly positioned a few feet apart, were four brass speed telegraphs rising up from the floor. They sat just above waist height, and atop were beautifully polished brass handles that the operators would move to change the speed of the great ship. Either side of each telegraph had black-backed gold leaf lettering divided into sections, denoting the speed at which the ship was set. There were five forward and five reverse speeds; dead slow, slow, half, full and flank. At this moment, in the middle of the day, they were all set to full forward.

"How fast can this ship go Chief?" Mary couldn't help asking.

"Oh a fair old miles an hour," Ginny replied gingerly. "There's one telegraph for each engine. When used in concert and with a good engineer looking after them she can put out about . . . sixty thousand horsepower, a little more with the cruising turbine."

"And where will that get us at full speed?"

"Well, at full speed almost anywhere." She glanced towards a window for a moment and continued to speak as she did so. "We have been heading due south east at full speed since you came aboard so - if we maintain course and speed all night - I'd expect to see the Med at breakfast."

"The Mediterranean?" Mary exclaimed.

"Yes, I believe that's what it was called the last time we were there."

It began to dawn on Mary that she might not even be in England anymore; the clouds were easing swiftly past the windows at an unnatural speed. She had never been further from England than Paris before. Now here she was, in another world put up in the sky, rocketing over Holland, or Germany or god knows where, much to the ignorance of all those down on the ground.

If ever she needed reminding she was in a very special

workplace, she had it now. With so many incredible locations she longed to see around the Mediterranean - Beirut, Egypt, Sicily - she was desperate to know where they might be going and couldn't help letting her enthusiasm show.

Ginny smiled at her. "I know a man who does know where we're going, and I think he'd like to get around to telling us in about five minutes - time to head to our assignment briefing."

Back through the bridge, past the chart and wireless rooms, was the wardroom. Long and narrow down to a window, walls strewn with maps, some had framed pictures of aircraft behind them. There had obviously been an attempt to make this meeting room a little more orderly than it was, but it had been well used and showed it.

Dozens of cast-off maps of numerous locations visited by this great ship were pinned hastily to the walls and adjoining small bookcases. In the middle, however, the long silver table surrounded by chrome-tubular chairs was immaculate. Mary and Ginny joined Colonel Gresham, who was at the head of the table, straddled by Walker, a delegation of bridge officers of varying ranks, Mary's fellow pilots and a couple of corporals.

Following Ginny's lead, Mary took a seat near the door. At the top of the table Gresham was conversing with Walker; the Colonel was gesturing to an area on a map on the table with a pair of pincers. Once they had finished, he chucked the pincers down; this was obviously some subtle signal that the briefing was about to start as the hum of chatter that lingered since everyone had gathered abruptly dulled into complete silence.

"Good afternoon gentlemen and ladies," Gresham announced. "Now we're underway I can put you in the full picture as to our new assignment and give you all, personally, my appreciation of the situation. As usual, being officers and department heads you'll be told the truth, your staff are only permitted to know as much as to permit them to fulfil their roles to the best of their abilities."

There was a pause, and he began to slowly pace around the large table, it was obviously a well-worn path, his eyes bearing down on the floor and his hands behind his back.

"One week ago," - in another career he would have made a reasonable storyteller - "a German battleship, the SMS Drakensburg, anchored in the Grand Harbour at our base in Malta. The ship was on a goodwill visit. On the night of the fifteenth, with most of the officers and crew ashore, including the captain, the ship unexpectedly raised its anchor and quietly steamed out of the harbour, onto the open sea. An alarm wasn't raised until the ship had long vanished into the night. The captain was understandably outraged."

He paused a moment, and continued walking.

"It was first suspected that the crew had mutinied, much to his objection. However this suspicion was quickly proven false as the dead bodies of the crewmen, who remained aboard the ship, began to wash up on nearby sandbanks and slipways early the following morning. Eventually, all the bodies of the 247 German crewmen that had remained aboard were found in the harbour. It has been established that they had been killed aboard the ship and the bodies disposed of."

He had reached the opposite end of the table; he stopped, turned to the assembled crowd, and his eyes danced a moment on a brown file he had left on the table at the opposite end.

"Officially they died of drowning, that's what will be reported at the inquest at any rate. Unofficially . . . well - Mr Walker, if you would."

Walker opened the brown file, and removed a large photograph. He began to pass it around the assembled crew at the table. As each individual held it and examined it for a moment, there was a shocked silence followed by a pained inhale from each individual as they passed it to the next person. Mary soon found out why; as it was passed to her, she almost couldn't look at it.

It was a photograph of three bodies, laid out, side by side on stretchers. The bodies themselves appeared unharmed; navy uniforms that were clearly soaking wet clung to lifeless bodies.

But it was their faces.

Each face was contorted into the most horrible twisted grimace imaginable. Their mouths were stretched open in a horrific grin, wider than seemed possible, with their teeth showing - violently clenched and long lines of stiff taught skin ran up their necks as if they were in extreme pain. It reminded her of a painting she had been taken to see once, that gave her youngest sister terrible nightmares, called 'The Scream'. She quickly passed the photograph on.

As it was making its way round the last few crewmembers, the Colonel continued.

"There was no water in their lungs; they had not drowned, so they died before they were thrown into the water. But not a single body had any kind of visible physical injury. They had not been shot or stabbed and no detectable poison was found. But as you can see . . . their faces; they had not been dead long before their bodies were recovered; rigor mortis had not yet set in. All their other limbs were limp, but these terribly distorted expressions would not relax, their contorted faces were frozen as if held in a solid mask, leaving them permanently deformed."

Mary was baffled and as disturbed as everyone else, but achingly curious to know more, so much so that she found herself interrupting.

"So, what killed them sir?"

He stopped pacing and held her gaze for just a moment.

"We don't know." He turned anyway, took the last few steps towards his chair at the head of the table and seated himself calmly.

"The German government is outraged, angry and are being unsurprisingly litigious. But that's hardly new to us. There is no proof whatsoever of any British agency being involved in the theft of their ship or the murder of their crew but, because it occurred in a British port, they have been using this incident to demand concession after concession. The one other baffling thing however is that as yet they have neglected to go through with pressing for any specific reparations."

He paused, and leaned forward.

"Our department in London believes they know a little more about this incident than they're letting on as a . . . compromise has been reached unusually quickly. The British Government has promised to track down and recover their stolen vessel. In return, the Germans will back down. So three days ago all British ships in the area were ordered to locate the Drakensburg. The search was initially concentrated to the east of Malta in the expectation that the ship was trying to make for the Atlantic. However, yesterday a British Merchantman off the Gulf of Taranto, southern Italy, sighted it and was fired upon by the Drakensburg, but they managed to get out of range and weren't pursued."

He stood quickly, and pointed to a spot on a map sprawled on the wall, his finger landed just at the heel of Italy.

"The Drakensburg was last seen heading northeast into the Adriatic." He retraced his path to his chair, slowly. "Our mission is this: the intelligence service wants us to find the Drakensburg; they want us to find out who stole it, why they stole it and stop it. My intention therefore is simple -to track her down, cripple her and re-lay her position to the navy via London. A thorough and large-scale search off the Eastern Italian coastline will begin tomorrow and upon sighting her we shall attack at once, day or night. She can out-range us but we can outgun and out-manoeuvre her so the moment we sight the beast, we'll dive to gunnery height and shell her until she's helpless. The Drakensburg's likeness will be circulated amongst the gunners; their primary targets are the gun turrets and rear magazine. If her engines stop, she'll be a sitting duck and our ships can board her at leisure. But if she gives us no option but to sink her, we'll sink her . . . I'll take questions now if anybody has them."

There was a pause; the assembled audience took a few glances at each other but nothing more. Of course, Mary was full of questions. Her apprehension at her extraordinary new circumstances subsided for a few moments as this startling mystery drew her in. Just what had happened to these poor sailors? Who had taken the Drakensburg and why? There was something chilling about it, but nevertheless it was a delicious mystery and she was very glad to be among the few people who had been given the task of solving it.

The silence continued. Gresham was tapping his hand lightly on the desk; he suddenly stopped and turned to the aide Mary had seen collecting his gloves in the hangar earlier.

"Staff, where's the sun?" he asked very seriously.

The aide smiled. "Just over the yard arm, sir."

There was a slight exhaling of relief and the hum of murmuring returned to the room. The aide left and moments later returned with two bottles of Glenturret scotch whiskey and a tray of glasses. Everyone was handed a glass. The conversation amongst the crowd turned to their assignment. Every now and then heads turned to the photograph of the dead sailors placed on the desk. It had rattled a few people. Mary wished she hadn't looked at it; she knew despite the thrill of last day she would have a hard time keeping those faces out of her nightmares.

A glass of scotch was given to her. The glass was cool, thick with a nice heavy base. She had never drunk scotch before; where she came from it was not within a lady's 'ken'. Smelling it, she got a scent of fruit, so she took a sip.

The flavour wasn't too bad but she was completely unprepared for what it did to her throat.

She tried desperately to muffle an uncontrollable cough but it slipped out. She knew she was trying a little too hard to blend in. It was not something that had ever bothered her before, maybe she had inwardly grown to enjoy being different; but here was a room of individuals who were all different, and sipping the scotch very easily.

Walker simply downed his and left for the bridge. Ginny had been snatched for a conversation by another engineer but smiled at her as Mary spluttered and regained her composure.

Suddenly she became aware Gresham was looking at her from his end of the room, his eyes fixed on her while speaking to an officer in front of him. She lip-read the words 'excuse me' and he made directly for her.

He wasn't wearing his hat now; she could see clearly his full head of fine blonde hair with a slicked back fringe. As he came closer his blue eyes never left hers, and he confidently held her gaze.

He reminded her a little of her instructor Jack, but this Lieutenant Colonel Gresham was intensely handsome, very clean and much broader in the shoulders. She had known a number of similar well-groomed young men, but this one was different. It was his eyes that seized her and suddenly fed her fascination. There was a calmness to them that was conspicuous in its persistence, she knew it hinted at great confidence but there was more; it was as if it was veiling a ruthlessness that shimmered just beneath the surface. The rest of him matched the eyes; he was well poised, and never seemed to move without purpose.

She knew there must be great danger ahead - he had talked of going into a pitched battle and pursuing the culprits of a mass murder - but the way he spoke about it, his confidence, to Mary, seemed to make it fun. For the first time, she was extremely excited to be in the presence of a man.

He was the first to break the silence. "I hope you'll forgive me for not introducing myself back at the airfield, but I wanted to see how you handled a plane."

"And how was I?" she found herself asking playfully.

"Quite satisfactory."

"I imagine that's high praise coming from you," she smiled.

"As a matter of fact," he went on, "you're the first person to land a plane aboard the Resurgence while we're in flight. Usually we launch and land planes by dropping to the ground and rolling them on and off but . . . something told me you might be a good test pilot for that particular manoeuvre."

"And why's that?" she asked.

He looked down a moment, and then back to her eyes. "I bet you don't blink."

For a moment, she forgot where she was; she kept looking at him, and she felt she knew what he meant by that, as if he knew more about her than he was letting on. She suddenly realised she had felt that way since the moment they met; something about him was drawing out her personality and the military respect was already floating away.

But the moment passed and he returned to a more conversational tone. "You must forgive the scotch, if it's not to your taste, it's just a little tradition when we get a new assignment - we're a good crew," he said, looking round the room, "- we just all drink too much."

"I was told to be sure to thank you for accepting me as a pilot in your squadron. I love to fly," she said, purposefully trying to be formal with him again.

"Well that's good Pilot Officer because if you get to stick with us, you'll be doing plenty of it. After we're finished here I'll get the Chief to go over your duties with you in detail, but the rest of the day will be your own to settle in. Be sure to get a good night's sleep - I'll need you at very early o'clock in the morning."

"I will sir."

He nodded and left the room. She felt the first proper conversation with him had gone as well as it could, but she usually had more to say for herself than that.

Another little tour was followed by an overview of what was expected of her and her duty pattern. It would appear most of her time would be split between her aircraft, which she was responsible for keeping operationally ready as long as she was an acting Pilot Officer, and taking her share of bridge watches in charge of the lookouts.

Each watch was four hours, once a day; she gathered she had drawn the short straw, as hers was 0600 to 1000 hours - but Ginny assured her it was one of the best as she got to see all the sunrises and nothing much happened at that time of the morning anyway, so it would be easier to learn the ropes.

Usually this would be perfectly true - but typically, not on Mary's first day at work.

CHAPTER VIII

DRAKENSBURG

Six in the morning was a time when the window-shrouded bridge of the Resurgence was bathed in gold.

Through the port side windows, Mary took in the majestic sight of a sunrise from above cloud level, something only a privileged few had ever experienced. She had arrived on the bridge after another surprisingly restful sleep; the dim hum of the engines which filled her thoughts as she settled into bed had become soothing after a while, and she had woken fresh and clear headed.

After a surprising breakfast in the mess hall of eggs, black sausage, bacon and potatoes asparagus, she ran over in her head the outline of the duties she was required to perform day to day, which seemed straightforward enough. Around them, she had been give something which, in it's offering, was totally alien to her; free time. A few hours a day of free time to do whatever she chose - without interference, obligation or having to run away to find it.

The idea of this new regime seemed like heaven; being paid to be in a place that captivated her and to know there would always be time for her to do whatever she wanted. She entertained this thought with pleasure; after her first spell of duty that morning, she decided she would go and sit at those magnificent windows in the corridor she had seen when she first came aboard, and watch the clouds go by.

For now, however, her attention was demanded by her duties. As she arrived on the bridge Captain Walker was just finishing his four hour watch and was being relieved by a young, skinny man with a baby face and a somewhat 'eager to please' way of standing - a bit like a spaniel waiting for instructions from its master.

"Pilot Officer Dane," greeted Walker formally, "this is

fourth officer Townsend - he'll be in overall charge during your watch, you'll be stationed forward on the observation deck and reporting up here to him with any messages that come to you from the lookouts. Follow me and I'll give you a quick overview of how it all works."

Forward on the observation deck were the five lookouts, spread around the huge semicircle nose of the bridge, all with binoculars trained on the horizon. There was a bollard rising out from the far wall of this observation platform with four white telephones attached at head height, facing out in four directions. The two on the left were apparently for communicating with lookouts stationed at the aft end of the ship and the other two were for lookouts amidships port and starboard.

"Any report from these Pilot Officer," Walker hammered home sternly, "goes straight to the officer of the watch - in this case it's Mr Townsend -whose position is always on the command deck where the ships wheel is. If it sounds routine you can go up there in person, if it's urgent you shout it from here up to him, understand?"

Mary nodded.

"Alright," he continued, "we're currently descending to just below the cloud layer to start our search for the German ship - we have just flown over Trieste and are reaching the open ocean, so stay alert. We're not expecting to find anything this soon other than fishing boats, but any sightings must be reported."

Despite Walker's strict tone, Mary thought it all sounded fairly simple; she knew there was probably a hundred things she could do to make the system go wrong, but she had the courage to wing it.

"Very good sir," was her confident response.

Walker didn't look particularly satisfied, he just looked at her a little hopelessly. Mary was beginning to wonder if she should take it personally, but he still took himself and his enduring moodiness away and off the bridge without another word.

Mary surveyed her domain; above on the other platforms about a dozen people slowly went about routine business, checking compasses, making subtle changes in direction and updating charts. Putting her hands behind her back and standing up straight and confident - a little like she thought Gresham stood - she positioned herself by the window at the very front of the ship.

They were indeed descending to the cloud layer; the gold-bathed expansive mass was approaching steadily, looking as solid and as impenetrable as the ground does when approaching it for landing. She couldn't believe how smooth the ship was riding, and how quiet it was considering the speed at which they seemed to be travelling. Further back towards her room the muffled hum of the engines could be heard, but up here the bridge was a hushed quiet place for the most part.

She tried for a moment to get her head around where they were; her geographical knowledge was excellent thanks to her obsession with travel writing. Trieste was on the northern tip of the Adriatic, where the narrow sea meets the only enclave of central Europe. To the left was the Austrian Riviera and to the right the coast of Italy. She couldn't believe where she was, in more ways than one. It was supposed to take a week to travel by land to this part of Europe and here she was having left English soil only the previous morning. It was unreal.

To live the lives led by all of her best-loved travel writers, was a dream of hers. If she could, she would have had this great ship stop at every port along the way so she could see everything, but settling for seeing them from the air was good enough for now.

Hitting the cloud layer was a little different in the Resurgence than it was in a small plane. It struck like it was made of something solid, there was a sudden shuddering of turbulence as the bridge was engulfed in a mask of white cotton. The room became much darker; she looked dead ahead waiting for the clouds to break, and slowly they did, a little glimpse of blue first, then a little more, and as the clouds faded away a huge, beautiful sparkling ocean stretched out before them. It was seamless. She couldn't see any land sadly but there were no ships to spoil the crystal glazed perfection of the calm ocean either. It was beautiful.

She began to hear some orders barked out by Townsend.

"Terminate descent, level her off here, increase to full, steady on one three zero!"

"Aye sir," was the response, followed by the ring of the telegraph bells as the big brass levers were adjusted to the 'full' position.

Mary felt the floor move very gently; she realised they had been on an almost indiscernible slant and were now coming level. They were flying just below the clouds, she was sure that the top of the ship must still be hidden inside them.

All the lookouts were silently sweeping the horizon, the telephones were silent and she couldn't see so much as a seagull down on the water. 'All clear for now,' she thought. Suddenly, a lookout took his eyes off his binoculars and turned to her.

"Horizon clear ma'am," he said.

"And here too ma'am," another piped up.

She knew they were talking to her; she nodded confidently and thought, just to be safe, to report it to the officer of the watch. It was not urgent, so she decided it was an occasion she should go up herself. Approaching Townsend, she tried her best to copy the professional tone of everyone else.

"Sir," she said, affecting her already flawless accent a little. "The lookouts have swept the horizon, all clear."

"Very good Pilot Officer," he replied and he swiftly turned away.

'That was easy,' she thought, 'nothing to this bridge duty lark.'

An hour of watching the day emerge over the ocean was her reward for getting up early. The sun got higher and the beams of golden yellow that had bathed the shiny silver furnishings of the bridge purified into clean, fresh daylight.

Mary had hoped to catch a sight of land. She had never seen Italy, and she knew so many places she had dreamed of seeing were close by. Thankfully she was well versed at imagining, and she thought of each one as being just over the horizon she was looking at.

"Smoke bearing red one eight zero! Smoke bearing red one eight zero!"

The sudden outcry from one of the lookouts startled Mary, she didn't like being taken aback and realised she probably should have been concentrating a little more consistently. She was halfway across the observation deck when a short sharp ring from one of the telephones fully brought her head into the here and now. Picking it up, a growly urgent voice also shouted, "smoke bearing red one eight zero!"

Upon reporting this by shouting up to Townsend, half the bridge crew trained their binoculars to the horizon off the Port side. Mary picked up an unused pair on the window ledge and looked for herself.

She saw nothing at first, but then became aware of a vague dark line that looked no thicker than a strip of cotton, rising up from the horizon. She suddenly regarded these lookouts she was in charge of with a newfound respect - their eyesight and attention span was remarkable.

Townsend, after taking a look for himself, hurried over to the communication pipes at the helm and shouted down one.

"Colonel sir! Smoke bearing red one eight zero!"

"Very good," came the echoed response from down the pipe.

Townsend moved to the next pipe. "Mr Walker sir! Smoke bearing red one eight zero!"

"Due south?"

"Yes sir."

"Very good."

Mary couldn't understand why everyone was saying 'very good' to each other in exactly the same dry routine way.

Everyone watched the little streak of cotton get larger and thicker as the steam ship it belonged to eased urgently over the horizon. At the base of the smoke was a little indiscernible dot that would soon start to take on more shape as it got closer.

After a few minutes, Walker arrived on the bridge once again.

"Well anyone can you make her out?"

Townsend reported to him. "It's a clear morning sir, visibilities about twenty miles but she's only just tipped over the horizon now. She's heading north and we're still on our south westerly bearing - if she holds her course we'll get closer very quickly."

"Very good Mr Townsend, double your lookouts."

"Aye sir," he replied and turned to face Mary.

"Pilot Officer, double the lookouts!" he commanded.

Mary responded immediately with a confident, "aye sir", not having the slightest clue what she was supposed to do next.

'Is there a button I'm supposed to press to make more lookouts appear?' she hurriedly thought, 'or do I saw the existing ones in half?' All these things rushed urgently through her mind, as Walker and Townsend stared at her expectantly.

She knew this was not one of those situations where she could ask casually, 'pray tell gentlemen, how does one do that then?' Nor did she want to. She suddenly realised she had spent all morning being amused by the curious habit of all of these people, of issuing instructions loudly from one person to the next. So that the same instruction would travel through three or four different people to get to whoever was to carry it out - even though everyone in the room could hear each other perfectly. It was one of those military quirks that was, to her, funny to watch.

Realising that just looking confident on the outside was working wonders so far, she took a wild stab at it and - still facing Walker and Townsend - shouted as commandingly as she could:

"Double the lookouts!"

To her immense relief, a number of crewmen at the back of the bridge instantly dropped what they were doing and bounded down to the observation deck; one brought a huge telescope and trained it on the little trickle of smoke.

The feeling of anticipation on the bridge was now palpable; Mary was buzzing. She knew they were going to attack this ship if it was the one they were looking for; she didn't really know what that would entail but she knew she had a ringside seat and watched the unfolding spectacle before her with fascination.

"I can see at least one funnel sir, and some upper works!" called the lookout with the huge telescope.

"Can you make out more than one funnel?" Walker queried.

"Not yet sir, she needs to get closer."

Walker paced slowly to Townsend. "Send for Ploughman," he said.

A few minutes later, Townsend returned with a huge hairy creature of a man in tow. At least six foot five, he was gruff and heavily bearded; however, his blue Quartermaster's uniform was immaculate.

Walker silently pointed to the telescope mounted down on the observation deck. Ploughman gripped it firmly with one hand as if he was about to strangle it, but as Mary observed, when he put it to his eye, his grip changed. He lay it as delicately and as pristinely on the pre-developed ledge of skin below his eye as if he were a master Swiss watchmaker placing the final hand on a delicate clock face.

Standing next to him, Mary saw the other lookouts

raise an eye from their binoculars for a moment to look at him. After only a few moments he turned to Mary and Walker, who by now were standing next to each other.

"It's a three funnelled warship," was his rich, pipe-tobacco laced pronouncement.

Walker immediately strode back up to the pipes at the helm. "Colonel sir, I think we've got her already, three funnelled warship off our port beam and closing fast."

"Very good," he replied calmly. "Sound off actions stations, sound the alarm."

Walker closed the lid on the pipe and immediately turned to the back of the bridge and shouted: "Bugler!"

Nothing happened; Walker's next command was twice the volume.

"Bugler!"

There came the urgent sound of a pair of little running feet and a young boy emerged, no older than fourteen, dressed in a dark red coat and holding a brass bugle.

"Aye aye sir," he chirped as Walker carried on shouting at him.

"Sound off action, followed by the double!"

The bugler turned on the spot, put the instrument to his mouth and let out a loud bugle call that Mary had thought only soldiers on horses made. At first she thought she heard the sound of the bugle call echo somehow, but it turned out to be numerous other buglers stationed all over the ship spreading the action stations alarm to every corner and crevice.

As the bugler finished, Gresham appeared on the bridge, marching briskly with his right hand doing up the top button on his uniform. Walker instinctively held out a pair of binoculars for him. Taking them, Gresham - without a blink or a hesitation of any kind - strode to the window, lunged forward whilst putting the binoculars to his eyes, took one quick look at the rapidly approaching ship, then stepped back up to his full height. He then began to issue loud words of command that got everyone on the bridge running all over.

"Hoist battle ensigns! Close blast proof doors! Increase speed to flank! Alter course thirty degrees towards her! Mr Walker, make your height two hundred feet! Staff, make to admiralty, am engaging battleship Drakensburg, give them our reference position."

"Engine room reports flank speed signal answered sir!" Walker shouted.

Mary felt the great ship ease to port and begin a steady nosedive towards the sea. They began to descend to two hundred feet - the optimal firing height it had been calculated the Resurgence could fire upon a moving ground target. All over the ship the crew were manning their battle stations. Dozens of gunners were populating the decks above, where the ports were opening and long gun barrels were being run out the side of the ship. The gunners then loaded them with eleven-inch armour piercing shells in a flurry of shouts and grinding machinery.

They descended fast and the ride became rough again as they levelled out. They were still two hundred feet from the ocean, but to Mary it looked like they were almost surfing it.

By now, the target was no longer a dot on the horizon, amongst the activity on the bridge Mary looked out at it again as they levelled off. Even with the naked eye she could now see its three funnels belching black smoke.

Gresham ordered a hard turn to starboard leaving both ships running parallel to each other, and bringing the Resurgence's huge line of guns to bear on the enemy ship.

Mary was staring at the Drakensburg when she saw what she first thought were camera flashes all over the ship; they were followed by puffs of smoke. She and everyone around her suddenly stepped back from the windows in surprise, as huge columns of water erupted from the sea right in front of them. She thought some dreadful giant monsters were leaping out of the water, but she quickly realised it was shells fired at the Resurgence from the Drakensburg, plunging into the sea.

Looking up to Gresham, Mary saw the explosions of water hadn't moved him at all; his eyes were fixed on the Drakensburg. He didn't even take his eyes off the enemy ship as he leant to a speaking tube at the helm.

"Guns open fire as soon as you're ready!"

Mary couldn't take her eyes off him for a moment, the way he stood - upright and commanding, his unswerving glare at the ship they were chasing. Mary though to herself 'He has seen what he wants and he's going to get it'. An excited shiver ran down Mary's back, she found the image of those hands running down her body flashing into her mind.

She smiled - as if she should be embarrassed and shook her head, telling herself she was being silly thinking such things at a time like this.

All attention had turned to a board at the back of the bridge with the outline of the airship across it, along each side were white circles with a number in each one, the port side had 1 to 15 and the starboard 16 to 30. These little white circles were beginning to light up one by one, indicating when each gun was loaded and ready to fire. Very quickly they were all lit and Walker turned from them to Gresham.

"We're opening fire sir!" he shouted.

There was the sound of a bell going 'ting-ting', which was followed by what sounded like the biggest crack of thunder Mary had ever heard. She wanted to cover her ears, but no one else did, so she just braved it. The thunderous bangs came in sequence one after the other as the eleven inch guns along the Resurgence's port side fired their half ton shells into the air, pummelling huge clouds of white smoke out from the side of the ship.

The recoil was incredible. The guns fired in sequence so as not to alter the direction of the ship too much. The guns at either end fired first, then the next two in from either end and so on until the last one, dead centre, fired and the guns began to be reloaded.

Mary felt like she was in some kind of huge children's cot riding an enormous rogue wave as the whole airship rolled to starboard with the recoil; it only rolled a certain way and then eased back level again.

The force of the guns could be felt in everything; the floor, in the walls and in the air all around.

She suddenly heard a high pitched whistling followed by more huge columns of water erupting in the ocean, this time they were much closer. One was dead ahead and they skimmed the tip of it as it dissipated, leaving water droplets on the windows.

There was only a fifteen second gap between the Resurgence's broadsides, so it wasn't long before everyone was rolling around in bangs of thunder again.

"Helmsman," barked Gresham, "steer clear of those columns - they are only water but if we hit one it might as well be concrete, understand? Walker, we've straddled her with our first salvo, but her gunnery's more accurate than I expected; put her to starboard for a minute and then back to port again, that ought to throw her aim out!"

Mary dared to position herself at the window again and looked for the Drakensburg. It was no more than a few miles away now and columns of water were erupting all around it. There was a sudden loud grumble from below; Mary looked down to see a giant circular wave ebbing out from an eruption of water shooting up directly beneath them. As it hit the bottom of the ship, everyone was thrown off their feet. It was literally like having the floor kicked out from under you. The nose of the Resurgence rose sharply as the solid column of water punched the whole ship up into the air violently.

Everyone scrambled to get up. As the ship settled the guns fired again. There was jubilation as a flash of flame appeared towards the stern of the Drakensburg; a hit had been scored and black smoke bellowed out from the source of the flame.

"We've got the range Mr Walker!" called Gresham. "Pour it in, rapid fire all guns!"

Resurgence's broadside erupted in a Mexican wave of smoke. Mary fixed her eyes on the Drakensburg to watch where the shells landed; there was a trail of water eruptions leading up to the ship and then two huge explosions directly amidships. A great cheer came from the lookouts and they all flung their caps in the air in triumph.

The Drakensburg stopped firing and, gaining speed, began to pull away all of a sudden. Gresham arrived at the window next to Mary looking urgently serious. It suddenly became apparent they were losing speed fast and the Drakensburg, though damaged, was getting away. The Resurgence's guns had also stopped firing.

Walker was yelling down a speaking tube at the helm.

"Bridge GCT! . . . Bridge GCT! . . . "

Getting no reply, he turned to Gresham. "Sir! Gunnery Control Tower out of action!"

"That's not all Captain," Gresham replied. "Our speed's plummeting - helm, take evasive action!"

The Quartermaster at the helm moved the great wheel but with some confusion on his face. He moved it some more, looked at the compass in front of him and began to appear panicked.

"She's not answering the helm sir, I've got no control!"

Gresham gripped the top of the window in front of him and with an almighty tug he opened it. There was a sudden and violent inrush of air, but it didn't stop Mary joining him in sticking their heads out.

Looking aft along the ship, there were huge clouds of white smoke bellowing out from the stern, obscuring everything from amidships aft.

Gresham suddenly turned to her. "Pilot Officer, get aft to the engine room now and find out what's going on - tell them we need more speed!"

"Aye sir!"

Mary darted across the bridge and down towards the rear of the ship. She weaved in and out of dozens of frantic crewmembers running all over with fire hoses, bandages and messages. Entering her favoured corridor with the scenic windows was when she first noticed the damage. All the windows were smashed to pieces and there were frantic flames licking the windowsills from the deck below. She felt the floor; it was scorching hot.

Running further aft she saw more fires, with people desperately trying to get them under control with hoses. The corridor to the engine room was thick with acrid smoke; she choked as she knelt to try and get below it.

The engine room, when she had seen it on her tour the previous day, was a glorious cathedral of pounding engines, dancing columns of metal and humming bulkheads. Now it was a hot, dark, noisy smoke filled mess. The floor was slippery with oil so Mary started to crawl on her hands and knees. She called out for Ginny but she couldn't be heard over the frightened and panicked voices screaming for help in every direction.

She suddenly heard Ginny's voice bellowing over all of them.

"The flows not too strong, plug the leaks damn it!"

Emerging from the smog, dressed in her dirty overalls and an oil-smothered face, Mary grabbed her.

"Chief, the Colonel wants to know what's happened - the enemy ships getting away, we need to get more speed!"

"More speed!" Ginny exclaimed. "Sweetheart, we aren't going anywhere, anytime soon, any bloody how!"

Their exchange was cut short as a broad pipe erupted next to them, spraying hot oil everywhere. Mary rolled away and looked back to see Ginny clamouring to her feet.

Shielding here eyes from the jet of hot oil, Ginny got as close to it as she could, then ripped off the top half of her overalls exposing the skin of her upper body, thinly veiled by a dripping wet white vest that was rapidly becoming transparent. She held the torn clothing out in front of her and, using it to shield her face, stepped into the jet of hot oil.

One powerful step at a time she pushed back the roaring force of hot liquid, her strong-arms rigid against the tide. She got to the pipe, wrapped her torn clothing round it and began to tie it up to stem the flow. With a powerful pull using both arms, she sealed it. Oil was still seeping from above and below the knot of material, but it wasn't flying out anymore.

"That was . . . bloody amazing," Mary blurted out.

Ginny strode confidently over to the stunned Mary on the floor. Her body was glistening with a mixture of oil, soot and blood from a cut shoulder, and white teeth shone out through a satisfied grin.

She grabbed Mary's hand and wrenched her to her feet.

"I hate heights, but I love my job!"

CHAPTER IX

DECENT COFFEE

To Mary, it appeared Gresham also liked to indulge in losing himself to his thoughts. Not for anywhere near as long as she was prone to do, but as she watched him gaze out of the wardroom window with a mug of coffee in his hand, she could feel he was somewhere else for just a few moments.

Mary had her own mug of inky coffee which she was cradling at the wardroom table with most of the other beleaguered officers and pilots. They were enjoying the peace, but with the echo of the battle of a few hours earlier still rumbling in their heads their thoughts were less than calm.

A somewhat tanned Ginny, now dressed in her green tunic and with a bandaged arm, stepped in quietly and sat down to pour herself a drink. Taking a sip, she then gulped it down in discomfort and looked into the mug with distaste.

Gresham slowly turned on the spot; gripping his mug to his chest, he calmly broke the peace in the room.

"Alright Chief, let's have it."

Ginny was in the process of quaffing her coffee, her head was tilted back and Mary watched with interest as she proceeded to gulp down another whole mug at once. Without so much as taking a breath, she then half threw the mug back onto the table, leaned forward and replied grimly.

"A shell from the Drakensburg penetrated deck two just aft of the engine room; it travelled through the ship and out the other side without exploding, but it caused a fire around the four inch ready-use lockers which has created one hell of a mess. Two prop shafts are jammed, most of the ship-wide electrics are shot, there is also extensive heat damage to the inner struts aft of the holds, so even if we could move I wouldn't recommend doing any sharp turns until we've had a thorough inspection up there."

Gresham nodded, as if he already knew what all this meant in relation to their next move, but it didn't stop him asking for the benefit of the group how long Ginny estimated repairs would take.

Ginny answered immediately and confidently.

"All in all sir, we're looking at two days, minimum, until we can get underway again - and that's working three watches round the clock."

Gresham put on an understanding half smile.

"I know you'll do everything you can Chief."

He put down his mug and spoke up to address the whole group. "Gentlemen and ladies, we succeeded in wounding the enemy today but they got away. Their last course was the one they held throughout the whole engagement: due north west. In spite of coming under attack, they didn't alter that course at all. That tells me they have a destination in mind, due north west of here."

He pointed to a spot on a map placed on the table.

"The only significant location north west of here is the Venice lagoon - as we all know, a labyrinth of islands and landing places. The perfect place to hide a ship, even one as big as the Drakensburg."

"Though we still don't know why anyone would want to." Walker commented.

"Indeed," Gresham replied as he threw down his mug, "the admiralty has ordered a concentration on Venice, all hunting groups but - Mr Walker, if you'll show everyone the chart."

Walker rose to a huge chart of southern Europe, the Mediterranean and the Atlantic oceans plastered over one wall and pointed to little red crosses at the end of black dotted lines.

"Second Battlecruiser Squadron," he began, "Inflexible

and Indomitable, six hundred miles south of Menorca, which puts them about twelve hundred miles way. Having to re-fuel at Malta, five days is probably the earliest they can be here. Warrior left Alexandria this morning, two and a half thousand miles to steam."

"Thank you Mr Walker, so as you see we're not getting any help for a while. We're currently drifting in a strong south easterly, which is taking us further and further away from Venice with every passing hour. If the earliest the engines can be repaired is forty eight hours from now we'll be over Greece before we can head north; by that time we'll never find her."

"So what are we going to do sir?" Ginny asked.

"Well Chief, like I said, she didn't retreat to Venice, she was heading there when we spotted her. I think we can therefore assume with some confidence that Venice was her intended destination, so it is my intention to travel there immediately, locate the Drakensburg and keep it under observation until the Resurgence is repaired or the fleet arrives."

Walker looked confused.

"Sir, even if we could get low enough to launch the sea boat, it doesn't have enough fuel to reach Venice."

"No it doesn't, Captain, but plenty of our aircraft do; I don't suggest this lightly Walker, but we need to locate that ship before it has a chance to disappear again. If we can get high enough it may be possible to launch one of the planes off the stern. A few pilot trainers back home have been experimenting with a new manoeuvre called a silent dive. In theory if dropped from high enough with its engine running, a plane can build up enough airspeed to pull out of the dive before it hits the ground. It's only been attempted a few times; I can't order anyone else to do it so I'll fly the plane myself. I'll need one volunteer to accompany me on the flight as navigator and on the mission in Venice."

A few of the pilots' hands shot up straight away.

Mary wasn't going to forego an opportunity to visit a place she had longed to experience all her life and dutifully stood up.

"Sir, I have some experience with this manoeuvre, perhaps I could fly the plane?"

Gresham had been silently eyeing the pilots with their hands up; at first he didn't acknowledge Mary's offer at all. She wondered for a moment if she had overstepped a mark in some way.

He slowly turned to her. He didn't question her or press her for further details of her experience with silent dives; he just nodded once, said coldly, "very good", and dismissed the meeting.

Mary was told to put a leather-flying jacket over her uniform, pack no bag and only take what she could fit into her pockets. Walker instructed her to report to a corridor amidships on deck two where she was told she'd find Quartermaster Dallyard.

Arriving at what she thought was the right place, she found a corridor that stretched the breadth of the ship. On one side was an entrance to a workshop and on the other were double doors labelled 'stores' with different numbers.

Wearing clean braced up overalls over a white shirt - a man with short prickly dark hair, a little older than Mary, stuck his head out of the workshop door and inspected her from behind his round glasses, which perched precariously at the end of his nose.

"Excuse me," she said, "I'm looking for Quartermaster Dallyard."

"Yes that's me." He approached her and made a point of checking the rank on her shoulder.

"Pilot Officer, is it? Yes I was told to expect you. Where is it you're going exactly?"

"Venice."

"Who's going with you and for how long?"

"Just me and Colonel Gresham."

His head turned to a door labelled 'store 3 / costume'.

"Right," he said slowly, deep in thought. "Follow me please."

He pulled a key delicately from one of his top pockets and unlocked the door. As it opened, the heady smell of carbolic soap and fresh linen washed out into the corridor. The room was already lit and as he strode on resolutely into it, Mary paused on the threshold to take in the store's contents.

It was row after row of hanging rails stacked heavy with the most eclectic mix of clothes she had ever seen.

"Over here please," shouted Dallyard, "and bring one of those bags by the door would you!"

Seeing a wicker basket filled with small empty canvas bags, she plucked out a brown one and tried to walk in the direction of his voice.

He sounded a little impatient so Mary did her best not to get distracted by the overwhelming array of eye-catching garments, fripperies and accessories that garlanded every inch of this immersive space.

They seemed to be divided up according to some kind of system and no region, nationality or ethnicity appeared to be missing. She passed frock coats and Vatican robes, fezzes and brown hoses, walking boots and French knickers. It was like a costume store that would have furnished every theatre in the world.

Seeing Dallyard again, part way down one aisle holding something on the rack, she made for him while he beckoned her over with his other hand.

"Yes just over here please . . . could you hold the bag open."

Mary did so and he pulled two full sets of clothes, tops and bottoms, from the rack, rolled them over one arm and slotted them into the bag.

"There must be thousands of costumes in here," she remarked.

"Disguises if you please, Pilot Officer," he snapped.

"Oh, I see."

"Yes . . . not that we can persuade the Colonel to use them as often as he should. We have anything and everything to cover all requirements in here," he continued with thinly veiled pride.

"Approximately ten thousand garments, arranged according to continent, region, country and then province, all handmade for us by Mr Clarkson of Wardour Street, Soho. There - " he said, finishing bagging up the clothing he had selected, " - two contemporary Venetian clothing sets, overtones - apprentice stonemason for the Colonel and silk spinner for you."

"What . . . what does a silk spinner look like?" Mary asked, genuinely intrigued.

He gave her a critical glare from under raised eyebrows and swiftly asked her to follow him out of the store.

"Armoury next," he said.

He led her through the workshop. The vast assemblage of tools and equipment lay silent but there was a pungent smell of recently cut metal in the air.

The far wall was covered entirely in locked roller shutter doors. Lowering one, Dallyard revealed enough meticulously stored small handguns to equip an army.

He plucked from the collection two gleaming Colt 1911 automatics, cast in silver, with black grip panels.

To her surprise, Mary was issued with one, and twelve rounds of ammunition. Having inveigled her way into the shooting at innumerable hunts, she had handled plenty of guns before; but never in this cavalier fashion. She felt very trusted. She loaded it straight away, slotted it into the inside pocket of her jacket and was told to take the other to Gresham.

Reporting to the hangar as ordered, she found Gresham already there, also dressed in a flying jacket and making some final arrangements with Walker.

It appeared a rendezvous location was set off the coast for them to re-join the Resurgence in two days' time and that communication would be via wireless, 'once suitable contact was made'. Mary didn't know what that meant but, for all the hastiness in which the arrangements were being made, she felt this was a well-worn path for these people.

The moment Mary climbed into the cockpit a deckhand was at the propeller ready to start the engine. Gresham swung himself confidently into the cockpit in front of her.

There was to be no protracted leaving ceremony; every second that went by they were drifting further away from their destination.

Ginny appeared at Mary's side and shouted over the noise of the air rushing in, as the hangar door was lowered for launching.

"We've stripped out a few bits to lighten her up, make your fuel go further! You've got a full tank which should just about get you there, but don't dawdle in finding a landing space!"

"Where do you land a plane in Venice?" Mary questioned in her first chance to think ahead.

"Don't worry about little things like that!" Ginny smiled. "You've got a good navigator! This is where you find out about that trouble I was telling you about - and if you don't find what we're looking for, for god's sake bring us back some decent coffee!"

CHAPTER X

MIA AMICA

Just under one hour's easy ferry journey north of Venice, sits the little island of Mazzorbo, supporting a manor house and an ancient walled vineyard. This methodically cultivated peaceful landscape received a rude awakening the night Mary and Gresham tore out of the low hanging mist onto its rich soil, using a path cut between its ripe vines as a landing strip.

The engine coughed itself into silence as the last residue of fuel was used up. They had only just made it. As they jolted to an untidy halt and removed their goggles, Mary was immediately struck by the colour of this new country. Though it was the dead of night, the moons gaze made everything a deep blue and it cast a white layer of dusted icing on the tips of every row of vines leading up to the distant silhouetted manor, straddled by the spire of a small monastery.

It was a serene place, but the gravelly vineyard ground crunched loudly even with a gentle tip toe as Mary eased herself down from the cockpit and instinctively made her way round the plane. Gresham was buttoning up his leather flying jacket and tucking his revolver into the back of his trousers when Mary made it round to him.

"What now sir, do we just leave this here?" she asked quietly.

"Yes Pilot Officer we do."

"But what happens when the people who live over there find a plane in their vineyard?"

"I'm sure they'll be confused and angry, but it has no markings on it - and they won't be able to get it off this island with no fuel in it for days, so for as long as we plan on staying in Venice we can be sure it's not going too far - now follow me."

She thought he had a point, but couldn't help feeling a

little peculiar just leaving the plane as she followed him through the corridor of vines.

There was no sign of life anywhere, not so much as the glimmer of a gas lamp or the twitching of a curtain; somehow, their landing had gone unobserved.

For a while, Gresham seemed to be leading them to a bridge; but before they could get to it a wide channel between two islands appeared, with a small jetty keeping two little motor yachts bobbing together side by side.

Gresham clambered into one; it was only a little white thing with a mahogany cabin at the stern, but the lack of a funnel meant it must have had a petrol or diesel engine of some kind, so it obviously belonged to someone wealthy. Mary didn't bother to ask him if they were stealing it - she was learning the score fast: they weren't here and that was that.

Gresham loosened the ropes and pushed the jetty away.

"We'll drift out onto the lagoon," he whispered, "then start her up. Less chance of alerting anyone in the houses on the other bank."

He instructed Mary to take the wheel while he disappeared down a hatch.

She was alone for some time, with nothing but the lapping of water around her as they slowly drifted from between the two islands out onto the open lagoon. There was the dark shape of the mainland off to the right, dotted with lights. Mary left the wheel for a moment, and moved up to the windows to take a look at it. As it disappeared away into the distance there was a gap of empty, black skyline between the mainland and something else; a huge island sat perched out and away, ablaze with tiny lights. It looked like a colossal, over-decorated Christmas tree had been laid on its side across the horizon.

There was a wet cough and a sharp vibration in the floor as the engine juddered into life. Gresham appeared and flung the throttle full forward as Mary took hold of the wheel again.

"You see that bonfire of lights out there, Pilot Officer!"

"Yes sir."

"Make straight for it!"

To anyone, the realisation of a dream is a truly amazing experience. As the horizon of a million brilliant lights eased closer, Mary began to see spires, domes and the criss-crossing of tiny boats, causing the lights to twinkle enchantingly. She could feel the life amongst these lights; a kind of impulsive energy radiating out, creating a vibrating, pulsating excitement inside her. These lights were telling her something new was about to happen, something that would leave a deep mark on her imagination and last throughout her life.

As they got closer, they motored smoothly round the wall of lights. It appeared a waterfront skirted the rim of the illuminated beige and crimson buildings that rose out of the water, as at their base were throngs of people walking in either direction. The hum of the crowds began to overtake the growl of the engine as they pulled into a jetty between hundreds of bobbing black boats.

The first moment her feet touched the grey flagstones of the Venetian waterfront, Mary felt the tangible sensation of arrival. Either side of them was a wide and proud promenade, carrying throngs of carefree people strolling and bustling in every direction.

There wasn't long for Mary to soak up this experience as on Gresham's order - "Stick close to me Pilot Officer"- she was following him down narrow streets with urgency, weaving in and out of an endless oncoming jam of people. They passed musicians; warm welcoming lights and a thousand tables out on the streets, strewn with wine and food. Whole flotillas of boats were moored up in front of goods stacked high on the waterside - sacks of salt, rice and cane sugar, piles of wheat and barrels of olive oil - even vast rolls of silk, cotton and one pair of lucky locals who were admiring a case of Peacock feathers.

Had she had time to catch up with what was going on

around her, she would have wanted to stop and take in everything; but right now she was so happily overwhelmed, it was enough just to be here.

They came to a canal; the water in it seemed to glow light blue even though it was night. As they turned off the main street and followed the canal to the right, the ebb of humanity seemed to start to flow away. As the other bank stayed light and dotted with people, Mary now found herself hastily following Gresham along a dark, narrow waterside street, empty of life. Ahead she saw the canal open up onto what looked like a great lake, with the lights of dozens of boats slowly floating by like stately carousel horses.

The little street ended and they jumped down onto a dank grimy surface that sloped away to the canal. It became difficult going as they eased up the slope, the slanting surface opened up and stretched inland, into what Mary recognised as a slipway for boats. Looking up the slope, there were indeed a line of little black boats resting side by side; beyond them, there was a charming row of boathouses with what looked like a higgledy-piggledy balconied wooden cottage, of about three floors, rising above and away from the boats.

They made for a small door in the cottage.

"Keeping up?" he suddenly whispered.

"Yes, where are we?"

"Hopefully our home for the next few days, if they're still here."

There was a moment's pause as he stepped in front of the door. He looked both ways and back down the slope but there was no one to be seen. Appearing reassured, he gave the door three gentle knocks, hardly loud enough for anyone to hear.

Nothing happened. He knocked again; no louder but still three knocks. Suddenly there was the grinding sound of wet wood rubbing together in the door. It opened a crack and a fine shaft of firelight shone out. Gresham put his face into the light, so the person inside could see him. The door was then flung wide open; there standing in the entrance was a tall thin Italian girl. Olive brown skin, jet-black hair and sultry deep brown eyes laced with astonishment glared out from the light. Gresham looked at her, both his eyebrows raised a little nervously.

"Ciao mia amica," he said in an unusually high-pitched voice, presumably in an effort to appear friendly and considerate. Her confused stare was replaced by a beaming smile; she flung herself at him, one arm around his back, the other wrapped around his neck and she kissed him passionately.

It wasn't a sight Mary was used to; though she had never actually seen it, she knew what kissing was supposed to be - at least in England. But this was different. This dark beauty had her whole body pressed against his and she seemed to be using it in unison with her mouth to embrace him thoroughly. She had never been easily embarrassed, and though she did feel somewhat voyeuristic, she couldn't look away and watched where this stranger put her hands on him with guarded interest.

Finally she released her clasp on Gresham's lips; still with her mouth open and nuzzling her nose into his, she spoke in a smooth and distinctive Italian accent. "I did not think I would ever get the chance to do that again, and maybe I still won't, so I do it now."

"I'm . . . ah . . . really quite overwhelmed to see you too, Arabella," he replied reservedly, conscious Mary was watching, "and I would love to elaborate further but could we get off the street please?"

"Of course!"

They were hurried through the door into a rustic little kitchen. It was mostly made of wood except for a giant metal range and a stone fireplace with a little flame, which cast flickering shadows across the room. Several large bolts were drawn to lock the heavy wooden door behind them.

"Who is this with you?" Arabella asked, finally noticing

Mary and looking at her with interest.

"Arabella di Tullio, meet Pilot Officer Mary Dane, a colleague of mine."

"Meraviglioso di incontrarvi Mary!" A warm and sincere kiss on one cheek and a firm hug from this dark stranger was Mary's reward for being there.

"I know I shouldn't know why you are here," Arabella went on, smiling, "but I take it you need somewhere to stay for some time?"

"Only for a night or two," Gresham replied. "We're . . . just shooting in and out. That is if you can mia amica?"

"Please! My aunt and brothers would be overjoyed to see you again, anything we can do!"

They were shown to an upper loft; it looked a little like a stable but as it was at the top of the building it must have been something else. There was lots of straw, bundles of cork, ropes, large cooking pots and a myriad of tools and objects scattered on the walls. A large flame lamp hanging from a beam was lit, casting a warm yellow glow over the whole affair. Arabella disappeared and then returned with two off-white sheets and an armful of ornate black cushions from a gondola with pink tassels around the edges.

"For you to make a bed," she said, offering them to Mary.

Taking them, Mary instinctively threw one sheet across an area of straw; the cushions became pillows and one sheet for warmth. Gresham watched her make up a cosy sleeping space, admiring her practical skills.

"Here," Arabella said, handing Gresham a canvas bag, "tomorrow dinner time you eat my aunt's cooking, I hope?"

Gresham smiled at her with a gratitude Mary hadn't seen from him before. "I hope so too," he replied warmly. They embraced, very firmly, still held each other as they came apart and after a few moments looking at each other Arabella let go of his arms and crept back down the thin wooden steps.

"Well Pilot Officer," he said, turning to Mary, "I suggest you get something to eat; we have a long few days ahead."

On that, she found herself copying him by changing out of their flying gear, down to white vests with their braces hanging by the sides of their trouser legs. With Mary sitting on the bed of straw, and Gresham on a wooden box, a bottle of unlabelled red wine, two wooden cups, a big round slab of crusty bread, pointy tomatoes and some cheese were pulled from the bag.

It was the simplest and most pleasant meal Mary had ever had in her life. She liked it but at first she wasn't quite sure what she was supposed to do. She watched Gresham produce a penknife; he expertly cut a tomato into small chunks, tore off a slice of bread, and then peeled off the block two wafer-thin slithers of cheese. Topping up the bread with both ingredients, he washed it down with a slug of wine from his cup and poured her a cup of her own. He prepared a few slices for her to do the same.

She took a bigger than expected gulp of wine as she tried to wash the food down and choked a little. As she tried it again, she looked at him and there was a glimmer of kindness in the hitherto universally serious eyes.

"Have you ever been to Italy before Pilot Officer?" he asked.

"My first time," Mary replied, preparing another mouthful, "but I have always wanted to. I used to read a lot about many places including Venice; I think I know roughly where we are right now."

"Good. More importantly, how was your first taste? Try a little sip of it now and see what you think."

Mary took another sip of the wine. This time, however, it was as if the first gulp had coated her throat; it was much softer now and to her amazement she tasted gorgeous, deeply ripe berry fruits. Her experiences up until then with wine mainly involved sipping expensive French offerings with dinner, but this was bold and moreish.

"It comes from the islands not too far away from here," Gresham went on, tearing some more bread. "Maybe even the one we landed on. Try a little of the bread and cheese, then take sip before chewing."

She did so and was surprised by the result; all the flavours seemed to blend together to create new ones.

"What do you think?" he asked.

"I think I have finally been proven right," she said, looking thoughtful. "You don't need hours of preparation and a ton of silverware to enjoy a meal."

He looked at her a moment, then a half smile emerged and grew into a genuine if slight laugh. He seemed to take a moment to regard her a little more; she would have loved to know what he was thinking but he seemed well practiced at being unreadable.

"I take it you come from what they call a privileged background," he remarked.

"Yes you could say that . . . but I was told it wasn't a good idea to discuss our backgrounds with each other?"

She found herself regretting that comment the moment she uttered it; she realised she really wanted him to talk to her and ask more questions, in the hope that he'd even talk a little about himself, but she had found that comment coming automatically. She felt perhaps she had said it as a way of asking permission to talk some more.

"Yes that's quite right," he replied, and seemed to leave it at that.

She didn't want to leave it at that, so after a little pause she went on. "Let's just say then, you'd need more than all your fingers and toes to count the number of our servants," she added.

He grinned a little again. "Well put," he said, "I never would have known from looking at you."

She was about to laugh as she thought he was being sarcastic, but as she looked at him, she realised he wasn't.

"Why do you say that?" she asked.

There was a gentle silence as he looked at her; he opened his mouth as if about to speak, then hesitated. After a little longer, what he eventually said was not what she expected.

"There's . . . more to you than most."

"I beg your pardon," she teased indignantly, "and what exactly do you mean by that?"

"Oh for god's sake, I didn't mean . . . "

He then shrugged as if he couldn't quite articulate what he wanted to say, shook his head and returned to his food.

She didn't know how to respond, but she liked that he had let her tease him and she didn't mind what he had said.

"Would I be wrong in saying, you could have had a very comfortable life?" He went on. "Easy even, comfort, servants, everything done for you - other than the circumstances you found yourself in when you were offered this job, what on earth attracted you to working for a living?"

"It was never that simple," she said curtly.

"What do you mean?"

"I . . . always saw . . . so many possibilities," she said slowly and thoughtfully.

She looked at him, hoping she was making sense. He was expressionless, but he looked down at his food again and cut up some more cheese - seemingly satisfied.

They sat in companionable silence for a short time.

"How about you," she eventually asked. "Did your family have more servants than mine?"

He raised his eyebrows and drew in a breath through his mouth, as if he could say so much in response to that question, but all Mary got was a very flat, "No."

"Well," she rounded, "I'd say there's 'more to you than most' too, but you're much better than me had hiding it."

"If you say so Pilot Officer," he answered dismissively, followed by a glimmer of an honest smile, acknowledging that he was aware he was being deliberately equivocal.

After a few more quaffs of wine he laid back, and when

he eventually spoke again the quiet, conversational tone had gone.

"We'll have to get up at dawn, if we're going to find what we're looking for; we'll need all the daylight hours we can get." He then turned over and closed his eyes.

Mary had never shared a bed with anyone before, let alone a makeshift straw bed with a man she didn't know. As she lay there with her back to him, it was a little uncomfortable at first as she tried not to move in case it disturbed him. As she relaxed, sleep eventually came but not before she found herself experiencing some new sensations that she found very satisfying.

As she lay there, thinking on what he had said about her, she began to feel the warmth from his body on her back and she gently worked her back closer to feel more. She found herself relishing the sensation of it just being him and her, together, and she suddenly felt she would be very jealous if she knew anyone else was lying here, next to him, in her place.

When dawn broke she found herself woken, at the same time as Gresham, by the noise of men shouting in the boatyard below, beginning their working day. Putting leather jackets on over their vests, the two of them descended to the kitchen again. At the sturdy wooden table in the middle were sat several young, athletic looking Italian men with a beaming elderly lady at the huge metal stove and Arabella bustling in between all of them.

They were very gladly welcomed at the table and these young men all introduced themselves as Arabella's older brothers. It turned out she was the youngest and only girl of five children, which explained a lot about her buoyant nature. Although, whilst kissing Gresham the night before she had been sultry and feminine, she otherwise carried herself with a physicality and energy that had almost masculine traces.

Sat at this welcoming breakfast table, Mary felt

comfortable and genuine warmth; she wondered how people could be so readily accepting of the stranger she imagined herself to be.

It appeared Arabella's brothers also had some history with Gresham; he was hugged and backslapped to the top of the table as though he was a guest of honour. They quizzed him constantly in Italian throughout breakfast; Mary didn't understand his answers but they received resounding laughter and hearty claps. They were served a delicious breakfast of chunky toasted bread rubbed with tomato and garlic, fresh apples and thick black pungent coffee that struck like a lightning bolt through the whole body.

Feeling very fortified and following Gresham's lead, Mary ventured out onto the streets of Venice after a cheery farewell from their wonderful hosts. The warm air hit them the moment they left the cool wooden cottage. She couldn't see where it was coming from but Mary could hear a close rumble of people and bustling life. It was nowhere to be seen, - the street they could see on the opposite bank had only a handful of people going about their business but she could feel civilisation was just around the next corner the whole time.

"Where are we going sir?" she asked as they were retracing their steps inland.

"A place called the Palazzi Barbaro, Pilot Officer. It's not far from here, there maybe someone there who can give us some useful information."

Gresham's stride was brisk and purposeful; he wasn't interested in taking in the surroundings, he seemed to be fairly well acquainted with them anyway. They began walking down a long narrow street; in the distance lay the steps up to a bridge.

Mary was still struck by the warmth she had received from the boatyard family, and the reception they had given Gresham, particularly Arabella. It all seemed so unlike the world he kept aboard the Resurgence, and she hoped to find out why.

"Arabella?" she enquired as they made their way, side by side, along this long street, "how is it you know her . . . was she a lover?" She had never used that word in conversation before, and hoped to sound a little worldly wise in her use of it, but it became obvious it hadn't worked.

Gresham's reaction was guarded, but he didn't seem to mind the question. "I . . . once helped her father and . . . she . . . was very grateful."

"Did you save his life?"

"Not exactly no," he replied, "he . . . is dead but..." he sighed, "I suppose, I saved his reputation."

She knew that was as good as it was going to get; anyway, the thought of more questions soon went out of her head as they ascended the steps of the tall arched bridge at the end of the street.

Mary suddenly glimpsed at where all the noises of bustling activity was coming from. She was stunned to a gaping standstill, and a total loss of control over her facial expressions as she saw the Grand Canal for the first time. It was just like every painting of it she had ever seen, but in real life - richer, fuller and immersive even just to stand and look at. The water was littered with a thousand boats, mostly little punts and gondolas jostling here and there, many of which looked too overfilled with people, cargo or both. Moored at the canal edges and stretching out onto the open water in the distance, were elegant crimson-sailed fishing boats of all manner of slender and curvaceous shapes and sizes.

Everywhere, there were people, extraordinary people, and to Mary living an extraordinary existence. To these locals, it was a normal day, but Mary felt she had stepped into the biggest celebration of life in the world. The throng of these excited, corporeal masses, and the rich, densely packed beauty of the city they lived in, seemed to rise up and blend with the sun's caressing heat, blanketing Mary with invigorating warmth.

Amongst those who were working, there were people eating and drinking, arguing, flirting, debating, reading, bartering or just simply trying to get somewhere. Sprinkled meagerly were slow moving over-dressed couples; they were, of course, the tourists.

They didn't stop long at the top of the bridge. Gresham allowed her a moment; he knew what she was feeling but eventually had to tap her on the arm. As Gresham marched on Mary followed him, but with an occasional unconscious skip of pleasure as her eyes fell on one stunningly rich sight after another.

The Palazzi Barbaro was, from the outside, innumerable floors of expensive warm-beige coloured gothic grandeur. It was actually two palaces in one and like many private homes in the San Marco district, bordered the canal on one side with its own private moorings at its base, above which hundreds of little windows dotted the building and faded pink blinds sat over balconies located on every few floors.

The street entrance was much less impressive than if you arrived by boat. A casual knock on one of the little crooked doors brought the glaring eye of a suspicious manservant, peering out through the black crack in the half open door.

"Che cosa volete?" was the foreboding greeting they received.

Mary expected Gresham to respond with something clever in Italian but he didn't. As casually as you please, and in perfect English, he said, "Hello, we've come to collect two cases of Glenlivet, the eighteen year old."

This dark manservant's pointed glare became even fiercer as his beady eyes flickered to either side of them, then he flung open the door and ushered them both in. They found themselves in a stone tunnel leading along to a bright opening halfway down the building.

The servant brought them through this opening to a

lush inner courtyard. There were balconies on each of the four walls that towered above them to the heat hazed blue sky. To Mary's amazement, trees stretched out from the centre of this stone courtyard, reaching up to the square opening above for sunlight.

"You will wait here," ordered their escort. The light tap of his shoes on the stone floor echoed between each of the walls as he disappeared between the many decorative plants that shrouded the centre.

Moments later he returned, beckoning again with his bony white-gloved finger. On emerging at the courtyard centre, surrounded by lush greenery, Gresham and Mary paused to take in the sight of a large portly man, perhaps just short of fifty, sat amongst a few fancy woven deckchairs and a small table. Caressing a long thin cigar between his lips, his eyes were resting on the affair that was taking place in front of him.

At the centre of this shrubbery circle were eight smooth-skinned hourglass shape women, perched completely naked on little three-legged wooden stools, all sat with their backs to him in a semi circle. In front of each of these ladies was an easel supporting a canvas, a small table with water, paints and brushes which each of them were using to paint.

"When someone has a skill in their hands," said the large man, "a skill they were born with and they know how to use it, I find experiencing them doing so first hand to be the most agreeable of pastimes."

The accent was American, a slow and melodic deep southern drawl.

Neither Mary nor Gresham responded; the large man didn't move, nor did he shift his gaze from the direction of the painters.

"In the middle you'll see what they're painting. It's the original; I wouldn't miss this opportunity to see it." Still not moving his eyes, he took the cigar out of his mouth and gestured with it towards the circle. Gresham played along; Mary followed him towards the painters.

Sat propped up on a small wooden stool in the centre of the semicircle was a small portrait of a young woman; it was unmistakably the Mona Lisa. Each of the female painters was in the process of copying it expertly.

Moving up close, they recognised the world famous brushstrokes of its creator.

"Sir," whispered Mary, "I remember seeing this at an exhibition in London, if it's the original it must be worth thousands."

Gresham didn't have a chance to respond, as there was a sudden unmistakable rattle of a dozen pistols being cocked at once that echoed around the courtyard. Turning around they found the artists now on their feet, each with a gun pointing directly at them.

"Now Pilot Officer," Gresham rounded calmly, "where do you suppose they were hiding those?"

Mary looked at him and he raised an eyebrow cheekily; she couldn't help but smile at him. She wasn't the least bit scared; she loved the way he was making this dangerous situation fun.

The large man was now also on his feet, strolling up behind the wall of barrels. "My late mother told me: when it comes to scotch, always stick to the oldest and the youngest. Never the stuff in between, it's going through too much . . . your pass code was out-dated," he said abruptly, "your presence here unconfirmed by your station in Rome!"

Gresham held firm. "The pass code is not out-dated, it's the first one we've used, and our station has never been in Rome. It moved from Genoa to Milan six weeks ago."

The man stopped strolling up and down and looked directly at Gresham. "Who are you?" he asked inquisitively.

"Lieutenant Colonel Thomas Gresham, and this is Pilot Officer Dane."

"Could you be the two peckerwoods who tore up a strip of my associate's vineyard last night with a light aircraft?"

"Yes," Mary interjected, "that would be us."

The large man looked at her keenly for a moment, then a congenial smile grew across his face.

"We'll I'm mighty pleased to meet ya, I hate that bastard. James Roquefort Delano, call me Jimmy."

A hearty handshake for both of them as he strode up was the welcome conclusion to their briefly hairy entrance. He shook Mary's hand affably, while his artists sat and resumed their work. Gresham tried to get a glance at where they re-secreted the guns - but missed it.

"Come and have a drink," Jimmy said, gesturing to the chairs. "Don't mind my 'artists', an eye for brushstroke translates mighty well to the trigger let me tell you. This is how we raise funds to keep our operation going out here, at least in the manner we're accustomed to."

"Where'd you get the painting?" Gresham asked.

"Well Colonel, things always have and always will fall outta the back of a safe, especially in these parts. Here, join me in a glass of Amaro," he gestured to his bony-fingered man servant, now standing obediently at a nearby table - topped with a very select array of alcohol. "Both of ya - unless Colonel you'd prefer yer scotch?"

"Oh no thank you, I'll drink Amaro." He turned amiably to the servant. "I'll take it over ice with an orange wedge please."

"I'll have the same," Mary said, "thank you."

"And I thought British intelligence was a contradiction in terms," Jimmy chortled. He turned his attention to Mary. "How about you ma'am, you 'partake' often?"

Mary was just taking her first sip from the thin vase-shaped glass she was handed; it was syrupy sweet and very tasty, her enjoyment was visible. "It's like all the best puddings in the world put into a liquid," she replied in delight, "I don't think I'll have a solid dessert again."

"That's the trouble with this stuff ma'am, means you have to work twice as hard to maintain a healthy stomach like mine." They all laughed and took a seat.

"So Colonel, Pilot Officer, why the sudden entrance?"

"We're in pursuit of a stolen German battleship, Braunschweig class, called the Drakensburg," Gresham began, producing a small black and white photo from his inside pocket. He flung it on the table; Jimmy gave it a quick glance.

"Big son of a bitch," he commented.

"We know she made for the Venice lagoon last night," Gresham continued, "probably arrived just as the light failed and entered under cover of dark. We suspect whoever stole her brought her here intentionally and we need to find out why."

"Colonel if this battlewagon was afloat and within a hundred miles o' here, I'd know," Jimmy assured them.

"We're aware of that, that's why we came to you."

"Well, I ain't seen her," their host concluded.

Mary didn't even think about whether it was appropriate to interrupt; she just did.

"What if someone had hidden her before sunrise? There are enough islands and landing places around here aren't there?"

"That's true missy but to hide a whole Battleship from view in a matter of hours? That'd take some doin'."

"That's why we suspect this was her destination," Mary went on, "if she's hidden from view already then there must have been associates of the thieves here waiting for her, with a plan to hide her ready to go at a moment's notice." As the last few words left her mouth she looked at Gresham; she could have sworn he was impressed as he gave a little nod of approval.

Gresham turned back to their host, thoughtful. "Jimmy, has there been anything out of the ordinary happening here over the last few months, anything suspicious?"

"This is Venice Tommy, its existence is out of the ordinary!"

"Alright . . . well, has there been any shift in the established lines of the extraordinary of late?"

The long thin cigar returned to Jimmy's lips, his eyes placed on Gresham's thoughtful glare.

"You been on a gondola yet?" he asked casually. "You might want to take one out to San Lazarro."

"San Lazarro?" Gresham responded, sounding surprised. "The Metikanist Order? They're just Armenian Monks who like collecting books, aren't they?"

"Well Colonel, our simple Armenian Monks have been uncharacteristically interesting of late. Once a week a small boat goes to and from their island carrying food and what not but about eight months ago larger boats started paying visits to the island, on an increasingly regular basis. They were carrying big loads of wood, scaffolding, tools, even steady quantities of refined steel, amongst other things. Enquiries placed amongst some local merchants by my well placed associates" - he nodded to the painters - "revealed the Monks claimed they were shipping these materials in to repair a large section of their monastery's undercroft which had apparently caved in. Once or twice, just this last month, larger vessels, unmarked and flying no flag have also been sailing in from the open sea and docking directly at San Lazzaro. That's never happened before and local authorities are unusually disinterested. Either they've got an undercroft the size of a small city or there's something else going on."

Mary was beginning to realise she loved a delicious mystery, even a dangerous one. She couldn't resist pressing him for what he thought might be going on.

"Search me missy, the Monks tend not allow anyone on their island uninvited, but I will tell you one other little detail that makes me think a trip there will be worth your while." He drank the last drop from his glass. "San Lazzaro has one wooded area that straddles the water's edge and shrouds a section o' the island from view." Jimmy leaned towards them slightly and added with emphasis, "this morning, a new one had appeared overnight."

Mary and Gresham glanced at each other; they knew what this could mean, and the urgency with which they had left the Resurgence was back with renewed vigour.

Gresham downed his remaining drink. "Thank you Jimmy," he said standing up. "We have been doing ourselves a disservice, putting off a gondola trip this long."

CHAPTER XI

WHAT YOU TAKE TO BED

To Mary, San Lazzaro wasn't much more than a thin, crimson topped slither of beige brick laid flat across the water.

There was little to be distinguished from what rose up out of the island's centre either. Tall trees bordered the entire square perimeter of the island; a few buildings could be discerned through the cracks and a white tower with a golden swirly top was the only structure peeping up out of the extensive greenery.

The gondolier at the boat's stern was somewhat reluctant to get closer; Gresham couldn't get him to explain why, other than landing at the island is by invitation only and is otherwise not 'a custom'.

There was an area where the perimeter wall rising out of the water was shrouded with greenery that had grown thickly over it, but there was nothing unusual about it as far as they could make out. While Gresham had their gondolier circle the island for them, all appeared very quiet, much like the other countless islands in the distance. No figures, no boats, nothing noteworthy at all - except the beauty of the lagoon and peaceful lapping of the water under this charming, unpowered little craft.

Mary had been taking some time after they initially set off from San Marco to note the design. There were a few aspects of it she didn't understand at first sight; the port side of the gondola appeared to have been made longer than the starboard side, apparently this asymmetry causes the gondola to resist the tendency to turn towards the left at the forward stroke of the punter. She may have dared to dream she would build herself a new boat one day. It was irresistible to entertain such thoughts and be able to think that maybe, just maybe, it could now happen.

As they edged round to the south of the island, another shroud of greenery protruded out and over the island's wall. This one was different to the last; it was much larger and very thick. Gresham firmly ordered the little boat closer but their pilot only made half hearted attempts to manoeuvre their small craft in towards the island edge. At a glance, it looked just like a huge clump of trees that had grown towards the water and arched over the wall; but it was huge, and there was no glimmer of the monastery behind it, no cracks of sunlight or glimmers of different colours between the branches. It all blended away into thick, impenetrable dark green. Under scrutiny, it certainly didn't look natural.

Gresham was on the verge of giving their poor gondolier a heart attack trying to get him to take them closer; as the man turned tearfully distressed, Gresham relented.

"Bene, torna a San Marco, grazie." He sat back down next to Mary. "I think we have seen enough to warrant a later visit - does that look big enough to hide a battleship in to you?"

"I can't see through it - that's the thing," Mary replied, squinting. "When do we come back?"

"Soon, just for a little look inside those trees." He looked out across the water, it was now late afternoon and the heat was beginning to ebb away. He let out a relaxed sigh. "This is our only lead, if it comes to nothing then that's it. There's no point in searching, even from the air - if it was visible to the naked eye Jimmy would know."

He turned to see her looking at him closely; Mary was usually quite good at reading people, but he wasn't letting anything show again. "I'm feeling hungry Pilot Officer, fancy trying some more local cuisine?"

"I assume you know all the best restaurants in town," she said a little playfully.

"No, I have somewhere much better than those places in mind."

A very gratifying walk through St Marks Square and over the Grand Canal again brought them, to Mary's surprise, back to the little boatyard. By now, it was a lazy golden summer evening and there were dozens of laughing, happy revellers lining the street on the opposite bank.

Arabella, her family of many brothers and a growing crowd of friends were out in front of the boatyard cottage with bottles of wine and a guitar that was being passionately strummed. Upon seeing them approach Arabella beamed and hugged them both at once, then put an arm round each of them and escorted them in.

"Bene! You're still here! Wonderful - no seriousness that will keep you from eating with us tonight I hope?"

"Mia amica," Gresham replied warmly, "your aunt's cooking is the only food in the world I dream about when I'm not here; there is no serious business when there is serious cooking to be enjoyed."

"She will be very pleased. Upstairs I have left some old clothes for you both if you like, you will find them more comfortable and less conspicuous than your . . . what is this?" she said, feeling Gresham's collar, "don't tell me . . . Cut-hler and Gross?"

Gresham laughed, genuinely, for the first time Mary had known him.

Upstairs they changed down to white shirts, then over that went black baggy trousers and dark brown suede leather vests that tied up down the middle with little strips of the same material. As she tied up the waist on the trousers, Mary realised she had got changed in front of Gresham and vice versa, but had thought nothing of it. He didn't seem to have either.

She suddenly remembered the disguises Dallyard had given them, still wrapped up in a brown canvas bag that had been left in the plane.

Upon warily telling Gresham this, he appeared delighted. "Good job Pilot Officer, what ridiculous getup did he issue us with?"

"I think we were supposed to be silk spinners."

He coughed up a snigger and shook his head.

"Why?" she asked. "Wouldn't they be any good?"

"How many silk spinners did you see in the street today?"

"I don't know . . . what's a silk spinner supposed to look like?"

"Exactly," was Gresham's reply.

Mary was really beginning to wish she had taken a closer look at those costumes.

"Spies sent abroad from England tend to have months to investigate whatever it is they're assigned to," Gresham seemed to conclude as he re-tied his boots."The advantage of the Resurgence is we can respond to problems that come up much quicker . . . but it means we have to think on our feet a lot more. Dallyard's much better with guns anyway."

Putting the day's events behind her, Mary smelt the amassing aromas from the kitchen downstairs - the kind that make you salivate - and heard the delighting laughter of happy people outside. For some reason she couldn't wait to get down there. It was her first real party; the kind she would come to realise had been missing from her life.

As Gresham finished dressing, Mary couldn't help staring at him and smiling. She had never seen an Englishman so underdressed for dinner in her life, and laughed at herself for thinking like that.

"What?" he asked.

"Nothing . . . it's just - back in England it would have taken a lot longer to get ready for dinner, that's all."

"Well," he said, standing up."We don't have to shun all our breeding - would you like me to escort you down?"

"How about I escort you!"

He took a few steps towards her. She wasn't sure what he made of her sudden teasing, but to her delight, even though he seemed to stay perfectly serious, he raised his elbow in a mock ladylike fashion.

Her laugh settled to a smile coupled with a momentary look of great warmth that hadn't beautified her eyes for a very long time.

Her heart skipping, Mary walked over, but didn't link arms with him; she instinctively put her right hand into his left and gave him a little tug towards the door. They descended to the party holding hands; Mary kept glancing at him like an infatuated youth. Arriving at the feast, nobody made anything of it, or seemed to notice in fact. It was thrillingly liberating for Mary.

Everyone was sat lounging in the cushioned seats of the gondolas that were lined up four abreast at the top of the slipway in front of the kitchen door. A glass of wine was pushed into their hands and they reclined in a cosy chair together with Arabella and a few friends sat opposite. Mary had never seen pasta before; she was served a bowl of it, and it looked to her like big wobbly worms. It was coated with a thin but heavenly flavoursome tomato sauce, filled with basil, garlic and onions. Big wooden bowls of cheese and bread were doing the rounds of each boat.

Arabella and her friends were hilarious company. They had all grown up in the area; Arabella's family had lived and worked in the boatyard for generations making gondolas, and she told Mary of her hopes for her children to live and grow around her in the same way as she had here, with her parents.

Watching some giddy young children run around the boats, and then get called up to the aunt at the house to be sat down for their food, Mary thought what a wonderful thing it was, for a whole family of many generations to all live together like this.

It dawned on her for a moment that that was how it was in England, in homes like the one she had run away from. But somehow, these people were a family in a way her own had never been. She envied it greatly - the strong, safe feeling of belonging all these people had.

A young boy, not far from his teens, with a wonderful smile and oak-brown eyes laden with an innocent curiosity, suddenly paused in his run up to the house. He gazed at Mary inquisitively for a moment, and then started to smile cheekily and pointed at her. A scattering of other children began to gather round him and they looked at her with fascination.

Arabella's aunt laughed and walking up behind them, she led the boy up to the house by the hand. He couldn't help walking the whole journey to the house looking back at Mary with fascination. She waved at him and he beamed at her, as he waved back a little bashfully.

"What were they looking at?" Mary asked her new friends as she turned back to them.

"Your hair," Arabella replied, "they don't get to see that colour very much."

They didn't seem to lack anything in these rustic surroundings. Arabella was a bright and effortlessly warm young woman, who, to Mary, wore her heart on the outside all the time. Watching Arabella talk was the way Mary learnt first-hand of how Italians speak with their hands as well as their mouths. Though her accent when speaking English was heavy, her voice was smooth and melodic; to be able to understand her in her mother tongue, Mary thought, must have been a beautiful experience. She told Arabella that she admired how comfortable in herself she appeared and asked how she did it.

Arabella just laughed, self deprecatingly and turned to her friends and said, "she thinks I'm comfortable in myself!" She didn't seem prideful at all and took the compliment in her stride; she playfully slapped her nearest brother on the shoulder and said, "I hope you are listening to this!"

"What she means is you never shut the fuck up!" her brother jeered.

She loved to laugh and loved to talk and was very

interested in Mary's life, and asked all sorts of questions about the rituals involved in everything back home. Mary had them all gawping in disbelief when she told them how many knives and forks they used at dinner tables in England.

She was thrilled to be getting to know these people, especially as they were mostly her own age. She had longed for friends such as these all her life. More and more bottles of wine arrived at each gondola. As the sun went down the divide between the party in the boatyard and the party at the bar on the bank opposite became narrower and narrower, until there really was no divide. Arabella tried to teach Mary, Gresham and a few revellers from the bar to dance; a few of the men from the bar turned out to be rather exceptional singers.

The evening's exulting was suddenly interrupted by two of them, their arms round each other, somewhat drunkenly standing rigid, looking out onto the lagoon, singing a bold and proud Italian opera. More and more people ran over to them, stood together arm over shoulder and joined in, swaying to and fro until the traffic on the nearby canals stopped to watch the spectacle.

Arabella grabbed Gresham and Mary's hands and they were pulled in too. Mary swayed side to side with the group all around her, and Gresham, his arm over her, doing his best to sing the words, with a huge rapidly growing smile on his face.

Mary didn't know a word of Italian, Gresham shouted to her over the tune to just make noises that sounded like the words and do her best to sway elegantly and nobly. She did, and they both nearly died with laughter at what they were doing, as the group seemed determined to rouse all of Venice to join in with them. Not that anyone seemed to mind - quite the opposite. It was the middle of the night but it seemed no one was in bed. The wine kept coming, and they laughed and they laughed and they laughed and they laughed. It was wonderful. No drinking culture that ever emerged later in history, that thought itself the boldest, wildest or luckiest would ever know the real truth unless they were there that night in Venice.

When the mass of howling tenors ended, a rapturous applause reverberated from all banks and even from a few boats away out on the lagoon itself that had slowed to take in the sight.

Mary moved away from the crowd, towards a wall that skirted one edge of the boatyard, on the other side of which was the canal. The warm night air became a little fresher as she stood close to the water's edge. She found it refreshing after standing amongst all those people, so she sat and looked out at the water and decided she would fill her lungs with some fresher air for a while, before re-joining the festivity.

Arabella must have noticed her, as she appeared at Mary's side with a thick corked bottle and a couple of small glasses.

"We cannot be too much for a person like you, Mary?" she laughed.

"Not exactly." Mary replied. "It's just," she said thoughtfully as she looked back at the crowd, "it's beautiful here, I've never known anything quite like it. You all . . . you all love being with each other so much, I think I'm just - enjoying being around that."

Arabella plonked the bottle and glasses down on the ground, and perched herself on the wall next to Mary.

"You know," she said, looking at her up and down. "You are a very strange person."

"Oh?"

"You look like . . . such a woman of the world, but you don't act like it."

"What's a 'woman of the world' supposed to act like?" Mary asked.

"I . . . I don't know but, if I see you passing in the street I would think - 'rich runaway'."

"You'd probably be right."

"No . . . you are too thoughtful for that - you have never been to Italy before?"

"No, never."

"You are missing home . . . because it is so far away?"

"Oh no," Mary exclaimed genuinely, "not at all in fact. There are very few places in the world I haven't read about and dreamed over and over of going to. I know exactly where I am and I wouldn't rather be anywhere else," she looked out across the water, "but . . . at the same time, I . . . don't know where I am."

She looked back at Arabella and was surprised to see her staring very knowingly and earnestly at her.

"Sorry, that's just a load of meaningless nonsense, isn't it."

"No," Arabella replied very sincerely. "It isn't."

They both looked at each other in silence for a moment.

"Do you not know what you want with your life?" Arabella asked quietly. "What your hopes are?"

In her mind's eye, Mary was suddenly transported back to the last time she was frantically running that question through her head. Standing on her parents' terrace, the night she tried to kill herself, and the hand of a stranger holding a glass of champagne; which had momentarily punctured the dismay that was consuming her, and said, "you die if you worry, you die if you don't".

It was still good advice now, and more than any worldly wisdom that had been imparted to her, helped her answer Arabella truthfully.

She sighed, smiling. "No, but . . . I'm very happy with where I am right now . . . I've never had that feeling before - and it's wonderful, I think that will do me . . . for now definitely." She smiled.

Arabella nodded slowly, and looked out across the water herself.

"What do you want?" Mary eventually asked, after a few moments mulling over her own thoughts, "what are your hopes?"

Arabella's warmth seemed to pale a little suddenly. "Oh . . . well," she said, still looking out across the canal, "to live again . . . would be good."

Mary found herself smiling sympathetically all of a sudden; there was a barely distinguishable trace of regret in those last few words, which seemed out of character.

Mary was surprised to find herself now trying to cheer her new friend up by gesturing at their happy surroundings and asking jovially - "How is this not living?"

Arabella looked at the crowd and then laughed affectionately.

"You are right . . . simple things," she said turning to Mary, nodding, seeming to rally again. "They are the best things."

"It seems everything about this life you have here is simple," Mary replied admiringly. "It's the most wonderful way of living I have ever seen."

Arabella looked at the ground modestly. "Well," she said slowly, "when you grow up here, you don't notice it much. I'm sure I would find your home wonderful in ways you may not think so."

"Oh I don't know," Mary laughed, "we wouldn't be having this much fun, I'm sure of that."

She looked back at the crowd smiling and she suddenly noticed Gresham. Her gaze became fixed on him, and thoughts began to crowd the smile on her face. "We wouldn't have any of this," she said softly.

"You love him, don't you?" Arabella said suddenly.

Mary snapped out of her trance. "What?"

Arabella just stared at her with a teasing smirk.

"I've only known him two days," Mary laughed self-consciously.

"Ha! You English, you all do that - you are so scared of your feelings," Arabella exclaimed, and began to look at Mary with a sympathetic smile.

"You want to know what there is beneath that don't

you," she continued.

"Beneath what?"

"Oh, you know what."

Arabella sat up rigid and broadened her shoulders, she put on a mock stern frown and pouted slightly, but with an air of seriousness that immediately reminded Mary of Gresham, and the way he had looked when he had first walked up to her aboard the Resurgence. Arabella was effeminately imitating him expertly and Mary fell back with laughter, pointing in recognition.

"That's fantastic!" she roared.

"You have seen this," Arabella beamed.

Mary nodded, struggling to control her laughter as Arabella went on, straight faced, and what she said stopped Mary's laughter in its tracks.

"You want to know what else there is, what more there is than what everybody gets from him . . . and you want to show him that part of you too."

Mary began to calm herself.

"Does that mean I love him?" she asked.

"What else do you think love is?"

Mary couldn't help but stare at her, as the laughter subsided and she thought about that question. She found she didn't have an answer.

"The two of you," Arabella continued, "for him to find that part of you, for you to find that part of him, you could spend a lifetime on that journey together, and it would not be a wasted life."

Mary didn't know what to say. She looked back across at Gresham, but what she saw this time, was different. His physical features didn't seem important anymore; her mind, carried on a flow of thoughts by Arabella's words, recalled feelings she had experienced when they had first met.

The shield of self-imposed stillness he seemed to have over himself and the few tiny moments she had been so thrilled to feel something more seeping through cracks in that guard. When he held her hand, without thinking, as they had come down from the loft, the way it had made her feel. The excitement and the promise of hope-fulfilled she had felt in those tiny moments.

Arabella only spoke again after letting Mary think for a little while.

"The only danger is, you may not like what you find when you get there."

Mary slowly began to smile again and looked at her.

"This does not concern you, does it," Arabella giggled.

Mary shook her head and began to beam at her.

"You like this," Arabella teased.

"Yes . . . I do."

"Ah, oh well then," Arabella said, sounding playfully sorrowful. "I offer you one last salvation."

She pulled up from the floor the heavy glass bottle, twisted out it's well-used ragged cork and began to pour the amber contents into the two small glasses.

When offered one, Mary realised it was a thick sweet wine not unlike the Amaro she had tried earlier.

"You must always end your evening with a sweet," Arabella announced as she tapped her glass against Mary's, "the sweet being the last things of a meal . . . the thing you take to bed."

Mary chuckled at her, and felt it was time to do some teasing of her own.

"Is this what you always take to bed with you?"

"Oh I have been known to take my sweet to bed," Arabella replied forthrightly. She looked over at Gresham and then purposefully back at Mary, this time with a definite sense of suggestion in her voice. "It is sometimes much less dangerous."

Mary instinctively returned to the gondola, linked arms with Gresham without asking - he didn't flinch for one moment - and found herself sat contentedly next to him. As they talked and laughed away with some friends, Mary grabbed a bowl of olives and nibbled on a few, somehow it made its way into Gresham's hands and he fed them to her like she was a Roman Empress while he talked. Each time he did so, she looked at him and smiled, with a slight mischievous pleasure. During one of these moments, Mary caught Arabella looking at her, she was observing the way she was looking at Gresham and seemed to take delight in something she saw. With a quick, cheeky flicker of her eyebrows, she looked away again.

As the evening eased on, Mary found herself being talked to by a pair of Arabella's athletic clean-cut brothers, who were evidently trying to impress her with stories of their skills with boats and macho conquests. Nodding unimpressed, she let out a yawn, which she saw was spotted by Gresham a few feet away. He gave her a sarcastic tired expression, she smiled indignantly but she was starting to feel tired and knew she would need her strength for tomorrow.

As Gresham walked up, she anticipated what he was going to say to the two Italian bucks and she decided it wasn't going to be him that said it, so beat him to it.

"Well gentlemen this has been a very stimulating exchange but I'm afraid this man requires escorting to his room so if you'll pardon my leave, duty calls." She gave a mock bow, took his hand and pulled him inside.

They arrived back in their loft, Mary was chuckling and Gresham, his guard down, couldn't help but laugh at her. She hadn't heard him really laugh properly before, but after the mood of the party it seemed more natural now, and made less of an impact on her than it would have a few days ago. As they approached their bed of straw, sheets and cushions, she realised she was still holding his hand. She wasn't tired all of a sudden, and found a nervous fluttering feeling of anticipation was clearing her head. She stopped and turned to look at him. She could feel the same strange expectant energy from him; he didn't seem to want to let go of her hand either.

He looked content, and relaxed; she looked into his

eyes for some clue as to what to do now they had found themselves in this situation. But they didn't need clues, it just happened.

They raised their held hands, still not wanting to let go, slid their fingers through each other's and as they did so, stepped towards each other and kissed, firmly and lovingly.

As he reached round her shoulders and pulled her closer, the affection became passionate. Mary hadn't kissed anybody like this before, but it seemed she had learned a lot in the brief moment she watched Arabella up close the day before; she liked what she had seen and wasn't disappointed by the sensation.

Falling to the bed, their brown jackets fell off too; Gresham took his lips away from hers and looked down at her with an honesty in his eyes she didn't expect. As if he was cradling the most precious thing in the world to him, he slowly put both hands delicately on her shoulder and began to run them down her arms, taking her vest with them. Reaching her breasts, he found their soft heights firm and expectant under his caress. She closed her eyes - determined to embrace every sense of what was happening, it was nothing like she imagined it would be, it was much better. He continued along her flat stomach, he went much lower than the sun had ever gone; as he did so she flung herself up, back to his lips and pulled him back down to the bed.

CHAPTER XII

SAN LAZZARO

When a gentle hand rocked her shoulder to wake her up, Mary expected to see daylight streaming in through the cracks in the wooden roof - but it was still pitch black outside.

Thinking it was time for an early breakfast, she rolled over with a dopy smile that quickly turned to confusion as Gresham knelt over her, fully dressed, and back in his leather flying jacket.

"Wake up, we have to get going. Get your vest and jacket on - it'll be chilly out on the lagoon."

"What? . . . Where are we going?"

"Back to San Lazzaro."

"Now?"

"Yes, now."

Mary stared fuzzily at him in bewilderment; it must have been pushing four in the morning and after the night they had both had, she certainly didn't feel like doing any work.

"Venice is a city that only sleeps for a few hours," he went on, "we have to get over there unseen and now is the best chance we're going to get - come on."

Limp and half asleep, Mary strained to pull herself to her feet, leaving the lovely warm sheets behind. She looked up at him as he was tying his shoes, hoping for some quick smile, a kiss, a touch - anything that indicated their relationship had changed as a result of the nights activities.

Nothing came, he almost went out of his way as he was filling his pockets not to look directly at her - Mary began to feel more vulnerable than even she could stand - sitting there looking at him, and began to feel upset with him, so she gave up for the moment and simply did as he asked.

The cold air in the room made her shiver. She dug out

her white vest and flying jacket. Gresham handed her the revolver she had been given, fully loaded.

"You keep that lodged in the back of your trousers - I'm hoping we won't need them but never leave anything behind that could get you out of trouble quicker than you got into it."

Still confused and frustrated, Mary followed him as quietly as she could as he expertly and silently crept down to the boatyard. The party had long since ended - the last few drinkers had clustered together in the first gondola outside the front door and fallen asleep where they lay; their limp arms hanging down the side of the boat and their heads flung back in a deeply refreshed state.

Gresham and Mary snuck past their gurgling bodies. They walked silently to the water's edge and then away from the town out towards where the boatyards inlet met the Grand Canal. Moored up at the last jetty was a thin slither of a steam launch; almost nothing more than a glorified gondola, with a little boiler and chimney in the middle that powered a propeller at the stern.

"The family use this to tow other boats around," Gresham said quietly as he swiftly untied the moorings with one hand. "I'm sure they won't mind us borrowing it for a few hours but all the same I'd rather not wake them. Here - " he handed her a punting rod, " - we'll shove off using this, I'll get the fire going again and once were out on the canal we'll use the engine."

The boat slipped away from the yard with them both aboard. It had been used that day and the boiler was still warm with a few simmering embers in the little firebox. This was what Gresham was hoping for; with a little tender loving care to the fire, they would soon have some steam. Mary guided them expertly out of the inlet and onto the canal. She had never punted a boat before, only rowed, but she had enough sense to understand the principal and she took to the feel of it very quickly.

This was indeed the time to find Venice at its most

peaceful, even out on the Grand Canal between two towering banks of civilisation. It was eerily quiet, like a great empty arena in the hours after a performance has finished and the audience long departed; the lapping of the water under the prow being the only reminder to them both that their surroundings were real, it was that dead.

When Gresham got steam up after twenty minutes or so, the chuff-chuff of the little pistons seemed obtrusive over the peace of the early hours. They were far enough from land not to be heard but it didn't stop Mary looking either side to see if they were waking someone up.

Settling down by the fireside and topping it up with fresh coal now and then as instructed, Mary watched Gresham as he took the rudder at the stern and guided the boat along.

He was standing looking right at her, but his attention never left the direction ahead of them. He didn't look at her once. She sat there hoping for a smile, even the plainest glance; but she was disappointed. The man she had spent the night with was gone again; she watched and saw the cold armour clad professional at work, the slight concentrated frown, and the calm eyes with that pointed ruthlessness boiling behind their glaze.

She didn't understand, and she suddenly started to feel a little lonely sat there in silence. She found herself unusually calm considering what was going on. As she thought about it, she felt as if a long and maddening ache had been taken away from her - she felt liberated from something but the aftermath was not what she had expected. Although they'd only been awake a few minutes everything seemed much more complicated between them now and she was baffled as to why; she wanted so desperately to talk about it, but he obviously didn't.

There was a small horse-hair blanket in the bottom of the boat, she couldn't help unraveling it and wrapping it around her.

It was a quicker trip in this boat to San Lazzaro than

the last one. The early morning air cooled by the lingering black night provided a sharp wake up call as it hit their bare faces. By the time the black outline of San Lazzaro was spotted easing up ahead the breeze had blown away the warm lethargy of the night before, and Mary was wide-awake and back focussing on why they were here.

The warm brilliance of Venice was behind them and San Lazzaro was a forbidding black mass looming up ahead. There wasn't a scrap of light to be seen anywhere, not even a glimmer through the heavy vegetation.

Gresham's sense of direction was excellent, they eased round to the great assembly of suspicious foliage and came in much closer than their frightened gondolier had. About fifty yards out, Gresham killed the engine and closed the firebox door to hide the glare.

A cold silence once again engulfed them; they drifted in on momentum with the water easing gently past. "When we reach the trees," he whispered, "grab a hold of one, we'll climb up to the wall and over the top."

It seemed to take forever to drift in close to the island's edge; when they eventually hit the trees, however, the noise they heard was the last thing they expected. There was a brief rustling of branches and then two heavy metallic bangs. They had obviously hit something solid; but the island wall should have been a good distance away yet. It even generated a resonating rumble making it feel almost hollow.

Gresham tied the launch to the strongest branch he could find and they scrambled up the twisted interwoven mass in front of them.

Mary began her ascent cautiously, feeling for a sturdy grip before she pulled herself up. She reached out and grabbed what she thought was a firm branch, but it was freezing cold and completely solid. Reaching up further she found another one. She pulled herself in closer to get a good look at what it was. Peering up she saw there were dozens of them, horizontal, stretching up towards the island, just a few inches in from the leaves and twisted branches.

"I think I've found a ladder of some kind," she whispered.

Gresham stopped scrambling and eased over. He reached out and confirmed her suspicion. "Very good, let's see where it leads."

The ladder poles were wide enough for them to ascend side by side; as they got higher the tree coverage over the ladder thickened until eventually they were inside it - engulfed and completely shrouded from the outside. They must have clambered a good thirty feet when they both felt the ladder stop. Reaching out Gresham found the wall behind the ladder had gone, but he couldn't see what was there as they both had a face full of thick leaves and branches.

"I think we've come to the top of whatever this is," he whispered, "these feel like railings rather than a ladder, time to climb inwards and over, ready?"

Scrambling forward over the railing top, both of them fell forward as the wall of branches and leaves instantly disappeared and they landed with a thump onto solid wooden decking.

They both breathed in suddenly at the sight they were now confronted with. Stretching elegantly away from them to form an almost theatrical spectacle was the smooth deck, guns and superstructure of the Battleship Drakensburg.

Looking up, the whole ship was shrouded in a giant patchy dome-like construction of foliage, woven into areas of netting all held up by an intricate arrangement of scaffolding. It was almost unbelievable the level of effort that had been undertaken to hide this stolen ship from view.

Cautiously getting to their feet, they both stood there in an almost reverential silence, as if they had just fallen into the lair of a giant sleeping beast.

All the suspicions they had had of the theft of this ship as being part of something intelligently and meticulously planned were now all too obviously well founded.

After gaping in awe at the cathedral sized structure that encapsulated this huge vessel, Gresham's attention fell on the Drakensburg itself. The ship was softly visible, tiny white lights were strewn at the base of the guns and superstructure, just enough to see it against the dark patchy backdrop - but he didn't like what he saw.

"Well," he said slowly, "we appear to have struck gold, but something's wrong."

"What is it?"

"Look at the guns," he pointed, "the tops have been removed and the barrels cut short. There are huge chunks missing from the superstructure, it looks like all the armour plating's been stripped off. We didn't damage her this badly. The smoke stacks have gone as well, and the glass from all those portholes!"

A loud scraping noise from a nearby open hole in the ship made them both dive for cover behind a big cold bollard further along the deck. There they watched with interest as a number of dark figures, a couple with lanterns, emerged from a hole in the wall of the nearby turret housing. The first figures stopped, looked back and appeared to light the way for more figures dragging out a large chunk of machinery. It looked incredibly heavy; as they rested it on the deck for a moment it made a substantial thud. They struggled to lift it and moved away again; taking small shuffling steps, they struggled along to a gap between the turrets and turned in with it towards the island.

"That looks like a bearing from the propeller shaft," Gresham said curiously as they crept out from the bollard. "Whoever they are, they've completely cannibalised this ship for parts; it's been absolutely stripped bare, she certainly isn't seaworthy anymore - I doubt they'd even get her out of the harbour."

"So now we know why she's been brought here," Mary replied, completely captivated by the unfolding scheme, "but what on earth would they want with the parts of a warship . . . I thought you said this island was home to a community of monks . . . are they warrior monks?"

"No they stopped making those a while back, but your points well taken. I've never known of any need to armour-plate an under-croft before, unless they're brewing particularly volatile altar wine down there. Let's see if these people can't lead us to the answer."

They began to follow the figures towards the other side of the ship.

As they made their way between the aft turrets they saw the island clearly for the first time. The figures were lugging the object down a gangplank, at the bottom of which was a clear path that led up across a vast pristine lawn to the monastery. The path was lit on both sides with tiny flame torches. The monastery itself was in darkness, save for a few windows showing a dim light.

Mary and Gresham waited aboard the ship until the figures were some way down the pristine illuminated path. They then descended carefully to the island, watching their targets intently.

Mary instinctively followed by staying in the black of the flat ground next to the path, out of the glow of the nearby lanterns, but able to follow the figures as they were silhouetted against their own lights. It was a trick she had lots of practice at, sneaking away into her parents' garden at night; but this was far more interesting.

As they rounded the path a long courtyard entrance to the centre of the monastery came into clear view; it was well lit and causing the back glow of light that made the silhouette of the monastery visible. The monastery itself was beautiful; even under the pale moonlight Mary could see it was an eye-catching, well cared for place.

For a while the figures looked like they were moving towards the grand courtyard inside the monastery walls but at the last minute they veered away from the arched entrance to it, and disappeared completely into the shadows of the outer edge. Daring to get closer, Gresham realised they had now vanished from view and he sprinted towards the spot.

Coming up behind him as he stopped at the monastery wall, Mary saw he was looking down. There in the ground was a rectangular opening; just discernable in its black centre was the outline of an ancient stone stairwell, wide enough for two people to walk down side-by-side, visible for only a few steps, the rest lost to the blackness. Gresham drew his gun, Mary followed suit.

"Let's be nosy," he said calmly.

They began their descent; pressing their hands onto the cold stone walls either side to steady their footing as the darkness overwhelmed them. Almost instantly, there was no light at all and the only comfort they had was the sound of one another breathing and the feel of the dank walls. Treading cautiously and feeling with their feet as they went, they edged further and further underground.

This went on for a long time; neither of them were claustrophobic but it got more and more unnerving. It wasn't just the dank black space in front of them, but not knowing how far down it went and the knowledge that lurking in it were some potentially very unfriendly people.

Finally, it levelled out and a glimmer of light through a wooden door appeared up ahead.

Gresham eased his hand round the doorframe, indicated with a beckoning gesture that it was clear and Mary followed him though. They entered a stone corridor, lit with flaming torches fixed to the walls. The whole space was now carved out of solid rock; there wasn't a wooden support or metal beam anywhere.

Moving down to the end, they came to a junction. Taking a moment to decide which direction to head in, Mary became aware of a deep rumbling sound, it could almost have been likened to the wind bellowing through a tunnel like the one they were standing in, but the air all around them was dead calm. The deep bellowing rumble felt as if it were behind every wall, under the floor and above their heads. It was an almost indescribable sensation.

They were both, somehow, drawn to this sound. It was deep and resonating, almost like it was a feeling as well as a noise. They moved left, as if some sixth sense was telling them that was the direction towards the sound's source. Turning another corner the corridor looked as if it opened up into a large room at the end. They approached it cautiously at first. But once they realised no one was in sight, they boldly went for it and stepped out into the open.

Once again they could only stand and stare. Nothing could have prepared them for what they were looking at now.

The air had changed, it was now much cooler and fresher, at first they thought they were outside again and looking up at a dark grey cloudy sky, but they weren't. They found themselves in a massive underground chamber. Either cut out of solid rock or a natural cave, they couldn't tell. It was monstrous, it reminded Mary of a time she saw the inside of St Paul's Cathedral at night, but bigger. The deep booming noise was the sound of the air travelling through this giant organ of rock. They were standing on an artificial wooden balcony, that stretched away both left and right around the cavern perimeter, surrounding the centre.

The sudden manifestation and sheer size of this huge underground chamber quickly paled into insignificance as they moved to the balcony's edge to examine what rested at its centre.

Over the edge of the balcony, there was a sharp drop of a good hundred feet. Some distance away and rising tall out of the centre was a huge object that almost defied description. Mary asked what it was, as if Gresham would know, but he certainly didn't. Together they stood dumbfounded - to the point they neglected to make sure they weren't being watched.

The object was obviously man made. It was almost completely light brown, as if made of wood. From the top it sloped down to round sides like the roof of a monstrous circus tent, except the top was wooden and made up of thousands of strips, like vertical venetian blinds, cascading in perfect lines from the pointed tip downward.

As the top dropped down and out to the round sides it came sheer for a while and around this rim were equally spaced out gun ports with barrels protruding out from the inside.

Further down the outer rim, the shape curved in again towards the bottom, the whole of this underside was perfectly smooth and a sickly light metallic silver colour. It was a strange, eye-catching colour of metal, it seemed to have a natural fluorescence and at points it looked as if it actually shimmered blue. For the entire object's eye beholding features and scale, it must have been hundreds of feet across; this strange metallic underside was the most hypnotic.

"Sir," Mary exclaimed, sounding breathless, "what is this place?"

"I don't know, whatever that is it's certainly the reason hoards of construction materials have been shipped here over the past few months. Judging by all those guns it's a weapon of some kind, but it's not got wings or wheels and it looks too shallow to float so what they plan to do with it, other than to keep it a secret, is anybody's guess."

The more Mary looked at it, the more she thought she had seen it somewhere before, and she said so.

"Where on earth would you have seen something like that before?" Gresham asked, implying that she was probably making it up.

"It resembles a drawing I saw, years ago" she replied thoughtfully, desperately trying to remember. "I'm sure it does. It was in a book . . . on exhibition in London. It was a book full of . . . amazing imaginative machine designs by some inventor. I think the drawing for this was supposed to be some kind of gun carrying car. But it was only a small thing, not like this. This is the same shape and has guns like the drawing but this is massive in comparison, I can't see any wheels either. This thing must be almost as big as the Resurgence . . . and I'm sure the drawing had a smooth wooden top not the stripy design this thing has."

Gresham still didn't quite believe her, but her descriptions were lucid and interesting nonetheless so he considered what she was saying very carefully. "And you say," he asked, "It was supposed to move across land and carry guns?"

"Yes, it was a way to protect men in battle and move guns."

"Well that's not moving anytime soon," he went on, "it must weigh tons . . . look down there - " he pointed, " - there's a structure of some kind. Let's do some more nosing around."

Off on the right hand side, down a slope into the trough this giant creation was sitting in was indeed a long, thin single story building with a flat roof. There was still nobody around, at least nobody they could see. Just the deep echoes of air moving though the cavern, and the chilling feeling emanating from the object neither of them could shake off.

The warehouse's small doors weren't locked. It was pitch black on the inside; Gresham struck a flame up on his lighter and Mary found a conveniently placed oil lamp for them to ignite.

Everywhere there was paper and piles of parchment strewn over long tables. Worn out pencils, rulers, and mathematical tools. They both began to realise they had struck gold; maybe this was where this monstrosity had been designed.

They began to rummage through the papers, holding

them up to the light. There was documentation of all kinds, in various languages, Italian, English, German, even some Georgian.

"This is it!" declared Mary, wrenching a huge beige parchment from a table of mess, "this is the drawing I saw!"

It was a design similar to the object outside, but, just as Mary had described, much smaller and with wheels. There was also no trace of the metal bottom. Gresham had never seen the drawing before, but he had seen many like it, and he recognised the designer's distinctive hand instantly.

"This is from a da Vinci codex," he said with a trace of admiration in his voice, "one of many of his futuristic technological ideas. Many people have tried to turn them into reality, so far without much success."

"Why's that?" Mary asked.

Gresham ran his hands slowly and smoothly over the parchment as he spoke. "Well, though astonishingly visionary most of them are just fantasy, they'd never actually work for the purpose they were intended. Don't get me wrong, there are exceptions, and knowing our luck this is probably one of them. If these monks have succeeded in building one of these that works, it would give a tremendous tactical advantage to any army that used it. That is, if it wasn't made of wood, which that obviously is. Modern artillery would make mincemeat of it, so what the hell are they playing at?"

They looked at each other; neither had an answer. Mary turned again to the sea of papers in front of them and carefully rummaged through the same pile this revealing design had been plucked from.

Another one emerged that displayed a large schematic sketch; it was made of the same material as the first drawing.

"Look, here's another parchment of the same colour," Mary whispered triumphantly.

The document looked like it was from the same codex,

but it was of something much different - and Gresham had seen this one before.

"I'd know that anywhere," he exclaimed. "It has fuelled the imagination of many of our best flight engineers." Mary couldn't place it or make sense of it. It appeared to be a tall rod, sticking out of a flat platform, at the tip of the rod were what looked like paper swirls cascading down and out from the top.

"Doesn't look like that could take much heavy artillery either," she said, dismissing it.

"No, and for a good reason. It was supposed to be a flying machine, but not like any we would be familiar with." Gresham took a hold of it; lay it lovingly down on the table and gently moved the oil lamp closer. Somehow this delicate paper and its contents seemed to be enriched and it glowed bronze under the candle's glare.

For a moment, he seemed lost to it, as if he was admiring it in a library rather than in this dark, oppressive atmosphere.

"It was an early theory of da Vinci's for a sort of a . . . rotorcraft I believe they call it. The idea," he went on gesturing with his hands, "was that if these multi-layered revolving platforms here rotated fast enough the machine would generate enough down force to actually gain flight."

He suddenly paused for an instant to think about what he had just said. He spun sharply to the window and looked out at the object. He felt Mary glaring at him, looking over at her he could tell they were both dawning on the same impossible realisation together.

Mary was about to try and say something, but became distracted as Gresham's eyes suddenly looked past her, settling on something behind her. His hand slowly lifted from the parchment and round to the revolver in the back of his trouser belt.

Mary felt a chill go down her back; she slowly turned to see what he was looking at.

Through the window of the warehouse door,

silhouetted against the dark grey distant cave wall, were dozens of statue still, black hooded figures. Their eyes couldn't be seen, but they could be felt.

Mary backed away. There was another door on the opposite side of the room and they both briefly entertained the idea of leaving the warehouse through it, but they soon realised the seriousness of their predicament as more figures appeared at the windows. They were startling as they didn't seem to move, they were just, all of a sudden . . . there.

Gresham spoke up quietly, "We're completely surrounded, walk away slowly as if nothing had happened." There was a tinge of sarcasm in his voice; he was acting as if they'd just been caught in the headmaster's office reading examination answers. She knew now this was the sign that their situation was serious.

Gresham kicked open the warehouse door; they darted out. Making for the entrance, they were stopped the moment they crossed the threshold of the door. The whole cavern was awash with black figures, stood creepily apart like chess pieces; perfectly still, dotted around as far as the eye could see.

"Well are we glad to see you!" Gresham shouted congenially. "Could one of you point us in the direction of the Cafe Florin?"

There was total silence; the figures didn't move.

"Do you think they'll mind if we just go around them?" Mary asked, trying to copy him in showing disdain for them with smart remarks.

They moved towards the exit.

The closest black figures enveloped them. As the first one reached Mary she threw herself backwards as it tried to grab her. She swivelled on one foot as she leaned back and bringing her other leg up she kicked it hard in the head; her heel made contact with a crunch and a whimper from the cloaked face. But even as this one fell back, she was engulfed from all directions; there was a momentary struggle, she felt something being pushed into her face, she suddenly felt incredibly drowsy . . . then, there was just blackness.

CHAPTER XIII

PRIVATE HELL

Mary first saw a dark wall, then three more, all with no windows, a heavy iron door, two wooden crates, a small barrel containing a few old tools - a shovel, a pickaxe and some broken hammers. That was the sum total of the small room she found herself lying in with Gresham as she slowly woke up.

They had no idea how long they had been unconscious, whether it had been minutes, hours or days; Mary tried to look at her watch but the room was just too dark to make out the dial face.

Mary sat where she had woken and had watched Gresham walk the edges of the room slowly for some time, while they discussed all possible measures of escape - not that there were many. The walls were solid stone, old but completely unyielding. There were no air vents, no holes in the door, and the rusted tools were no good without a more pliable surface.

Having come so close to finding out what all this was about, neither of them wanted to relent and resign themselves to the fact that the only thing they could do now was wait - but that was inevitable. Now they were shut away; and it was all happening without them.

Gresham's pacing was slow, but relentless. He didn't seem occupied, so Mary didn't ask what he was doing, but she couldn't stop watching him. He had one hand gently skimming the wall as he walked round and round; she couldn't tell if he was feeling for something or just passing the time.

"I don't think we'll have long to wait," Gresham suddenly said.

"What do you mean?"

"Up until now these people, whoever they are, have

had it all their own way. Having gone to great pains to keep their operation a secret they'll want to know how we came to be investigating them, who sent us, what we know and who else knows."

"But no one knows we're here, on this island I mean. I know they don't know that but, what hope have we of rescue or escape from here?"

Gresham stopped pacing, he was facing the wall with his hand gently placed on it, his head down. He didn't reply.

"So there's no hope is there . . . what's going to happen to us?" Mary asked quietly.

"You're in His Majesty's Royal Flying Corps Pilot Officer," he said with a sudden undertone of casual sarcasm. "It's not just an occupation, it's an adventure - until you've breathed your last breath there's always hope."

"Don't feed me that adventure story drivel!" she snapped. "I know what it's like dammit . . . I know what it's like to have no hope . . . that . . . maddening vacuum of emptiness, I know it can happen and how frighteningly real a thing it can be, so don't patronise me! I mean it, what's going to happen to us?" She stopped as the echo reverberating around their cell told her she had started shouting.

Her words didn't seem to have any effect on him anyway; there was no reaction. The man she had shared herself with, who had made love to her with all encompassing and sincere feeling, was now buried away; simmering somewhere away behind this exterior and she was struggling to find him. She didn't understand what was wrong with him, or if she had done something wrong, but all the same, she wasn't willing to be dealt with lightly anymore.

"What are you doing anyway? If you know of a way out of here . . . just say it," she rounded.

He looked at her silently for a moment. He didn't have to reply, he could have ignored her, or told to her to shut up. He was still her commanding officer and that was that.

"Last night - " he began to speak, then stopped abruptly. He turned again to face the wall. Mary could see the side of his face. Whatever it was he was trying to say it was creating cracks in the surface; it was something genuinely difficult for him.

But then as quickly as it appeared, it vanished; he returned to running his hands along the wall.

Mary gave up. Everything about this man was cold and practiced; but he had chosen, for a moment, to share feelings with her that were so much more genuine - at least she thought so at the time. Now it was different. There was no evidence of what they had shared in his face; his attitude seemed almost cruel. For a moment she was about to turn away, and torture herself with the realisation that this man was a brutal cad. Maybe he was. But at the last moment he reassured her, in his own way, that there was something between them.

He didn't ignore her, he didn't dismiss her, he gave her the answer she wanted. "There may be hope of getting out of this room," he said calmly, "but, I'm not quite sure yet. In any case, it may be worth us sticking around here a little longer. In their attempts to find out who we are, we may be able to get them to slip up and tell us who they are."

He knew he sounded over confident, and it could be heard in his voice. He quickly turned and caught her shaking her head and breaking into a smile; she tried to pretend for a moment that she wasn't amused but kicked herself for not being able to help it.

Their moment was shattered by a loud sharp grind as the metal bar of the door to their makeshift cell was pulled back. They both instinctively moved to the centre of the room to receive their captors.

The door was quickly flung open; it struck the stone wall with a painfully loud bang. Two large men entered. They were dark skinned and had short prickly beards.

One glared with hostile intent at Mary; he appeared to

have recently broke his nose. Pausing for a moment, their rifle barrels trained on the prisoners, they took two big steps into the cell, and then sidestepped to make way for other figures waiting outside the door to enter.

Gresham stood upright, with an impatient expression on his face, evidently to show their captors contempt. Mary watched his expression turn from this cool practiced sureness, to barely concealed unnerved astonishment and bewilderment - as one of the dark figures outside the room, stepped into the light.

It was Arabella.

She stopped just inside the door; she glared penetratingly at Gresham.

Mary gaped at her in confusion; it was obvious she was not here to rescue them.

Mary looked at Gresham, then back to Arabella; confounded. Arabella's face had no traces of the warm glow Mary had been so used to seeing in her. There were tears being desperately fought back in her wrathful eyes - the only evidence of the suffering she was feeling below the intense anger and hatred that was pouring out from her entire body.

Gresham frowned questioningly at her; he couldn't hide his astonishment.

She held his gaze defiantly; she shook her head side to side, slowly. As she did so she looked like she was desperately controlling an urge to lunge forward and tear him apart, but the effort required to fight back the tears seemed to keep her still.

"Why you make me do this, you stupid English bastard?" Her voice was pained and sour, as if by speaking she was ripping out her own insides with each word, but there was rage in there too, so much rage. "Why can you not go and fucking police the world somewhere else!"

Gresham struggled to respond, "Arabella, what are you . . . what? What am I making you do?"

"You came here to find the ship for the Germans . . .

you have orders to find out why it was stolen and stop whoever did it. Well I did it, but I cannot let you stop me, I can't you stupid bastard!" She began to breathe heavily and a tear trickled from one eye as she balled at him. She wiped it away very quickly, as if it was showing weakness, and that it had been a while since she had allowed herself to be seen like this.

"Why! Why could you not have been somewhere else, doing something more useful instead of forcing me to . . . you're the last human being in the world I wanted to find here, for fuck sake!"

"Arabella," he continued slowly, "whatever it is, I can help, we can help. You don't have to do anything you don't want to."

"You wouldn't help! For all you have done, you are the same as all the rest in the end. You would think it too bad, but never mind. Stop what you are doing and let us lock you away so you can never get what you want, no! I know better than that. You have seen what we have here; you are clever enough to understand what it is. As long as you are alive, you will not stop. . . so you force me to . . . "

She fought back more tears, her face was crimson with rage, and the conflux of emotions inside her was overwhelming. The room fell deadly silent. Mary looked with gut wrenching grief at the enraged face of the dear friend she thought she had made. It seemed they had more in common even than Mary had first thought. A body full of overpowering rage and soaring pain, she recognised those feelings and had thought her own experience with them had broken new boundaries for a human to endure.

Now, she was learning otherwise. Looking at Arabella, she began to feel an unexpected surge of guilt and humility.

Gresham's face dropped to the floor. He was still trying to do his job, but it had taken an unexpected turn. He spoke slowly. "Arabella, what have you done . . . I thought I knew you, mia amica."

"You of all the people can never say that to anyone! You never knew me!" she raged cruelly. "You knew . . . what I used to be . . . long ago. But now it's just a face, a mask that covers the . . . nothing that lies beneath." After an icy silence, her next words to him were slow, cold and pitiful.

"Just like you."

Gresham still didn't look at her; he seemed to be fighting for an inner composure, and after a moment he seemed to rally.

"What did you do to the crew of the Drakensburg?" He said flatly.

Arabella looked at him for a moment, and a part of her anger seemed to fade as if she was surrendering herself to the situation. She turned and beckoned with her head to a figure still outside the room. It came in, a dark hooded shape, clutching what looked like some sort of lamp. It had a golden stand, a rising neck, but at the tip of the neck there was no bulb, instead it had a small silver cylinder, hollow, with wires coming out of the hollow inside and disappearing down the neck.

The strange colour of it was not lost on Gresham or Mary; it seemed to shimmer with a dark blue glow, the same as on the underside of the huge creation in the cave.

Arabella held it up to the light. "This, is a . . . well, we do not quite know what it is. We think it is some kind of weapon experiment - but, as you would say, who knows these days."

She was now speaking softly. "When turned on this silver part creates a powerful electric area which gives horrible painful seizures to anyone near it. They writhe, scream and convulse, then it kills them. Leaving them totally disfigured, frozen in horrifying pain. A friend of ours stole it from a German hospital in southern Africa. A place called Lüderitz. They had rounded up thousands of native people, imprisoned them in this camp and - can you believe - we found them testing these things on them.

They would invite ten or twelve people at a time, into a surgery room, as if to get medication. Then they would turn on one of these that sat on a doctor's desk. They would watch, and record what they could see, then cut the bodies up and send their bones back to Germany, to universities. What is 'your Majesty's Government' doing about this? What are you doing about this?"

Gresham didn't answer.

"You see," she went on, "you're no different from the rest, you would only lift a finger to solve problems for your little island, for it to have its millions of knives and forks - " the last sentence was directed at Mary, "- so, when we needed a ship for materials, we chose a German one, and used this on them. They have gone to where their victims were waiting for them now."

Gresham wasn't giving much away. He looked at her coldly. "You have put these things on your - 'creation' - out there?"

"Enough to send thousands to Hell at once, and we intend do that very soon."

"And who would be these thousands?"

"We are taking it to Constantinople; when we have rid the world of them, we will simply carry on. This time next week, you'll have to go to a museum to find out who the Turks were."

"You're going to use it . . . to wipe out the entire Turkish people?" He asked, barely containing a look of revulsion. "Arabella . . . in the name of god, why?"

Arabella handed back the little weapon and beckoned her companions out of the room. When the armed men objected, she barked at them fiercely and they retreated to just outside the door.

She turned back to Gresham.

"I am not Italian. The man you thought was my father was only my step father, he was from Venizia but my mother," she let out a longing sigh. "My mother . . . my mother was Armenian, I was raised by her, not my step

189

father like I told you. I lived with her, all of my life, I came to Venizia only once before, when my mother married my step father - that was when we first met. After - I went back home, until four years ago." She looked straight at Gresham, and breathed quickly as if she was about to shout again, but she didn't. She continued, quieter and colder. "Adana . . . our home was Adana."

The name meant nothing to Mary, but she knew it was of great significance; she heard Gresham breath out through his mouth.

"I watched," Arabella continued slowly, "as she was . . . she was bathing when it happened, we had a tin bathtub . . . the roof fell and a beam kept her from getting out . . . the fire from the rooms below acted like . . . a . . . stove for the water." Her breath became short as her chest tightened and her entire body began to shiver. "I tried to get her out . . . I tried so hard . . . I couldn't . . . but I couldn't leave her . . . I couldn't leave her! I . . . I watched . . ."

Her eyes had fallen on an empty corner of the room; Gresham and Mary knew that blank stone wall was now a theatre on which the horrific images from her memory were being played out.

There was a long, and solemn silence. Arabella eventually closed her eyes tight and a tear was forced out that ran down her cheek.

It felt like the extreme of disrespect to say anything, but to the aversion of even Mary, Gresham spoke up.

"Arabella, she wouldn't have wanted this for you, none of them would."

Arabella angrily grabbed him by the neck, and shoved him hard against the wall with a bone-breaking snap. She tightened her grip around his collar and seethed at him.

"Is there nothing left in there, you bastard! You cannot tell me," she raged, "how I should feel! Don't tell me revenge won't bring them back. You know! You know what it is - to be a vessel of vengeance . . . retribution you know to be right. You know how it feels when there is nothing beyond it, and enjoy it, enjoy the freedom that feeling gives you - to do what is right!"

"Tell me then! Tell me you're not about to become exactly the same as the people who killed your mother!" he rallied.

Arabella reached round to the revolver he still had tucked into his back, grabbed it and thrust it violently into his chin, with the barrel poised perfectly to blow his jaw off.

"Stop trying to do your job!" She was now, almost frothing desperately at the mouth. "You push me to this you bastard, you fucking push me to this!"

"Arabella!" Mary roared, "don't, please!"

"Why not!" Arabella continued to rage.

"Because I don't want him to die . . . I love him don't I!"

There was another silence; Gresham tried to look at Mary but his head was forced upwards by the gun.

For a moment Arabella didn't move, then slowly her grip on the gun became slack and her head rested on Gresham's shoulder as she began to laugh desperately.

She then lurched round to Mary, bringing the gun down to her side as her arms flopped and her laugh echoed throughout the underground caverns.

She laughed at Mary, almost pitifully, and pointed at Gresham.

"You love him . . . silly girl! There's nothing in there!" She sneered, mocking. "What do you know about love, 'spoilt runaway', about anything? You say my life is 'so simple and wonderful' . . . fuck you - fucking idiot."

Arabella threw the gun at her half heartedly, and slowly walked to the door.

Stopping on the threshold, without looking back, she spoke one last time. "You will be sealed in here, and it is far underground. Soon there will be no one down here."

"Even if we don't make it out of here Arabella,"

Gresham said hoarsely after having a gun barrel shoved into his neck, "they'll try and stop you."

"Not unless they can learn to see in the dark they will not."

Her party withdrew; the door was sealed again with a grinding metallic shudder.

The draught of air created by the door closing, caused the little paraffin lantern hanging from the ceiling to flicker. Gresham walked slowly up to it, pulled it down and peered at it. "This will burn for another hour or so, then that will be it."

He put it down on the ground, dragging his feet as if exhausted. He came to rest against the back wall, leaning on it with his shoulder and sighed heavily.

Mary stood, where she had last spoken, frozen. Like someone who had been shot through the chest, and, in deep shock, was only slowly beginning to feel pain.

They had found the Drakensburg, but that didn't seem to matter anymore.

They now knew they were the only hope millions of men, women and children had from a mass genocide, but the cold resignation beneath Arabella's rage was infectious.

Mary was the first to break the long silence, speaking bluntly, where she stood. "What is Adana?"

By now, Gresham was sat with his back to the wall; he was gripping the tip of the fingers on his right hand with his left and picking at them, staring down. He didn't look at her as he answered.

"It's a city in southern Turkey. The area is largely populated by Armenians, has been for centuries. It's now part of the Ottoman Empire. A few years ago some Armenians from that area decided they wanted to be treated a little fairer by their Turkish masters, the Turks didn't agree so they sent troops to Adana to restore order. But the troops went too far. Something like thirty thousand Armenian Christians were massacred in their homes - though it was probably a lot more. As we have witnessed this evening, far from subjugating the Armenians, as in all these cases, it has simply bolstered their resolve for independence. And now . . . vengeance for Adana."

He looked at her. "We sent warships to the black sea coast, and we helped thousands of refugees escape the horror. But that's all we could do - after that it became just another barbaric atrocity from the east to be given a few column inches in the Times, worthy of a few ounces of removed pity over breakfast tables . . . and then, forgotten about. Except, of course, by those who were actually there. As long as that's all that us, supposedly good people, do about these things . . . they'll always be another Adana."

He got wearily to his feet, walked over to Mary and spoke, almost tenderly.

"Mary . . . look at me." She slowly turned from the direction of the door. "An awful lot of people are going to die soon . . . I'd rather not be in a room like this if I think I can do something about that, I'd like to think there's still something in me that keeps me from doing nothing about anything."

Mary looked at him, confused and unsure if he was being genuine or if his gentle persuasion was just something he turned on and she gave him a sort of a desperate half laugh. "Do you really believe that? Is there anything in the world that you actually believe that brings you hope or are you just saying that because you think I'm going to stop helping you?"

He leaned back in surprise and looked stern, "it's your job to help me Pilot Officer."

"Was it part of your job to make love to me last night Lieutenant Colonel? . . . Because that's what it feels like now."

Gresham frowned in reflection. "You still think you know what it's like to be truly without hope?"

Mary looked in the direction of the door again, and her head fell.

"I think," he continued, "you'll get some comfort from that thought at some point - perhaps not yet."

"That'll be about all the comfort I get I think," she mumbled, "but what do I know about anything anyway . . . I'm just a spoilt little rich runaway."

"Maybe you are," he said loudly.

"And maybe last night I made a terrible mistake!"

Mary looked down at the dirty floor. She couldn't look at him all of a sudden. It was too confusing. She thought about those perfect moments they had shared earlier that evening, of the amazing wisdom she thought Arabella had shared with her, when she spoke on the nature of love and seemed to have drawn out Mary's true feelings. Now, after seeing what was actually lying beneath the shell of that wonderful person, Arabella's warning of not actually liking what you find in someone when you get that deep now seemed like the only genuine advice given to her that evening.

She eventually looked back at Gresham, stood up, straightened her tunic, breathed in and rallied more than she had ever done in her life.

"I may be a rich runaway, but I'm a rich runaway with a job, a job I intend to do and I don't need any persuading thank you. Now are we going to try and save thousands of lives or is your occupation really just to fly around the world being moody and sleeping with 'silly girls' like me when it pleases you?"

He looked at her, irritably, and marched over to face her directly.

"So Arabella was right about you too?" Mary went on, undaunted, "there really is nothing more to you either?"

Gresham's expression settled defiantly into unreadable again.

He moved to the centre of the room, and stared straight at the back wall. "Hand me that pickaxe," he said coolly. Confused but keen to see what he was at, Mary plucked the rusty old tool from the barrel in the corner. It was heavy and sturdy enough but it was smothered in rust and the end was blunted from years of use. Gresham took it; he twirled it round in his hands and examined the end. "It'll do, stand behind me, but slightly to the left - I don't want to hit you."

Mary did so, but was still puzzled. She didn't bother to press him for an explanation. She knew it would all be clear shortly. The room fell eerily silent again; she watched him just standing there, staring at the back wall. He was paying it the most studied regard, as if it were a priceless piece of exquisite art. His attention to it was palpable in the air. It was like watching a great painter in front of a blank canvass, sizing up on what spot his brush was to land first.

After a while, he raised his thumb to his mouth and licked it, and then taking a single step forward he used the moisture on his thumb to make a small mark on the wall. He stepped back; Mary could feel him putting his weight on his back foot. "Take hold of my arm, don't let go. Wait for the room to fill, then swim for your life."

Mary didn't have a chance to invite him to elaborate. As the last words calmly left his mouth as if it were dinner table conversation, he raised the pickaxe above his head and with an almighty force, slammed the tip at the spot on the wall, hitting it dead on.

The wall exploded at them. A roaring mass of bricks and ancient mortar came apart with astonishing ease after hundreds of years of being merged together. Mary was struck in the face and thrown back; she thought it was a brick it was so strong. Very quickly, she realised it was water gushing in.

The water was black and freezing. The room filled in seconds and as Mary was just coming to terms with being thrown back against the door, she was lifted from her feet and the ceiling came down on them with unstoppable force. She still had a hold of his arm, and she had the sense and nerve to operate automatically on the simple instructions she had received.

The water engulfed them. It was inky black and bitingly cold; she could see nothing, she felt Gresham pull her forward, and she could still feel the force of water coming at them so she knew it was the right direction to swim in.

She kicked hard and scooped the water past her as hard as she could with her left arm. For a moment it felt hopeless, the force of the water was too strong, it actually felt as if they were going backwards, but it was so black they couldn't tell. Mary took comfort in the fact that as she kicked she couldn't feel the wall behind her, so they must have been making some progress.

Suddenly it got easier, but they were running out of air, as she kicked harder in desperation she could feel Gresham shaking as he did the same. Then the hard regular thumbing of her heart crying for air took over. Harder and harder it throbbed, she began to feel its desperation all over her body. It felt like it throbbed right up to her head, there was a moment of panic as if it was about to overtake her, and she was about to cry out in desperation. Then, the wonderful tell tale sound of water rushing down her ears signified they had reached the surface.

They both emerged silently screaming for air. Deep gasping breaths settled their pounding hearts. They were free.

They both trod water for a few moments, flapping like butterflies, coming to terms with their new surroundings. It was still dark; they hadn't been unconscious down in the bowels of the island for too long. Turning on the spot, they saw the rocky shoreline of the island a few yards away and swam for it.

The huge walled perimeter was almost unassailable, but as luck would have it a nearby collection of jagged boulders rested up against the island edge, and gave them some chance of getting back on to dry land.

They clambered up, breathless after their experience,

stopping on top of the biggest boulder to rest before trying to clamber over the wall.

The panting eased and the pain in their chests died away. They both looked at each other.

"Well done, you're a damn good swimmer."

"Where did you learn to do that?" she replied.

Gresham gathered his breath some more before he responded. "My father, was miner, in Yorkshire - all his life. When I was a boy, I spent the early hours of every morning carrying his tools for him and watching him work, down in the mineshafts. He knew a coalface better than he knew the face of his own son, he would stare at it for hours, getting on intimate terms with it. Then he'd make his mark, ask me for whatever pick he wanted, like I was a golfer's caddy. Then if he hit it just right, tons of coal would come collapsing out. Saved hours of digging. I hated it, but learned a few things over the years. As soon as I felt the wall down there I knew there was water behind it, it was so cold and . . . well, you bang your elbow on a table a thousand times and it just hurts a little, but bang it with the same force in just the right way and you break it."

"Well," Mary smiled, "I'm grateful to your father right now."

"Me too, another of life's genuinely new experiences encountered this evening."

Mary was aware she still had her watch clipped to the inside pocket of her jacket. She took it out but couldn't make out the time. It was useless anyway - she held it to her ear and realised it had stopped ticking. The water must have damaged it.

They eventually clamoured to their feet, there was now a tinge of light blue in the sky, the sun was just coming up and the blackness was lifting from the lagoon.

As Mary stood up, she looked back down at the water, confused. "Look," she pointed inquisitively, "we seem to have climbed up from the water a lot further than I thought."

Gresham saw what she meant instantly. There must have now been a dozen boulders visible beneath them. As they looked on, another emerged very quickly, and then another. The water level was dropping rapidly.

"What is it?"

"I don't know," he replied, "I've heard of flash flood, but flash droughts?" He suddenly became transfixed by something further out on the lagoon. "Look, out there!"

The water appeared to be streaming past them and at the same time the level was dropping as it did so. Further out, about half a mile away, it seemed to be gushing in the opposite direction. Faster and faster until the giant swirling mass of water literally roared, it kicked up a breeze that washed over them. Then it became clear what was forming, a black hole emerged dead in the centre of this melee; it was a giant whirlpool.

The eye of the whirlpool opened up, and grew wider, as it did so it sucked more water down into it to form its swirling walls. It was like something out of a biblical tale. Mary and Gresham could only look on in horror as it grew to huge proportions. The giant terrifying eye began to suck in air as well as water; they could feel themselves being pulled towards it. They threw their bodies flat against the boulders and kept their grip firm. The eye of the swirling mass seemed to growl, as it grew bigger, it was terrifying.

Gradually the growling roar of the water was overtaken by something else, the only thing Mary could relate it too was the sound she imagined a billion bees would make, swarming in anger all at once. The deep resonating hum got louder. Then, as it became deafening, it appeared.

Rising out slowly from the eye of the whirlpool, came the great creation they had seen in the cave below. Its gun ports were now open, and cannon barrels stretched out all around its perimeter. The eerie deep blue metal smeared all over its base, ebbed and flickered in what was left of the moonlight reflecting off the water. On top, the cascading dome of venetian blinds was now an eye-dazzling blur of motion. It was indeed what they had suspected, a flying machine. The deafening humming was coming from the layers of swirling blades stretching from the top, creating a hurricane like down force that propelled its huge mass out and away from its underground lair.

For a moment, it hovered perfectly above the water. The roar of the whirlpool dissipated further as the huge eye began to close. As it rose higher, it became difficult to see against the dark and began to move off to the east. As it eased away, at about two miles the shimmering glow of its underside became too faint to make out. It was now invisible and as the swarming hum ebbed away, the spectacle was over.

Neither of them had any words left to describe what they had just seen; they stood there frozen to the rock as the peace of the lagoon returned. As the eye of the whirlpool closed, there was a huge upsurge of water from its closing spot; the surge settled into a vast rolling wave.

"Get over the wall quickly!" shouted Gresham. They scrambled to the top, but they weren't fast enough. They did get onto the pristine lawn of the monastery grounds once again - but were thrown there in a surge of water crashing over the top of the island's walls.

Getting to their feet, shaking the cold water off again, Gresham, standing closer to the water's edge began to stroll towards Mary, wiping the silt off his sleeves. He strolled past her in the direction of the shell of the Drakensburg. She called after him. "Don't tell me - walk away slowly as if nothing had happened!"

CHAPTER XIV

ONYX

"Jesus wept Tommy! Reminds me o' something I once saw after I had my first taste o' that Irish Poitin. Are you sure they hadn't drugged you or something?"

"Quite positive, thank you Jimmy," Gresham replied. "Otherwise I'd be a lot less anxious to forego a few days of your excellent hospitality - as it stands we don't have long. Did your people come up with anything?"

"Italian army stormed the island a few hours ago, that whirlpool bullshit wrecked a ton o' moorings, some of which belonged to some right influential locals. I told them about all the strange river traffic going on over there and then some malarkey about weapons, so they finally went to see for themselves. All they found were a few old monks, an abandoned cave system, and these." He clicked his fingers at a waiting line of his 'artistes'. A long curly haired brunette with a swagger produced a small wooden box. Jimmy lifted out of it the codex pages they had seen under the island.

"These things have been missing for over a year, they suspected I might have had something to do with it but, not usually to my taste. Anyways, I said I'd see they were returned to their rightful custodians - eventually. Avoid the embarrassment of official channels; their disappearance is still pretty hushed."

Jimmy gave a sly wink and went to see the codex put away to his satisfaction, leaving Gresham and Mary alone in his serene courtyard garden. Having bathed in Jimmy's private pool, washed and been fed a hearty breakfast, they were now in bathrobes, thoroughly warm and dry after their exertions.

Gresham noticed a smattering of papers on a nearby table; he took one, and a pencil and began to scribble. "I'm going to send a signal to the Resurgence; all being well they should have engine power back about now. I'm updating them and ordering them to proceed directly to Constantinople and take a defensive position over the city - that's if they're not too late. It would be the best part of a day's round trip to pick us up. I'll instruct them to inform London about what we know, and to contact the Turkish army."

"Will they be able to do anything?"

"Probably not; granted this is all guesswork, but it's all we can do. We don't know how fast this da Vinci inspired flying monstrosity can move. If it's any quicker than the Resurgence, they'll know as soon as they get there. We don't even know how high this thing can fly; if they can't get above cloud level to hide during the day, there's a chance the Turks - if word can be got to them in time - could shoot it down before it did too much damage."

"But if it can stay above cloud level?"

"Then we don't have much hope of stopping them."

Gresham finished scribbling his coded message, tore away the page, slotted it into a little pocket in his gown and let out a peaceful sigh as he looked around at the still trees; as if getting the story down on paper had helped calm his thoughts.

Mary reclined in her big cosy chair; the tranquillity of this lovely courtyard was very welcome after the last twelve hours. She felt now, that maybe their part in this affair was over and they could leave it to the Resurgence. They were too far away and stuck in a beautiful city - why not be thankful to be alive and wait out the situation from this safe distance? The thought crossed her mind; but the pace of her thoughts told her that if there was still a chance they could help, she wanted to try.

"Is there anything more we can do now?" she asked, half expecting him to call her absurd for thinking so. Instead he looked thoughtful; he seemed to feel the same way she did.

"Well," he began slowly, "if we can get to Constantinople quick enough, there might be a chance of rendezvousing with the Resurgence in time to be there when that death machine arrives." He didn't sound too optimistic. "To hell with it," he suddenly said defiantly. "Even if we can't get there in time, I don't want to stay here . . . how about you?"

"I would like to be there very much. I left many people I hope to call friend someday aboard your ship . . . and it's our job isn't it"

He nodded firmly. "Alright. Jimmy! What's become of the plane we flew in on?"

Jimmy was in the process of emerging from the building. "Ha! Well Tommy, it's like this; the family who owns the vineyard you tore it up with, were a little quicker at disposing of it than I thought. They have actually sold it to the Italian Army; it's been fuelled up for immediate use and is under canvas, strapped to a flat railway truck in a siding over on the mainland."

A natural idea suggested itself to Mary. "Jimmy, what's the quickest way from here to Constantinople - please tell me it's by train."

"Well yeah ma'am I guess so, all depends on when you're leaving."

"As soon as possible."

Jimmy rolled his eyes up in thought; he didn't seem confident in the idea. "Well, I'm afraid there's no direct train between here and there this week - you'd have to change all over the place and that'll take days. Your best bet is a train leaving in an hour or so from Chioggia, get you direct to Varna at least, on the black sea by . . . sometime late tonight. Only stops once."

Gresham jumped in. "Jimmy, how far would you say Varna is from Constantinople?"

"Bout . . . hundred fifty miles."

Gresham turned to Mary. "If you're suggesting what I think you are, that's about two thirds of the operational range of our plane on a full tank. We wouldn't have much time to find the Resurgence once we got there, but what the hell!"

Mary smiled and nodded. Gresham turned back to Jimmy. "My friend, is there any chance you can get that truck our planes strapped to attached to this train to Varna."

"Yeah . . . why?"

"We'll travel with it to Varna, then fly on from there - it's the best we can do. If you could get us two tickets as well - charge it to His Majesty."

It was agreed. Gresham gave Jimmy his communication for the Resurgence - to be transmitted via a British intelligence control in Milan. Mary and Gresham rushed back to the boatyard on Gresham's instruction. They were going to get their belongings and uniforms. Mary was a little apprehensive about going back, but Gresham assured her he didn't think there would be any trouble.

He was right. They found the boatyard deserted; the front door to the cottage was open but no one was inside. What had happened to Arabella's family? Who knew? Maybe they had gone with her, maybe not, but the life Mary felt when she first arrived at this place, wasn't here anymore.

Jimmy had leant them each a few clothes, packed up tight in a brown suitcase, and was going to have some sent ahead to the train.

Opening the suitcase back in the loft bedroom, Gresham found Jimmy had procured for him a dark grey pinstripe suit from Turnbull and Asser. Even Mary was astonished by the generous resourcefulness of their host; she happily pulled a long beige sports coat over a white shirt with a tall stiff collar and a narrow crimson necktie. A very recent fashion trend for travelling women, though she still thought about wearing her leather-flying jacket over it. She was desperate to put her whole uniform back on but knowing they probably looked less conspicuous than 'silk spinners', she thought it prudent not spoil the effort Jimmy had made.

After they had gathered what they were taking and packed their case, Gresham performed a final and thorough check to make sure they had left no evidence of them being there, and Mary took stock of their little attic home. So much had happened in such a short space of time, she knew the memory of this room would be with her for a very long time. She had a feeling she wouldn't see it again, so she took a little stick of straw from the pile that had been their bed and stuck it in a pocket.

A little steam launch with a local sailor, courtesy of Jimmy, was waiting for them at the bottom of the boatyard. They unceremoniously hopped in and immediately chuffed away from the quayside. Mary took one last look back at what now seemed an empty stage, which had been the scene of one of the happiest nights of her life. She never saw it again, but the memory of that beautiful little boatyard in Venice stayed with her.

When they both hurriedly approached the station from the quayside, Chioggia was awash with activity. They were now on a little peninsula that jutted out from the mainland and amongst the throng of carts and bicycles in front of the station, they even saw a motorcar parked up on the pavement.

On the cusp of walking through the station building to the platform, a very well dressed young woman, all in deep bearskin brown and with a black centre-creased soft brimmed hat pulled down almost over one eye, approached them quick footedly.

Her American accent came through strong as she pulled an envelope from her bag. "Jimmy says the only compartment left on the train was in first class. You have it all to yourselves. You're up front but the plane is coupled at the very end behind the last carriage. He said you may also need these."

She produced a slim wooden box with gold hinges. Gresham knew what it was as he owned a box very much like it.

"We're not here for the hunting season," he said sternly.

"Maybe you aren't," replied their chic messenger, "but someone else is. After we booked your tickets there was a last minute cancellation for another compartment in the next carriage; it was swiftly taken by two men, travelling together. It's a single bed cabin."

Gresham took the box, opened it just a crack and peeked in. It was two silver pistols fitted with Maxim Silencers, a recent American invention.

"Tell Jimmy thank you, we'll watch our backs. And should we go hunting, which cabin should we be paying particular attention to?"

"They are in seventeen."

Gresham nodded in thanks, took Mary's arm and led her along the crowded platform towards the train. She found she didn't mind being on his arm but she was a little confused. He noticed her glancing at it purposefully. "Mary, these gentlemen could be a million different things other than what Jimmy suspects, but just in case he's right that means we're being watched, so let's act like the young travelling couple we look like."

"Does that include in private, Thomas?"

She watched his face and hoped for some kind of response; anything would have done to help clear the air between them. To her disappointment there was none - he didn't register the comment at all, his eyes were scanning the bustling crowd on the platform. He had called her Mary again, for the second time, seemingly without thinking, but he hadn't noticed.

The cabin was indeed first class; two spacious bunks with duck feather pillows and blankets, sandalwood panelled walls inlaid with decorative tulip and purple wood flowers, a generous wardrobe, an alcove for washing, two velvet-upholstered armchairs and a table perched at a large window. On top of the table was an ice bucket containing a bottle of champagne, two glasses and a plate of smoked salmon, horseradish and dill crostini.

Mary was a little wary. "How do we know it's safe to drink? Perhaps those men sent it and it's poisoned."

"I'm certain Jimmy sent it for us," he replied dryly.

"How can you be so convinced?"

"It's a Perrier-Jouët seventeen."

The carriage gave a rattled sigh and a brief shudder, as it was pulled from its comfortable standstill by the brooding black locomotive up at the front and the train eased out of the station. The creaking of the carriages being urged into motion was accompanied by the ubiquitous heavy breaths of a powerful locomotive inhaling steam into its cylinders to heave the cumbersome load out of its resting standstill.

As they trickled onto the mainland proper, leaving the peninsular with its view of the distant lagoon behind, the train began to weave north, picking up speed. The breaths of steam at the front became more regular and less pronounced as the driver skilfully wound in the piston intake to use less fuel now the train was moving and pacing up to a sprint.

The welcoming snack was pleasant, but they both preferred the hearty quaffable fare of the place they were leaving. Mary had found a new appreciation for the pleasure of eating: one that didn't involve dressing or nibbling at dollops and smears on a plate.

They sat restfully in silence, relieved to have made the train. All they could do now was wait, let the train make the effort of delivering them to where they needed to be and worry about the rest when they got there. Mary could have almost kidded herself that they were safe for a while, but thoughts soon turned to the rushed warning about cabin number seventeen.

"Do you think they're in some way - working for the

Armenians?"

Gresham's reply was slow and considered. "Jimmy is right to be suspicious about two men travelling in a single compartment, booking moments after we were booked onto the same train. Though it could be a coincidence in any number of ways. Maybe they're just desperate to get where we're going for some reason and one doesn't mind sleeping on the floor. If they are after us, I'd be more concerned about how they found out about our plans so quickly, given that we didn't tell anyone . . . except Jimmy."

He suddenly stood up, reached for the wooden case containing the silenced pistols. Removing one he loosened the cylinder and took out a few bullets. After jiggling them in his hand for a moment he returned them seemingly satisfied. "We can't afford to take any chances," he went on, "we have ten hours to Varna, we can have food brought here so there's no reason to leave the cabin . . . except the plane."

"What about it?"

He looked at her, thinking quickly.

"If I was intending to stop us reaching Constantinople, the first thing I'd do is go to the rear carriage, open the end vestibule and uncouple the wagon carrying the plane from the rest of the train, but . . . only after it was too late to do anything about it. Just after the last stop this evening, I'll make one trip to the end of the train and hang around a while."

A few hours rolled by, watching the warm glow of northern Italy turn into the lushly forested mountainous landscape of the southern territories of the vast Austro-Hungarian Empire.

A delicious three-course lunch was served in their cabin by white-coated stewards.

Mary didn't know what to order. She barely recognised anything on the menu, but it was everything anyone with a palate could hope for from a first class menu on a train in this part of the world. It relied on ingredients from all the locales the train was travelling through to make it work.

Piedmontese peppers and white anchovies arrived as a starter; all roasted in their sweet, generous juices. For their main course Gresham had ordered them both Fegato Alla Veneziana, a bowl of calf's liver, with melted onions and sage. It was delicious.

Mary wanted to try a wine like she had tasted at Jimmy's for dessert, so they had catuccini with a glass of Vin Santo to finish.

Black coffee at the very end of proceedings provided a welcomed balance after their one hour of sleep, - but it didn't last long. With the hypnotic cradling the movement of the train provided, Mary was soon having trouble keeping her eyes open. Gresham told her to get three hours sleep and he would stay awake, then they would swap.

Five thirty came and all was well, sounds could be heard of passengers withdrawing to their compartments to begin the long process of dressing for dinner. Mary, now sat quietly at the window while Gresham slept, was thankful she was stuck from doing the same. Even if it was potential assassins keeping them from leaving for the restaurant car, it was still like gaining the right to avoid dull school lessons to Mary.

Though she sat by the window, she couldn't help but watch Gresham as he slept. She had never seen him quite so vulnerable; she enjoyed a momentary feeling of being able to be protective towards him.

She watched his face; it was relaxed and restful, natural, she thought. No hint of guard, calculation, or any forced barriers; as she had seen him only once before.

She desperately wanted to talk about everything that had happened, but during lunch they were too tired and now she didn't know what to say. She knew she was still making sense of her feelings too.

By seven the sun was well and truly gone, and the view from the window was a shroud of black, occasionally obscured by fleeting streams of white smoke passing by from the engine up front.

The train entered a tunnel and the echo of the wheels hitting the rail joints woke Gresham.

He rolled over on the bottom bunk to face a small clock over the wash hand basin.

"You let me sleep for too long, I should have checked the plane by now."

"I didn't want to wake you, I enjoyed watching you sleep."

He huffed, unsatisfied and rose quickly, moving to the basin and splashed his face with some cold water. Drying himself off, he hesitated for a while, staring into the sink. It was as if he didn't know what to do.

There was awkwardness. Mary could feel it. She stood up and went over to him, she placed her hand very gently on his shoulder; he moved instantly to the window, without looking at her.

She sighed and leaned back against the bunks.

"You know," she began slowly after a while, "there's something curious about human beings I've always strangely enjoyed experiencing. Not that it's happened to me a lot. When you're alone with anyone, for a long time, with nothing to do. You can do the chitchat, or the 'meaningless pleasantries', with them for a little while. But then, once they are exhausted - you actually have to talk to each other, and it's amazing where that can lead."

She watched as his head, still facing away from her, tilted a little sideways. She had not forgotten the moments in Venice when, even in the middle of something important, he had stopped, surprised by something she had said and let loose a little trace of being vaguely impressed.

She was sure that was what was going on now.

"That's a very perceptive observation," he replied quietly.

"Well . . . I've . . . been alone with my observations,

more or less all my life. Nobody's ever given me the opportunity to have them listened to before, not quite like this. You're the closest thing to the first but . . . right now, I can express any feelings I want, but . . . there are certain ones I just don't want to, voluntarily. In case I . . . get something back I couldn't bear to hear."

He didn't say anything else; he just kept looking out of the window.

"I felt," she said at last, "last night I got close to someone, someone I liked very much and someone who I felt knew me, and I them. But you're gone . . . what is it? Please tell me, tell me now, if last night didn't mean anything . . . that it was a mistake."

He still didn't speak; his head bowed a little.

Mary had poured out enough; she felt a little tearful but kept it in. She gave up and sat down on the bottom bunk.

"Mary," he eventually said solemnly. "Yes it was a mistake but the mistake was not yours. Sex . . . just happens when it has to on an assignment, when it has a purpose towards getting the job done. But last night was much more than that . . . it meant just as much to me as it did to you and I didn't want it to."

"Why didn't you?." she asked slowly.

"Mary . . . a long time ago, I swore to myself, I would never get emotionally attached to another human being as long as I lived. That is the only reason I'm still alive." He turned to her and looked at her sincerely. "For years that has enabled me to do this job, and this job is what I am, all I have left and it's all I want . . . because I found I couldn't . . . live any other way anymore."

"What about Arabella?"

"She's the last, the only one left from . . . before."

"And me?"

He smiled sympathetically. "That's just it. I didn't count on meeting - someone like you."

Mary began to beam at him but he interrupted her instantly. "But Mary . . . Arabella was right, there really is nothing behind this - " he gestured with his hands to himself, " - only the job . . . I promise you - I mean, what on earth do you see?"

Mary paused, but she didn't look unsure of her conviction as she eventually answered, "I see the man who has the courage to ask me that question . . . and wants to know the answer."

Her words gave Gresham pause. He searched himself with thoughts but he couldn't see it.

"Anyway," she continued, "your job is a way of life in itself, isn't it? I mean for god's sake - flying all over the world, travelling to these places, trying to undo these - horrible things these people do . . . "

He signed, again almost sympathetically, and she stopped.

"What?" she asked exasperated.

"You're right about one thing, Mary, my job is a way of life but . . . what you just described isn't my job. The Resurgence, the travel - Venice, this train . . . this is all just my - commute."

Mary shook her head and shrugged her shoulders at him as if to say 'start making sense please.'

He didn't say anymore. He reached out slowly, and put his hands on her shoulders for just a moment - and almost protectively, left it at that.

"I'll be a few minutes - it's a long train," he said turning away. "Don't open the door for anyone unless you hear three knocks. Are you hungry?"

"Yes . . . a little."

"I'll see about having some dinner sent here."

He moved again to the basin with its little cubicle and put his suit back on, so as not to attract attention, and moved to the door.

Just before he left, he walked over to the box Jimmy had given them on the end of the bottom bunk. He took out one of the silenced pistols and expertly slotted it into the back of his trousers, keeping it fixed in place by his trouser belt.

He looked like he was posing in front of the mirror for a moment. He was checking it couldn't be seen, but Mary somehow found it in herself to let out a little snigger as she watched him.

"When you're wearing a tailored suit," he said indignantly, "it's where you keep things like that. You'd be surprised how easy it is to spot if you haven't thought about where to put it."

He opened the door and stepped out, leaving Mary, still grinning, sat on the bed.

Looking left and right, the dim sandalwood corridor was empty and he began to walk unconcernedly towards the back of the train. It was about thirteen coaches away and would involve trying to get through several dining cars; the last few he was certainly overdressed for.

Entering the next coach, he began to count the compartment numbers.

As he approached number seventeen, he stopped a little further up from it. The door was shut and there were no signs of life. The corridor was still empty.

Just as he was about to move on, the door opened suddenly. He instantly relaxed and made to look as if he was staring out of the window. In the corner of his eye, a figure stepped out and turned to close the door. As this individual had their back to him, Gresham stole a glance - but what he saw was certainly not what he expected.

A tall, slender and shapely woman stood in the doorway, wearing a long tight figure hugging black dress with a delicate black chiffon train cascading from her lower back to her feet.

She finished locking the door and turned to face him immediately. Her long, straight black hair fell silkily behind her; she looked straight at him, revealing the tip of her dress that rose to cup her upper body, an area she didn't need to draw attention to with additional venetian style lace appliqués. There, the expertly tailored dress ended.

Supporting her neck was a chest of pale white flawless skin. Perched on her jugular was a black onyx teardrop held in place by an almost invisible white gold chain. This alluring presence was rounded off with what Gresham thought was one of the most perfect faces he'd ever seen. Her skin was almost doll like, and though it was a pale white, it had a natural glow - like ice when in direct sunlight. A perfectly sized, pliable mouth was awash with an almost woody dark rouge lipstick; her long European cheekbones led up to two stiflingly hypnotic eyes. They were shaded with dark eyebrows and lashes but were of diamond like light blue in the centre.

She confidently took a few steps towards him. Her voice was deep and laced with proposition. "Good evening, you are looking for someone?"

"Yes," he replied, "and I'd like to think I just found her."

She smiled lazily; she had heard it all before.

"You are travelling alone?" she asked.

"Regrettably yes."

"Regrettably for me too. I book this cabin at short notice. I am told my table at dinner however seats two; I don't suppose you'd care to make this trip a little more interesting for me? Unless - you have already eaten?"

"Actually I was just on my way, I'd be . . . more than delighted to join you - thank you."

She smiled approvingly, placed the small black purse she was carrying into her right hand and accepted the arm he had offered her with her left.

The softness of her body was palpable even from underneath her clothing. She was an effortlessly elegant woman, fascinating, confident, even in the simple way she moved - but these impressions did not linger long on Gresham's mind. While he smoothly entered the dining car and courteously escorted her to their table, this practiced exterior was performing its task of masking the thoughts being processed fiercely beneath its surface.

Whoever she was, she was almost certainly involved in this situation somehow.

Two men supposedly took that single cabin; one of them now seemed to have miraculously turned into a woman, claiming to be travelling alone. Assuming Jimmy's agent had been correct, this woman was, therefore, certainly lying.

He thought quickly of Mary alone back in the compartment. If this woman were travelling with someone else they would either have to make a move on Mary or on the plane. This restaurant car was specifically for passengers from Mary and Gresham's part of the train, so if a lone diner passed them and went through towards the rear, her travelling partner would be revealed. If not, then no move had been made on the plane and only Mary was a concern. That is if someone happened to give three knocks on the door. Unlikely, he thought, and she knew how to take care of herself if she didn't hear three knocks; at least, in theory. Professionally she'd done all right up till now by his reckoning - not that he was willing to tell her that just yet.

They arrived at her table, beautifully set with silverware and crystal on a starched white linen tablecloth. He pulled out her chair for her; she gracefully placed herself on it. As Gresham took his seat, she spoke again.

"I'm afraid I didn't catch your name sir?"

"Gresham - Thomas Gresham, and you madam?"

"Vasilisa Zolonerwich."

"A pleasure Ms Zolonerwich . . . your accent, Pomor?"

"Very impressive Mr Gresham, you have travelled in Russia?"

"I have had the pleasure of sailing on the White Sea itself, more than once."

Her bejewelled eyes lit up. "I was raised on its shores, a village called Vorzogory. I left in my early teens. It was a wonderful place to grow up - " her eyes suddenly dipped to the table for a fleeting moment, " - it is different now."

"And where is home for you these days?"

"Tsarskoye Selo."

"You must be one very well connected woman, most of Tsarskoye Selo is a royal estate - I don't suppose there's any relation?"

"Only by association," she smiled genially. "Is it the sailing which takes you to Varna?"

"Actually yes, and you?"

"Onward travel home, I was in Venice for La Biennale."

She pulled a thin slither of a cigarette case from her purse; it was chrome and like her necklace, had a single onyx teardrop set dead in its centre.

She removed a beautifully flawless handmade cigarette, and slowly clamped it between her two lips. Gresham slipped his unmarked silver petrol lighter from his inside pocket, lit a flame and held it out for her to light it.

Keeping two fingers on the cigarette, she leaned forward to the flame. As the cigarette took light, Gresham observed it closely. The paper was tight around the tobacco; it couldn't have been made all that long ago, two weeks at most. She took a slight draw and exhaled a light cloud of smoke.

Gresham returned the lighter to his pocket, taking trouble to place it carefully back in his jacket to allow him a moment to breathe in the tobacco smoke.

It was so harshly earthy and rich it was almost cloy, but very quickly the sickening edge to the aroma smoothed out dramatically and became extremely mellow. Gresham had had a smoking experience like this before; it was unmistakably Shirazi tobacco, only to be found in Iran.

There was no way the cigarette could have been purchased in Venice. She was deliberately lying about where she had been. There was now no doubt in Gresham's mind; this was a woman who had been sent to kill them, and he now took a singular interest in her.

She was a very unique creation; one a man only meets

once in a lifetime, if he's lucky. Gresham was convinced many men had given much to merely have the pleasure of dinner alone with her - but not many had succeeded in doing so.

While keeping a watch for anyone passing them towards the rear of the train, he kept up the pretence of the lone travelling man, captivated by an exotic stranger. She made it very easy, almost too easy.

Dinner was a French inspired seven course tasting menu. They started with the ubiquitous melon, then pate with a fruit jelly and a rich sauterne. The fish was turbot and the meat, lamb. The conversation was exquisite, and easy. The fantasy of the situation didn't seem lost on either of them.

Before the final sweet arrived, he caught her staring intently at the flickers of crystal in her glass. She looked at him.

"You will have to excuse me for one moment. I will only be a short while, my apologies." She made all the right moves of a woman needing to withdraw to a rest room. And though there was one at either end of the carriage, she headed back in the direction of their cabins.

At least the plane was safe.

The train suddenly entered another tunnel with a series of long screeches from it's whistle; the tranquil background rumble of the wheels over the rail joints once again became louder and conversation in the dining car halted for a moment.

He decided how long he would give her, before he pursued under the guise of being concerned for her wellbeing. As the train left the tunnel, she returned much quicker than he expected and they finished dinner.

He offered to take her to the lounge car for another drink.

"No thank you, they don't serve what I drink."

"And what would that be?"

"Vodka of course, what else, all my life; but now I only

drink one type, it is made in Tsarskoye Selo. It is very strong, it has a . . . kick, that is hard to leave alone for too long."

"Reminds me of someone I know, not too far way," he said, almost to himself.

"I always travel with plenty, perhaps I could interest you?"

"I'd like that very much."

They got to their feet; he pulled out her chair for her and took her arm. Exchanging slow and considered "good evenings" with fellow diners as they passed, they reached the compartment carriages once again.

Outside number seventeen, no one had passed them and the corridor was deserted. Gresham stole himself for the entrance to a room that would finally establish what this individual's role in all of this was. One way or the other, some proof was going to be in this room somewhere.

She let go of his arm, pulled open her little black purse and took out a key. She stood with her back to him, unlocked the door and opened it in front of them. The room was lit, beyond her he could see no one. She took a step in and then turned to face him, leaving him on the threshold.

The train hit another tunnel; her compartment window was open and the noise was almost deafening - but it didn't distract him from what happened next.

She put both her arms behind her back, pushing out her beautifully cupped chest. The dress suddenly lost its tight grip and fell an inch as she undid the buttons down her back.

She stopped halfway down, reached up to her armpits and eased the top of the dress down to her waist, leaving her smooth pale white breasts to the caress of the warm night air forced in to the window by the tunnel.

She stepped forward and, keeping her eyes locked on his, embraced him with her body and pulled him slowly into the compartment. Her stare was excited and intense; it was impossible to look away. They reached the middle of the room and Gresham was suddenly surprised by the sound of the door slamming with considerable force behind them.

Before he could turn to see how it had closed, she brought her strong arms round to his chest and pushed him back forcefully. He tried to stay on his feet, but fell away backwards towards the corner on the right hand side of the door. He braced himself to hit the floor, but he didn't.

Instead he landed with a startled clunk in a chair. It took a moment for him to work out what was happening. As he sat there, he heard a murmur to his right. He turned; sat next to him, in another chair, was Mary. A huge, ugly muscular man knelt behind her, with one large hairy hand firmly over her mouth and the other holding a short sharp oyster knife at her throat.

Looking up at Zolonerwich, she was smiling alluringly, still topless, but was producing a small silver pistol from her little purse; she cocked it and pointed it at his face.

Gresham remained cool and his tone was still conversational. "Alright, I see. So what about the two men who supposedly booked this single cabin?"

Zolonerwich giggled behind the smile. "That was us, a simple disguise," she replied.

"Why?"

"How else were we to attract just enough attention, to make you leave your cabin in fear of your precious plane?"

"And what do you want with us now you have succeeded in apprehending both of us at once?"

"I do not want anything with you. Our employers, however, want you out of the way; another unsolved murder on a long distance train through unholy lands."

As she talked, Gresham put his hands to his back and squirmed a little as if in pain from landing backwards on the chair. To his delight, she didn't think the move conspicuous; he now had his hand gripped firmly around the butt of his gun.

The large, bald thug to his right was holding Mary more forcefully than was necessary; he had obviously had some trouble restraining her. Not that it required his full attention at the moment. With both his hands in place, he glared at Gresham; it was an arrogant angry sneer, like a bully about to take pleasure in causing more pain to his victim.

Gresham matched his glare with a relaxed gaze, almost complacent. The huge bulk didn't seem to like this very much; he was a creature that spent a lot of time maintaining his physique and liked the natural intimidation he instilled in people with it. He wasn't very happy to see it wasn't working on Gresham, especially in this situation. His angry sneer grew more acute as the two of them stared at each other, Gresham refusing to blink or look away.

Gresham could see the savage fire in this creature's eyes, and the thin layer of control that was keeping it at bay - 'excellent,' Gresham thought.

"Ms Zolonerwich," he began, "was your colleague here abused as a child?"

The bulk's sneer dropped briefly to a glare of shock; then a fresh wind of growing anger began to flicker in the eyes. Such a response to this kind of situation was something Zolonerwich was also not used to hearing.

"I beg your pardon?" she asked, sounding slightly incensed.

Still holding the bulk's gaze, and putting on a charming smile, Gresham continued in his conversational tone. "He has that certain look of one of life's victims about him; I've known quite a few."

The bulk's face began to turn crimson with anger at Gresham's provocative arrogance. Gresham saw this, and assured his words were having the desired effect, he leaned right over to the great sweating bald face, and eye-to-eye he said, "What is it about yourself that you hate the most?

The fact that your dad fucked you, or the fact that you enjoyed it?"

The pupils in the bulk's eyes contracted to pinpoints and he started to salivate as Gresham delivered his last line.

"Give us a kiss."

The bulk roared with anger; using the hand round Mary's mouth, he yanked her and the chair she sat on behind him with a crash, and lunged with all his might at Gresham. Gresham flew back on his chair; the bulk came at him with the knife with such force that as Gresham leaned back, the bulk missed and landed with his stomach over Gresham's chest, where the silenced pistol had already been brought to bear.

There was a muffled thud. The bulk's back exploded outward as the bullet passed through him; blood struck Mary in the face. She cried out.

Gresham instantly threw the convulsing mass off his lap onto the floor and leapt to his feet.

Zolonerwich wasn't smiling anymore. As Gresham got to his feet, he barely had time to bring his gun to face her when she pulled the trigger, twice, rapidly.

To her horror, the gun merely clicked. Even though the train was still rumbling, the room seemed to fall deathly silent.

Her confidence had left her; she looked at the gun in confused fright. She pulled the trigger again in panicked frustration. Nothing.

Gresham, standing perfectly still with his gun trained on her, still didn't alter his tone when he broke the silence. "You keep those things in your underclothes. If you put them in expensive purses, the material has a tendency to absorb any lubricating oil left on the piece. A lady's purse shouldn't smell of such things."

A look of horror began to creep across her face as she realised what had happened.

"In your haste to inform your associate here," he went

on, "that I had left Mary alone during dinner, you left your purse behind at the table. I removed the ammunition while you were gone. I found the conversation was already quite sufficiently . . . loaded."

There was a louder muffled thud as he put a bullet into her pristine chest; it hit just right of centre causing her to spin around, her face frozen in terror. Another thud and he put a bullet into her back, dead centre. She flew forward and smashed through a glass-topped table, the dead weight of her body coming to rest face down with a bone cracking thump.

Gresham pulled the silencer off the end of the barrel, gently blew away the hot smoke stemming from it and turned to Mary. She was looking at the bloody scene strewn across the lushly carpeted floor. This wasn't a delicious mystery anymore.

She looked at him.

He outstretched his arms and gestured to the beautiful, luxurious room that he had turned into a butcher's slab, scattered with cuts of bloodied, raw meat.

"Well here it is Mary, my job," he announced. "That's my work - that's the sum of it. Nothing there of any interest to anyone but myself."

She didn't move.

He stepped across to her and helped her to her feet.

"Are you alright?" he asked sincerely.

"It's not my blood," she replied quietly.

"Did he knock three times?"

"No he just kicked the door in when the train went through the tunnel."

" . . . I'm sorry I left you alone."

She didn't reply. She just looked at him - in silence.

He turned back towards the bodies.

Slowly, he moved over to Zolonerwich, kneeling as he approached her body.

She was lying face down, her head obscured from view, but the glistening white gold chain around her neck was still visible.

He carefully took a hold of it with four fingers and began to pull it to one side, moving the immaculate onyx teardrop pendant round into his hands. Holding it over his fingers, he stroked it with his thumb, considering it carefully. He seemed to frown a moment and he stopped stroking it. Pressing it firmly between finger and thumb he tugged it clean off her neck with one determined pull.

Standing up, and not taking his eyes off the body, he carefully pocketed it and then turned away.

CHAPTER XV

GOLD VOLCANO

The railway line into Varna, for its last few miles, straddles Lake Varna, a stretch of water with a foreboding depth and temper - not unlike one of the more rugged lochs of Scotland - but bordered by gently sloping scrubland rather than thick greenery. Nevertheless as the train from Venice weaved along its shores, interrupting the gentle stillness of the summer night, it all blended to make an eye soothingly idyllic picture.

Gresham had been here before, many years earlier, but it had been quite different then. He couldn't see much of the lake from the window, only a stream of reflection cast by the moon on the water. When he had last seen it, Lake Varna had been a freshwater lake, lacing the surrounding hills with flowers and plant life that covered the otherwise unexciting dark landscape. However, a few years ago Varna had been turned into a major port; the work caused the ocean to back up into the lake and now the salt water supported quite a different, dry look to the area.

As the train rounded a long curve, the straight run into Varna eased into the driver's sight, as did something more unexpected. Strewn across the track ahead was a line of miserable looking labourers showing red lamps; a couple of stout officials in waist length capes stood patiently next to them.

The engine's whistle was blown with an icy persistency as the driver shut off steam and brought the train to an abrupt and clumsy standstill.

The safety valve loosed on the locomotive, puncturing the clear starry sky with a roaring jet of steam. The unexpected halt and thunderous roar brought many passengers' heads poking out of the train windows, and a few climbed down from the carriages to see what the delay was; including Gresham and Mary.

Walking the short distance to the crowd now gathering around the engine, Gresham tried to speak to one of the footplate crew. After all the frowning, arm waving and hand signals that were the classic accompaniments to a language barrier, he returned to Mary.

"Driver only speaks Croatian of all things. Apparently, a local train has derailed up ahead. We're not going to get into Varna tonight unless we walk."

"How far out are we?"

"About eight miles. If I remember correctly, there's a concrete road that runs parallel to this line just over there; that's going to be as good a place as any to try and take off. We don't have much choice - let's go and hope Jimmy wasn't exaggerating when he said we had a full tank!"

They had already changed back into their uniforms; they had left the train in a hurry and the railway officials with the labourers were very confused to see a female officer of the Royal Flying Corps. Returning to their compartment one last time they donned their leather flying jackets and packed up their few belongings, including the pistols into their case.

The jog to the back of the train was long; there was little light at the rear as the last coach was a brake end with no inhabitants.

It was a difficult affair getting the plane off the truck; it was fixed side-on to the carriages so its wings wouldn't be clipped by other passing trains - this meant that once the tarpaulin was off and the intricate ropes loosed, they had to pull it by the tail, the only bit light enough for them to lift. They turned it and rolled it down the sloping back end of the wagon, with its wheels either side of a rail. With Mary pushing at the back and Gresham lifting at one side, they just about made it clear of the track.

Mercifully the ground between the line and the road was mostly flat and free of vegetation.

Mary clambered into the rear cockpit, thrilled to be

224

back in a familiar place and checked the instruments. Gresham took position at the propeller.

"Mary! I don't know how straight this road is once we get to it; if we have to taxi too far we could use up valuable fuel!"

"I'll do my best!"

"I know you will - Pilot Officer!"

"Contact!" she bellowed.

The plane was stone cold from travelling in the cool night air for hours; the propeller took four pulls before the engine coughed into life.

They taxied forward up to the road. Seeing it was clear, Mary accelerated down it in the direction of Varna.

The road was straight enough initially, but they entered a long curve as they hit seventy. It was unnerving to be travelling along the ground so fast, not knowing what was in front.

Mary held her nerve. Gresham was certain they would have to abort the takeoff until the road straightened out but to his pleasant surprise, he felt the plane lifting even as they were easing round to the left.

To the shock of both of them, a truck, its headlights blinding, suddenly appeared hurtling towards them around the bend.

Mary didn't hesitate for one moment. The plane left the ground at an angle, the tip of the bottom port wing scraped the ground as they gained height and they jolted violently as Mary tried to compensate. They were both sure the truck would hit them but it passed under the nose by inches, and they were safely airborne and climbing.

The plane gained height a little swifter than usual; they both felt this, and Gresham lurched over the cockpit edge to look at the underside of the plane. When he sat back up, he turned to Mary with his eyebrows raised - a look of being pleasantly surprised, which she knew didn't mean good news.

"We've lost our undercarriage, truck must have ripped

it clean off."

"How are we supposed to land without wheels?"

"We'll get to that later," he smiled.

'Nothing like living in the moment,' she thought.

The liberating feeling of being able to fly again re-charged Mary. Varna had been some distant inaccessible location beyond the horizon while on the ground; as they gained height rapidly, she could see its dim lights a few miles off.

Gresham didn't have a map, but he did have a compass and that's all he needed.

"Forget Varna," he shouted. "Steer south east, then when we hit the coast come south ten points and stay there!"

He gestured with his arms, she nodded and struck south when the grey and silver shaded patterns the moon picked out on the ground turned a resolute sheet black and Varna promptly disappeared behind them.

It was a clear night, not the clearest she had ever flown on however; this night had a few whispers of cloud blotting out the stars here and there. It was beautiful. The moon silhouetted distant mountains to the west and a sheet-glass ocean below and ahead.

Knowing time was of the essence, Mary pulled every trick she knew to average the highest speed without using too much fuel. The fuel gauge did indeed indicate a full tank, but every drop was precious.

The ocean and jagged coastline reeled under them rapidly. There was no sight of any living soul, save a few blinking lights just inshore; that is, until Constantinople came within twenty miles.

At first Mary thought she had made a mistake and was heading west into where the sun had gone down and that the yellow glow cast along the whole horizon was the last of the sunset. But it wasn't; it was that great and ancient city shining its defiant light of survival out into nature's darkness.

As the lights grew nearer they picked out larger collections of flat bottomed chunky clouds. Gresham turned to Mary. "If the Resurgence is here, she'll be above one of those clouds. We'll go down and take a look at the city first; if we're too late and they've already used their weapon, we'll know once we get low enough."

Mary lowered them to a few hundred feet as they came in over the great city.

Lit up from the air, it looked like a volcano, spewing a lava of crown jewels that cascaded down from its high crater, on which was perched the Hagia Sophia; the domes and spires of the colossal mosque dwarfing all the lesser jewels that basked in its light.

Below, they could quite easily see the throng of the city's thousands of inhabitants milling around like little black ants in a nest of gold.

They weren't too late.

But just as relief met with awe at this immense spectacle of civilisation, a deep rumble, almost a groan, which could be heard over the plane's engine, erupted and then subsided with a vast sigh. As it did so, the shining lights of the city below, flickered, and then died.

Gresham and Mary found themselves in complete blackness. Their eyes had become accustomed to the light of the city; now they couldn't even see the flicker of the ocean to guide them.

Gresham looked out at the black mass that had, moments earlier, been a sea of life.

"Only if they can learn to see in the Dark," he muttered to himself, remembering Arabella's words. He turned to Mary. "We're just in time, the attack must be imminent. We have to find the Resurgence or the enemy flying machine quickly - are you alright flying on instruments?"

"I think so!"

"Alright, we're as good as directly over the centre of town, start circling out from our current position, long and wide. Concentrate on keeping us from crashing - I'll keep my eyes peeled!"

Mary did as he said. The air seemed colder now, and the warmth of the city below had disappeared. Mary was sure she heard screams.

She watched Gresham scour the darkness, there were twinges of light from the ground here and there, gas lamps unaffected by the blackout and small fires people were lighting to see in the streets.

Then he stopped turning his head and leaned forward, Mary saw it too, a light of a different kind parallel to them, which was burning constantly. At first she thought it might have been a building on a hillside, but as they eased closer she saw another - evenly spaced from the first and moving. They were only pinpoint in size to the naked eye, but Gresham quickly recognised them as masthead lights and another as the unmistakable green starboard light of the Resurgence.

He knew that's all they would see given the situation, when safely hidden above the clouds the Resurgence was a dazzling spectacle at night, her electric lighting shining out of every window and porthole.

"There she is, Mary!" He pointed. "Stay on this heading!"

"Why are they so low?"

"With the blackout there's no need for them to hide and it's the best way for them to spot the incoming enemy machine!"

There really wasn't a light in a single window, everyone aboard was probably on the lookout for the attackers, but the Resurgence's huge dark silvery mass became visible in the moonlight as they flew under her belly and turned to fly parallel off her port side.

"Mary! I'm going aboard to coordinate with Walker for a moment, bring us up just aft of the bridge and get as close as you can. After I've gone stick to her like glue - I'll be coming back, understood!"

"I don't think I can get that close in the dark!"

"Oh you can," he replied confidently.

Mary hadn't a clue how he was going to manage it, but she liked the easy confidence he was displaying in her skills, so she didn't hesitate to return his faith.

The moon was off the port side, so at the distance they were, Mary could make out the window arrangement along the hull of the Resurgence, and the large ones of the bridge coming up fast.

Gresham climbed out of the front cockpit and leaped at the starboard wing, landing on it firmly. This upset the airflow and the weight distribution dangerously. Mary began having a hard time keeping the plane level; it was manageable as long as he stayed inboard rather than on the wing tip.

The Resurgence's hull was now only a few feet away; Mary took some time to match the great ships speed, but was fairly even with her when a boarding ladder strapped to the hull appeared just behind the wheelhouse.

Gresham gestured to her to ease closer; she was already closer than she dared.

She did her best with the tilt in the plane from his position on the wings, but for a moment she was certain the wing was going to strike the ship; if it did, it was all over. She eased away after this split second fright, but as she did so Gresham leaped at the wing tip like it was a stepping-stone and after another big step, flung himself onto the ladder.

He had made it. Mary eased away a little, as Gresham grabbed the window rail that ran towards the front of the ship and began to ease himself along towards the bridge.

On the bridge of the Resurgence, the lookouts had been keenly monitoring the situation.

"CO's coming aboard sir!" one announced.

"Very good," replied Walker. "You there!" he barked to a junior officer, "stand by to open that window!"

Just as the young officer took position, the lookout bell rang twice, indicating something had been spotted. Third

Officer Townsend grabbed the receiver. "Sir, the lookouts have spotted a large mass dead ahead!"

"Is it the enemy craft?"

"They can't tell sir."

All eyes fell on the direction ahead. Almost immediately, a huge light flickered up from the ground. The inhabitants of Constantinople were obviously trying to restore the power and the silhouette of the central dome of a huge mosque appeared directly in front of them.

Mary saw it as well but stuck to the Resurgence's side, Walker shouted out instant orders. "Helmsman hard to starboard, reverse port engines now!"

A junior officer dived on the port side brass telegraphs and rammed them astern; the helmsman frantically fed the handles of the huge wheel through each hand.

The mammoth ship began to turn. Gresham froze and watched the huge ancient mass of stone and glass, rapidly ease closer.

"Come on turn, turn!" he seethed through clenched teeth. He eased his head to one side; the ship was only just starting to alter course. It was obvious the huge structure was going to hit. Gresham frantically pulled himself along to the first window of the bridge.

"Jesus Christ, turn for god's sake!" he shouted, as if it would make a difference.

He pulled his hand inside the sleeve of his jacket and rammed his fist through the bridge window, smashing a portion of it through and stuck his head inside.

"Turn this fat bastard to starboard Walker!" he roared.

Walker marched over to the wheel and rounded angrily on the helmsman. "Give it 'ere, Quartermaster!"

The helmsman, still feeding the wheel through his hands, backed off. Walker grabbed the wheel at the bottom of its left hand side and with his full body weight, flung it over to the right. It spun wildly and with a wood splintering crack came to a halt, as the rudder turned as far as it would go. The Quartermaster gingerly took back the wheel as Walker withdrew and announced a little timidly, "Helm's hard over, sir."

The great ship lunged as the light shining up at the mosque died away again. Gresham had finished climbing in through the window and though a little grinding was heard aft; it seemed they only just missed the ancient structure.

"Welcome aboard sir!"

"Thank you Mr Walker, any sight of the enemy ship as yet?"

"No sir, but it was spotted off shore at dusk, flying very low; probably only about 200 feet."

"If it's coming in that low we'll never spot it. In this blackout from the top and sides, it's as good as invisible. What might just give us a chance is the underside; it's plated with an unknown metal that's partially florescent, a shimmering deep blue, even in the dark. I'd say that's our only hope of locating it."

"How do we spot that from up here; should we use starbursts?"

"Absolutely not: that would immediately give away our presence and position. That thing's armed with some conventional cannons and given enough time to sneak up in the dark while you're lighting up the landscape, it could ambush us. No, Mary's our best bet."

"Mary?" Walker inquired, almost sounding more puzzled by the familiar way Gresham was referring to her, than the suggestion itself.

"Yes. Give me some distress rockets, I'll get back to the plane, we'll hug the ground, low enough to see the machines underside. If we spot it, we'll light it up with rockets and you can take care of the rest. By the way, have you been able to coordinate any of this with the ground? How has it managed to get all the way here without being stopped if it's only flying at 200 feet?"

"Grey informed the Ottoman government of a threatened aerial attack . . . but they didn't believe him."

"And what did the organ grinder say?" Gresham said straight-faced.

"Well our department did go straight to the Turkish Army after that. They've rustled up some heavy artillery on the shoreline east and west but they don't know what they're looking for."

"Well don't stand for any nonsense from them; be ready with the main armament when you see our rockets."

"Yes sir."

Mary saw Gresham clamour back out of the bridge window with few long implements in his arms. She again got as close as she could to the ladder, but he gestured for her to come closer to the window. She was in the process of easing in the last few feet when he leapt wildly at the plane and gripped the fuselage with one hand.

She couldn't help looking a little distressed at him, he threw himself between the flying machines without warning and in such an unconcerned way, it was as if he didn't care if he fell. She didn't like it, - because she did care.

"Take these!" he called. The rockets were then thrust onto Mary's lap and she stuffed them into the cockpit edges either side of her. He crept along to the front and climbed back into his seat.

"What's our fuel situation?" he shouted.

"About half an hour at best!"

"That'll have to do. Turn back towards the city and get as low as you dare - we're looking for that blue metal on the enemy craft's underbelly; it's flying low and that's our only chance of spotting it. It's likely coming in through the Dardanelles, so come south west!"

With the blackout, Mary could now see all the stars as clear as day, she found the 'big milk saucepan' she was looking for, and the north star at the tip of its handle. Using it, she determined a rough south-westerly direction.

They curved away from the back of the Resurgence and

dived for the ground. Mary began to see silhouettes of structures ahead against the stars and worked out an average height she hoped would keep them from hitting anything. Now heading in the right direction, she just had to concentrate on keeping them as low as possible - and alive - while Gresham scoured the night.

The air grew cooler again as if they had crossed the coastline, and the silhouettes disappeared, so they must have been over the ocean.

Gresham was circling, glaring in every direction. Suddenly, the wind picked up; briskly at first, and then it was overwhelming. Mary could feel it pushing the plane down and she had no choice but to try and gain height to avoid being sunk into the sea. The strength of the wind became unnatural and frightening.

Gresham turned to her slowly. "Look up!"

She expected to see stars but there were none. What she could just about see above them, her eyes squinting at the force of the wind, was a sky of cold shimmering blue. They were directly underneath the enemy flying machine, and the downdraft that kept it airborne was almost killing them.

Something struck each of them in the face; the top wing in front of them had split and was in the process of sheering off.

"Mary get up to that monstrosity now; we have to get a rocket off before the plane falls apart!"

Mary rammed the nose of the plane up at the sky and they slowed. They came out of the enemy ships downdraught just before the plane stalled, but it was too late for the wing. There were only a few seconds left before it would come apart; it was obvious to both of them that nothing could stop that now.

They turned and rose up further, parallel to the craft's side; the underbelly disappeared and all they had to go on was that unmistakable swarming growl up ahead.

Gresham grabbed a rocket, but it was too late; the wing

cracked off, the plane spun and took a nosedive. The rockets fell out of the cockpit as they spun a whole three sixty. Mary did what she could to compensate and turn into the dive, she clenched her teeth as the stick almost juddered itself out of her hands. She briefly regained a moment of control to keep the plane from spinning, but it was too late.

There was an almighty crash, they both felt themselves thrown forward as more objects flew past their ears, but to the confusion of their senses, they then came to a very sudden juddering halt in mid air.

The motion of the plane stopped. The engine noise was gone, just the dim humming of the enemy craft's rotors.

Mary brought her head out from between her knees and looked up. In front she saw a dimly lit wooden wall, illuminated with a few small electrical bulbs fixed to hooks. She looked over and saw Gresham, also instinctively with his head in his lap.

Behind them were the remnants of the fuselage and behind that, a large wooden opening. By nothing short of a miracle, they had crash landed though an open gun-port in the craft's side.

CHAPTER XVI

LUCK OF THE IRISH

It was like the inside of a gigantic wooden sailing ship. Parts of it reminded them both a little of the Resurgence's gun deck, as there were plenty of cannons sat with their barrels poking out of the ship's side, except this room curved round out of sight in both directions and everything, floor, walls and ceiling was made of wood.

Their striking, and loud, entrance didn't appear to have roused any attention.

The immediate area was empty; the distant hum of the rotor blades spinning in the roof and a whistle of air past the open gun port they had entered from, were the only things to be heard.

Jumping down from the wreck, they both surveyed their new surroundings.

"Well Mary, you appear to have the luck of the Irish - well landed."

"Well, Ireland is where I get the blonde from," she replied. "So what now? Create as much trouble as possible?"

"That's it exactly; let's see if we can get closer to the middle of this thing, and see what's driving the rotor blades."

"Then what?"

"Then we shove something in the machinery. No point in trying to be clever - breaking something's easy."

He handed Mary one of the silenced pistols that had still been stuffed into his belt and they moved off slowly, round the curving room.

The guns arranged around the rim of this craft were a little older than the ones on the Resurgence, and appeared to be muzzle-loading cannons. They sat on rope pulleys for running them out through the ports, just like in an old ship of the line.

The Resurgence's interior was bright, clean and modern and tended to blend together, but all this was more a direct contrast of ancient and new.

Gresham paused and looked up at the ceiling, "It's all wood . . . I imagine that's what enabled them to build this in secret for so long, if all they needed was wood. That is, up until the very last stages, when they needed parts from the Drakensburg."

She followed him as he gingerly made his way around the inside wall.

"It's a pity we have to try and destroy it," he remarked quietly, "the technology that makes this thing fly could revolutionise many things."

"A grandmother of mine once said young gentlemen can never have enough toys. Can't you just make do with the revolutionary flying ship you've already got?"

Gresham ignored her comment as an opening appeared in the inner wall, which led to a long corridor, stretching inward towards the bowels of the machine.

"I can't see anyone down there so let's go for it," Gresham said quietly. They ran briskly down it, Gresham held his gun before him and Mary copied him without thinking.

The humming grew louder; they were certainly headed towards whatever was keeping this monstrosity in the air.

At the end was a dark room. It had caged netting dividing it up into compartments and in each were stored round barrels and square wooden crates.

Gresham made his way to the room's far wall and placed his hand on it; it was vibrating. He took two paces back, held his gun to the wooden wall and pulled the trigger. The bullet went straight through but dislodged one of the wooden planks that made up the smooth curving surface. He managed to get a hand around it and pulled it free, opening up a gap.

The noise through the gap was a horrible ear piercing

metallic squeal. He looked through.

"What can you see?" Mary whispered close to his ear.

"It's a huge vertical chamber," he replied, trying to turn his head partly towards her so he could be heard. "Looks like one of the Drakesnburg's propeller shafts. It's running the length of the ship, top to bottom; must be what's driving the blades above us. Looks pretty solidly made. I take back what I said - there's no easy way of sabotaging that!"

He forced the broken slice of wood back into place over the hole in the wall to drown out the noise. Turning back to the room, he made his way to a cluster of large dark barrels in a caged compartment. Removing the stopper on one, he took a sniff and smiled.

"Petroleum. They must have it aboard to run a generator for the lighting or something. Give me a hand getting these barrels back to the plane; four should be enough. We'll pile them up against the outer hull then set them alight - that'll be visible enough for the Resurgence to shoot at."

Mary grabbed a barrel and tipped it over to roll it. Gresham was standing further over towards the door they had entered through, in view of the corridor leading back to the plane. He suddenly dropped the barrel he was moving and stared straight down the corridor. He raised both his hands in the air. Mary heard men shouting and loud footsteps running towards them.

Gresham looked at them and spoke to her quietly out of the side of his mouth. "Mary, there's too many of them - but they can't see you. Hide in one of those crates, first chance you get to blow those barrels, do it . . . don't worry about me - just get the job done. Understand?"

She nodded reassuringly and made for the crates. Ripping the lid off one, she found little sealed silver cans at the bottom, and just enough room to hide. She climbed in and pulled the lid back down, just as the unwelcome company arrived. She watched through tiny slits in the wooden sides as several armed men grabbed Gresham, struck him hard in the chest and shouted at him.

Dragging him away, a few stayed behind to search the room. Thankfully, after only a quick glance here and there, they also made to leave. As the last three moved to the door, the one in the lead said something to the other two Mary couldn't make out, and then left them as they turned back into the room.

They split up and began to walk around, silently; a rifle each, held ready in both hands across their chests. It appeared they were searching the room more thoroughly, perhaps to see if anything had been tampered with. One found the loose top on the petrol barrel and screwed it back on.

For a while, Mary couldn't see or hear either of them. She began to think they might have gone. Shifting herself around, she accidentally rattled a few tins underneath her.

She froze.

She had moved to see out of some of the slits in the lid and wished she hadn't; the sight made her jump.

Standing inches away was one of the men. From the angle Mary was at his face was shrouded by a dark shadow; she couldn't make out his features, but she could feel his eyes staring straight at her. She reached for the gun lying next to her, and brought it up to her chest.

The man moved towards her. She told herself over and over that he couldn't possibly see her through the tiny slits in the crate, but he was looking fixedly at something. For a moment, he leaned forward as if he was going to remove the lid.

Mary tightened her grip on her gun.

He stood leering over the top of the crate, tilting his head in confusion. Then slowly he gripped his rifle and pointed it straight at her. He squeezed the trigger.

Just as he did so, the chunk of wood Gresham had stuffed back in to the wall fell out again, letting the piercing metallic whine of the engine into the room.

This alarmed the man, who swerved to look at it.

Mary kicked off the lid and rose to her full height; she pointed her gun straight at him and then immediately froze.

The figure was much clearer now; he was startled by Mary's sudden appearance and jumped back clumsily.

Mary had it in her mind that she was going to shoot straight away; but she could see him now and she made the mistake of noticing the fear in his face, this led to her looking at him more closely, and she was alarmed at what she saw.

He was almost a boy; he couldn't have been older than twelve. His face was pale and very soft; he probably hadn't even reached the age where he needed to shave. The old brown jacket he wore was slightly too big for him and the sleeves covered a little of the backs of his hands.

Looking either side of her head at her long hair, he seemed to relax a moment; keeping his gun pointed away from her, he breathed out a sigh of relief and smiled.

As he looked up at her and grinned, his eyes were almost kind. This was the last thing Mary was expecting to see.

His bright smile seemed familiar to Mary - then it struck her; it was the lovely boy from the boatyard who had admired her hair.

The room then seemed to go very quiet; the noise from the engines ebbed away and everything fell silent.

Mary stood with her gun pointing right at him, holding her breath and glaring at him with a mixture of distress and confusion.

This went on for what seemed like an eternity.

Slowly his eyes moved to examine her uniform; his beaming smile waned a little as puzzlement grew across his face. He looked at her gun and then back up to her eyes.

Then, it all happened as if in slow motion; his smile steadily dropped, his mouth opened and his face recoiled in horrified shock. He seemed to hesitate for a moment, then hurriedly strengthened the grip around his rifle and stumbled backward, bringing the gun round to face Mary.

Mary pulled her trigger. A bullet went straight through the right of his chest and flew out his back, spraying a fine mist of blood into the air behind him.

As it did so, his head flew back. Mary saw his taut expression of horror slacken as the life went out of him and his eyes drained of substance, becoming completely purposeless in an instant as his face flung back and rested, looking up at the ceiling.

Listlessly, he keeled over backwards and his body crunched as it hit the floor, his rifle slipping from his hands and falling with a clatter on his legs.

As the sound returned to the room, Mary forced herself from her frozen position. Now panting and straining hard to keep herself calm, she clamoured down from the crate, looking anywhere except at the body.

As she regained her breath, she quickly realised there was no one else in the room.

She didn't look at the body. She knew what she had done, but didn't want to think about it. As she passed it on her way back to the barrels, she wondered if that's how Gresham did it; but she knew that he had looked at the bodies on the train.

The corridor was empty; she automatically forced herself to re-focus solely on the task in hand, and set to work on the barrels once more.

CHAPTER XVII

GO SEE YOUR MOTHER

Gresham had been vigorously escorted further round the curving perimeter of the craft. The inner wall eventually sloped inwards to widen the corridor out into a huge room. In the middle were a number of communication tubes, a little like on the bridge of the Resurgence; they all went down into the floor, probably to a room where the craft was operated. On the outer wall was a huge window from floor to ceiling, looking out ahead over the city.

Several people stood around the tubes, dividing their attention between them and the window. One of them was Arabella.

She looked calm but her chest was breathing in and out heavily. She was probably very surprised to see him, but was hiding it.

They held him in front of her. She approached from the huddle slowly and looked at him, up and down.

"Where is she?" she asked casually.

"Who would that be?" he replied.

"Your future wife, of course."

Gresham frowned; his response was slow. "I beg your pardon?"

"My aunt told me I was the result of the last couple she overheard making love like that."

"Yes well," he began, as his captors released their grip on him with a little goading snigger, "I don't think that's terribly likely thank you."

"I don't think you will have a choice in this matter in the end," she smiled dryly.

"And what would you know about that?"

For a moment she didn't reply; her little smile faded faintly but her next words still held traces of irony. "I saw the way she looked at you that night . . . she can see you, and I think she can reach you too."

There was a silence; they both looked at each other. Neither of them could help smiling; her last words had been almost playful. They had enjoyed so much teasing like this throughout their friendship; a long friendship that they had both cherished.

Right now a part of them both longed for the simpler times that had brought them together; but here and now, standing in this place, they both knew those times had all gone, and neither could lose themselves to the memory for very long.

"She's dead," he suddenly said bluntly. "She was killed when our plane crashed into your machine here."

"That is a pity. I don't believe you, of course. We shall continue to search this ship, but if it is true, that is sad." She sounded strangely genuine. "You should have both stayed in Venezia."

"Even if we had, your hired Jekyll and Hyde would have finished us anyway - hardly the actions of someone who wishes we had kept out of the way."

Arabella's head suddenly tilted to one side in curiosity, a trait Gresham knew meant that she was genuinely confused. "What is Jekyll and Hyde?"

"The assassins you sent after us on the train."

Arabella's face became blank.

"The man and the woman sent to kill us on the train," Gresham went on.

Arabella shook her head, "I sent no one after you. I should have known even an underground prison cell would not hold you, but we had no idea you had escaped until now."

A flurry of thoughts went through Gresham's head - because he believed her.

"You left us to die in that cell, so why wouldn't it have been you?"

She moved closer to him, and spoke deeper and slower.

"If I did not leave you there, if I did not try - I knew you would be here somehow anyway, just like this. I know you . . . remember . . . tell me . . . does 'she' know who and what you are?"

Gresham didn't answer, Arabella looked at him up and down and turned when her name was called out from the crowd behind her. She suddenly became gripped by something in the direction of the window and moved towards it slowly without looking back at Gresham

Constantinople was still in darkness; Arabella and her companions gazed out of the gigantic window and the craft tilted a few degrees as it was manoeuvred into position.

Gresham, still with a guard watching him, stood at the back of the room, looking on.

The crowd of thirty or so were calm and solemn, looking down judgementally on their prey, waiting to watch their vengeance enacted.

They didn't look evil, or murderous. Standing motionless, as if sapped of life and energy, they had the quiet, collective expectation of victims of a crime; come to the execution of those who had wronged them, to see their sentence served. Their tired brown and beige clothing made them look like hungry prisoners standing, staring out from behind the barbed wire fence of their prison; judging an unjust world with their lifeless, condemnatory glare.

As they all remained transfixed, Arabella suddenly turned and looked at Gresham from within the crowd. There seemed to be a conflicting mix of excitement and extreme nervousness in her now.

When she saw Gresham at the back, calm and with a look of disappointment on his face, her nerves seemed to become more strained.

She moved back across the room to him. The rest of the crowd remained oblivious. He looked up to see her breathing heavily, trying to contain her uneasiness. She looked like someone who was about to go on stage in front of thousands of people for the first time and didn't like the thought.

"It will begin soon," she said as she breathed out. "You want to see?"

"No, thank you," he responded coldly.

She looked away; her breathing intensified; she was beginning to seem upset. Gresham stole a look at her. It was as if she now desperately needed reassurance. He somehow knew she still couldn't be talked out of it, but it didn't stop him going through the motions of trying.

"Don't do it," he said quietly.

She didn't look back at him when she replied. She held firm to the direction of the window. "I would not stop it now - " her voice was pained again, " - even if I could."

There was something about the disappointment in his eyes that had brought her over to him, but she couldn't bear it and kept staring back at the window. Her breathing became heavier; he could see tears welling up at the base of her eyes.

Despite all she had done, god only knows how, it could not stop Gresham from reaching to comfort whatever it was that was left inside her, which was now crying out.

"Well then," he sighed " . . . you got any good Sambuca?"

She turned to him straight away; a deep pained laugh followed by a very loving smile caused a tear resting on her eyelid to run down one cheek. She reached with her lovely olive skin hands into the inside pocket of the dark waist jacket she was wearing, and pulled out a small pewter flask.

"I am afraid I do not have three coffee beans to put in it," she said, handing it to Gresham.

"No matter," he replied, raising it to his lips. "I don't think this is a good time for a toast to health, happiness and prosperity anyway."

They looked at each other a moment, he then took a good gulp. Returning the flask to her, she did the same.

"What will you do when all of this is over, Arabella?"

he began slowly.

"We move on, and continue our work inland."

"No I mean when it's all over, when you have - I assume - exterminated the entire population of the Ottoman Empire. Leaving aside all the other ethnic groups you'll kill for a moment, when you have eliminated all the Turks?"

She looked at him tearfully.

"Literally," he went on, a little more earnestly, "let's say you have got every last one, what are to going to do with your life then?"

"Don't bother trying to provoke me."

"I'm not," he said genuinely. "I promise you I'm not. That's what's wrong with revenge you see, that's why it doesn't work in the end. When it so . . . utterly fills your life, you have nothing left to live for when the object of it has gone."

"You have had your revenge, you are still here," she said provokingly.

"Am I?" he asked honestly.

She looked at him tearfully again, her jaw went limp.

"So, what will you do when it's done - end your life? . . . tell me . . . I wouldn't mind knowing even just for myself . . . we've both of us already killed ourselves, isn't ending it completely all that's left?"

"I do not know," she replied painfully.

"Do you think your mother will be there at the end?" he continued calmly.

"I do not know . . . damn you!"

Reaching out to grab a nearby communication tube, she leaned forward as though there were a great pain in her stomach.

Gresham stared away into nothingness, slithers of emotion began to seep out from behind his armour, his voice became laced with a drop of helpless longing, leaking out from a well he kept it sealed up in. "I only want to know . . . I'd hope the people I wanted to see were there . .

. if I knew for certain . . . I'd go with you now."

There was a sudden electrical hum; it was deep and resonated through the floor of the whole ship. The gathered crowd at the window began to exclaim - the weapon was obviously about to be activated.

Arabella looked over at the crowd near the window. She rose to her full height again and seemed to compose herself, but she looked far from satisfied. She wasn't feeling the way she had expected to at this moment.

She looked back at Gresham one last time, their eyes met. "You are supposed to be the world's policeman," she said accusatorily. "Why do you not stop us?"

The electric hum intensified into a thunder like rumble as Gresham walked right up to her.

"It would appear, I can't."

He was still calm; he looked down at her in disappointment. She was hunching over again as if she was in pain.

He reached out, put the tip of his right hand under her smooth dark chin and turned her head to face him. He spoke now, deeper than he had in years and she could feel it. "Even after all of this, when I look at you, I don't see a murderous crusader for vengeance, righteous or otherwise . . . I see my poor frightened friend, who . . . " His voice pained almost into a whisper, her eyes began to build up more tears as she saw water begin to glaze his. " - got lost . . . trying to find a way back home again after she lost her mother . . . mia amica, for everything you have done . . . and for everything you are about to do," he rose his hand from her chin to her cheek, "I forgive you!"

She gasped deeply, reached up, flung her arms around him.

"What the hell ever happened to us two eh," he strained to say through walled up tears.

"Sei il mio cuore," she whimpered softly in his ear and he held her tight, but only for one precious morsel of a moment. A huge explosion suddenly deafened them; the room shook violently, so violently Gresham and Arabella were thrown apart. The giant window shattered; some people near it were blown out into the blackness, screaming.

The barrels had exploded.

Someone grabbed a communication tube and called out, panicked. "They have breached the hull, they're going to see us from the ground!"

Gresham, dazed, got to his feet. He had hit the floor headfirst and his mouth was bleeding. He wiped away the blood that was trickling from his lips and scrambled back to where he had left Mary.

Looking back, he saw Arabella, awake but making no attempt to get to her feet. She didn't notice him walking away. The room was listing heavily and another explosion a few feet out and away from the ship got everyone else's attention; they ran back and forth in a blind panic.

"We're being shot at!" someone cried.

The wall to the right of the great window blew in, as one of the Resurgence's shells struck the side of the ship. Gresham tore round the curving room to escape the flying wood splinters.

He passed several people as he ran, all of whom were too horrified by what was happening to notice him. He thought he came within sight of where their plane had been, but now there was simply a gaping hole shrouded in flames. The roof above him creaked and began to split in two; debris started falling and it became difficult to stand up.

The huge craft was crashing in the direction of the barrel explosion and Gresham found he had to turn away and try to put some distance between himself and the flames he was being slowly tipped towards.

He couldn't see Mary anywhere. He made his way back towards the front of the ship. The list became steeper. As he passed the last gun, its chocks couldn't hold the strain of keeping it in place; it fell sideways and rolled into the bowels of the ship, crashing through walls as it went.

He reached what was left of the great window again. It was deserted and fire was licking up through a hole in the floor made by the shell impact. The ship shook again as more explosions ripped through its core.

Arabella was still there; she was on the floor, clinging to a communication tube. She was almost hugging it, staring blankly at nothing with tearful eyes.

He crawled over to her; he tried to pull her away, but her grip was firm. She didn't intend on leaving.

He lost his grip and slid down. The wall at the back of the room had gone and a hole had been blown clear into the ship's core, exposing a number of decks and rooms including the spinning centre, which wasn't quite spinning as smoothly anymore.

Bodies lay everywhere.

Gresham had nothing to hold on to, but he didn't feel the urge to do anything to try either. He slid to the precipice of a huge drop, down into a chamber of flames. He knew there was nothing he could do now and let himself slide off the edge and calmly closed his eyes.

As he fell the heat engulfed him, he was shrouded in searing pain and he waited for the impact.

It came, he landed on his side and began to slide again, except, this time, uphill and away from the flames.

He opened his eyes in confusion, looking down at his feet he saw the well of fire he had expected to be in the middle of, but he was being dragged away from it at considerable speed.

Something nudged his cheek, he moved his head to see a hand with a fiercely determined grip on the collar of his tunic. Following the arm up, he saw strong shoulders and long blonde hair cascading down the back of a Royal Flying Corps uniform.

He couldn't look away as with unstoppable determination she lunged at a hole in the roof with one arm and pulled him and herself up through it at the same time.

Coming to rest on the floor above, they were back in what was left of the huge windowed room.

"Well that took long enough!" he called out. "I was running out of things to say!"

She smiled. "I take it, it worked?"

He pulled her up to him and held her for a moment. "I couldn't have caused more trouble myself," he said sincerely. "You know what we need to do now, Pilot Officer?"

She nodded. "Walk away slowly as if nothing had happened. Well I was just doing that, if you'd care to make room!"

They got down on their chests and began to claw their way up to the window. The heat was getting unbearable and Gresham felt a shooting pain in his right arm; it looked burnt. May began to help pull him up again.

It seemed hopeless. The huge craft felt as if it would collapse in on itself before it hit the ground.

They did eventually reach the window as the craft became vertical; they almost lost their grip on the edge when a sudden shock vibrated through the ship. It had obviously hit something.

They climbed up to the outside. The air was soothingly cool and the intense heat that had been burning their skin ebbed away. In the light of the fireball the huge ship was rapidly becoming, they saw it had crashed into the sea and was quickly plunging down into its inky depths.

Gresham looked back into the ship one last time; he looked at Arabella, still hugging the metal tube tightly.

"Arabella! Arabella!" he called out earnestly.

She didn't move.

Gresham found a block and tackled from one of the cannons, blown out of the side of the ship, resting next to him. He jammed the block in a jagged edge of the window, threw the rope back down into the ship and lowered himself back inside. A coughing and exhausted Mary perched on the outer edge couldn't believe what she was seeing.

Gresham knew he shouldn't have gone back in as soon as he descended. The heat was unbearable. His clothes began to steam as the moisture was forced out of them; he knew they would catch fire any moment.

Almost unable to see, he came level with Arabella. She was still clinging to the now scorching hot tube. Her hands were burning, what skin was not searing blood red had already turned white; but when she turned to him - he had never seen her look more content in her life.

He reached out his hand. "I'm heading into town tonight, and I know this great place - open all night. Fancy coming?"

She smiled kindly, then slowly and carelessly shook her head.

He looked at her, one last time; he took special note of her eyes. They looked just as they had, the day he had first met her: kind, full of certainty and free.

Risking falling again, he reached out with one hand and lovingly cupped her cheek. She leaned into it and tenderly closed her eyes a moment.

"Go see your mother," he said softly.

She beamed at him and nodded.

Stealing himself from her gaze he wrenched the rope towards himself and pulled his way back to the tip of the window.

He didn't have to climb the last few feet; an explosion from below blew him up out of the craft.

As he hit the outer deck again he rolled away from the window. The cool air was like a blanket of ice compared to the temperature of the flames, now licking at the rim of the gaping hole.

Gresham felt Mary pull him away. As she dragged him, he let the cool ocean breeze wash over his nearly boiling skin.

They had escaped; but as they both collapsed on their

backs, wearied and wondering how they were still alive, they both noticed the stars above them were moving.

One side of the craft had struck the water and was sinking, leaving the rest sticking up vertically, hundreds of feet into the air. With Mary and Gresham perched precariously right at the top.

They cautiously stood up. The coastline was only a couple of miles away, lights were returning to the city and they could see the shoreline was almost within swimming distance. None of which, however, was much help given their position.

The huge mass didn't stay upright for very long; it began to fall over, slowly at first but then building up to breakneck speed.

Mary and Gresham gripped the floor with their hands.

As the belly of the beast crashed down steadily on the water's surface, it began to produce a huge wave underneath it.

"Mary! That wave - we jump just before it reaches us, then if we're lucky it will wash us clear of the suction as this thing sinks!"

"What!"

"It's about all I can think of right now!"

Mary could feel the giant tidal wave rearing up underneath them; she didn't know much about the ocean but she had never heard it recommended that anyone should jump into one of those.

"From burning to drowning in no time at all, sums up my life really!" she exclaimed with an exacerbated laugh.

He smiled at her. "I know how you feel." He took her hand. "Just don't stop swimming - I won't as long you're with me!"

His last words were drowned out as the roar of the wave overtook them.

They jumped.

CHAPTER XVIII

THE WINDOW

Slowly the clean silver ceiling took shape and became clear as her eyes opened.

She thought she had drowned, but it turned out she was still breathing, slowly, and was waking from a very deep sleep. The ceiling looked vaguely familiar to Mary. The grogginess she felt was heavy; she was desperate to find out where she was as her last memory was of diving into a tidal wave, but it was a while before she could move.

Her body felt completely sapped of energy and she felt aches in her back and neck. At first she thought she had been injured, but it felt a little more like overstraining.

She eventually sat up and smiled, relieved, to find herself in a long, thin white gown, on the top bunk of her room aboard the Resurgence. A beautiful crystal blue sky shone in though the window, the distant hum of the engines reassured her that it was all real; she hadn't in fact dreamt the last few days, and she had come home, alive.

After sitting up a while and enjoying the peace and quiet, she clumsily climbed down to the easy chair at the dresser and sat, admiring the view through the portholes.

She found her beloved watch sitting on the table; it was ticking again and showed two thirty.

The door suddenly opened and Ginny walked in. She stopped and did a double take when she saw Mary.

"You're awake, she's awake! She's awake!" she shouted excitedly as she ran out of the room. Mary laughed a little in surprise; she was pleased to see her too, but in no condition to follow her and find out what all the fuss was about.

Ginny quickly ran back in beaming, with a briskly striding Captain Walker and Doctor Kilgallen.

"Welcome back," Walker said, unusually sincere. "You

gave us some great fireworks last night."

The doctor didn't have much to say. He pulled from his white coat a little silver torch and shined a light in each of Mary's eyes, a procedure she should have been used to by now. "How are you feeling, Pilot Officer?" he asked routinely.

"Like I've been tenderised and grilled, but much better for being back here."

"You inhaled a lot of smoke," Kilgallen went on, sounding almost judgemental, "so you may have some pain on your chest for a few days. I'm confident the rest will heal; you're on light duties for two weeks just to be safe."

"Lucky dog!" shouted Ginny. "You should see what I inhale in the engine room every day," she said playfully. Kilgallen didn't react.

As the doctor withdrew, Walker stepped up. "The Colonel wanted to see you as soon as you woke up - he's in his office."

"He's ok?" Mary asked keenly.

"A little overcooked like yourself but no less . . . than when he left." A smile almost crept across his face and with a twinge of admiration, he said to Mary, "Good job out there."

With an approving nod, he left them alone.

"I fixed your watch," Ginny said as she perched herself on the dressing table.

"Oh thank you," Mary replied, clutching it gratefully, "what was wrong with it?".

"It just had dirty water in it and needed cleaning out so the parts could move, haven't ever seen one like it though, clever person whoever made it."

"You know how it works?"

"Well sort of, the instruments inside are all made of some kind of magnetic ore, magnetite or something; they're painstakingly carefully positioned so they repel each other just the right way so they keep themselves turning. As long as there's nothing clogging it up I don't think it'll ever stop ticking - where did you get it?"

Mary cradled it in her hand with great curiosity. "A gift, from my grandmother."

"So," Ginny went on enticingly, "I'm working daytime watches only this week. I've got about five evenings worth of gin under the bunk - maybe we can have some time to get to know each other properly now . . . and you can tell me all about what happened."

Stunned, Mary looked at her in amazement and her mouth opened as a huge wide smile enveloped her face. She remembered fondly her grandmother and her best friend - sneaking away from the dinner table for just such an activity.

Ginny didn't understand. "What?" she asked.

"What did you just say?" Mary beamed.

"Oh I know we shouldn't discuss missions but I promise you it's not the mission I want to talk about. Besides, who gives a fuck about that anyway when you're sharing a bunk with Mrs Interesting."

"No no," Mary interrupted, still astonished. "What did you just say about gin?"

"Just that I have a stash . . . that's been waiting for good company . . . why? Don't tell me you don't drink after all?"

"I have never had gin before but I can't tell you how much I'd like that!"

"Great!" replied Ginny, still a little confused as to why that had made her grin so inanely - but very happy that it did.

"You know," she went on, looking at Mary, "your trip's put some colour in those pale well bred English cheeks of yours."

"Oh?"

"Meet someone you liked in Italy, did you?"

"I'm sure I don't know what you mean," Mary replied, barely hiding a look of guilty pleasure.

"The mission seems to have done the Colonel some

good too. I can tell; he's only snapped at twelve people since he woke up this morning. If I thought I'd get an answer, I'd risk asking him the same question."

Mary grinned, embarrassed, and tried hard to make her mock indignation look as real as possible - but Ginny wasn't fooled for a moment.

"Well we're not allowed to talk about all the other interesting stuff so . . . we'll see what gin night brings," she rounded gleefully.

They both laughed. Ginny then smiled sincerely at Mary. "I'm really glad you're back safe. I've got to get back to the engine room but if you need anything, call through the open door - there's plenty of people about."

Mary took it easy for another half hour. She knew her presence was required but given everything she had been through, she thought they would understand if she didn't snap to it like she would have when she first came aboard.

She went down the hall to the bathroom and washed a little, which made her feel fresher.

Returning to her room she realised this was the first opportunity since she came aboard this ship to get her head together. She looked around wondering what to wear. 'Do I even have any clothes?' she thought.

Opening the wardrobe, she saw she had two of everything that made up her uniform so she dressed in the next, unworn set; buttoning up the stiff, firm new tunic like it was the first time. She tied her hair back as best she could and strode out into the ship.

She felt a little taller than she did the first time she walked these corridors. Having been through everything that her job had thrown at her over the past few days made her feel like she had earned the very special right to be here just a little more, and that was really worth something.

With her aching joints keeping her walking slowly but confidently she was greeted, smiled at and even saluted by everyone who passed her. 'Welcome back ma'am,' was followed by hails of 'well hello, nice work,' and a few tongue in cheek, 'great show you put on for us last night Dane!' She tried to take it all in her stride and smile professionally, but inside she was buzzing. It felt wonderful to be so accepted, at last. Plus the notoriety wasn't doing her any harm either.

The atmosphere that greeted her as she arrived at the entrance to Gresham's office, however, was a little different.

The door was open and she stood on the threshold; the office was opposite the wardroom, just behind the wheelhouse and identical in proportions.

The immediate space was a taken up by three bottle green chesterfield armchairs around a table, presumably for more casual meetings. A wooden steamer trunk with wheels against the right hand wall and a bookshelf just inside the door faced the curved window at the far end, where Gresham had his desk.

He was thumbing through the mass of papers that were strewn across it. Walker was standing dutifully, with his hands behind his back, to the right of the table, making objections.

"Sir, if the Doctor gave me two weeks of light duties, I'd get him to put it in writing and take it to bed."

"Pushing pens is light duties, Walker. Besides, are you really going to sit here and do something about all this rubbish?"

"No sir."

"Exactly, so someone has got do some bloody work around here." He noticed Mary in the door. "Dane!" he shouted. "I was told you woke up two hours ago - where the hell have you been?"

Mary wasn't expecting this heated tone; the last few days seemed a little like a dream now she was back in this official atmosphere. She wasn't quite sure what she'd done wrong and back in Venice she might not have accepted his protestations, but here it felt very different all of a sudden.

"I'm sorry . . . sir - I had to wash and . . . "

"Stand before me at attention when you report to my office," he interrupted sharply.

He pointed to a spot just in front of his desk; she strode over and stood as rigid as she could to attention with her aching limbs.

She glanced quickly at Walker; he was staring at her very sternly. This obviously wasn't some sort of a joke.

Gresham walked across to the other side of his desk and thumbed through another few papers. "You may be interested to hear, Pilot Officer, that we're returning to England for full repairs. The engines are working but at reduced capacity so it's going to be three days journey, amongst other things we'll also take the opportunity to get a replacement plane for the one you crashed."

'Back to England' she thought. She knew her probationary period still had four weeks to run but if extensive repairs were needed, she might be stuck in England for that whole time and not be required. That might not bode well for her chance of being kept on; she had thought she had proven her worth but it didn't seem to cut too much ice, being curtly treated as she now was. A whole stream of sobering thoughts began to race through her mind.

Gresham went on, still thumbing though papers. "Doubtless had you been paying attention when flying in action last night, the plane would not need replacing."

"And what exactly is that supposed to mean?" she sharply interjected.

"I beg your pardon?" he replied.

Walker turned his head away from them; Mary couldn't see if he was laughing or appalled.

"You were there," she continued, "the plane got smashed up because we flew it under that thing and I resent - "

"You resent!" Gresham barked. He frowned at her angrily and strode round the table to her side.

"Damn your impertinence! I will not lose aircraft to clumsy flying! As long as you are under my command, you will remember that - understood?"

He had her very worried now, so she bit her tongue. "Yes sir, as long as I am a Pilot Officer aboard your ship, I will endeavour to do all I can to adhere to your orders."

By now Walker had turned back to them and he was nodding approvingly at what she had just said.

"Good!" Gresham replied, suddenly very calm. He then paused, Mary saw out of the corner of her eye that he was looking at the ground, and then he slowly strode away to the window, standing with his back to her, looking out at the sky.

"I'm very glad to hear that," he continued, unnervingly calm, "but . . . I'm sorry Dane, I really am . . . I'm afraid you're no longer an acting Pilot Officer with the squadron aboard my ship."

Mary looked at Walker; she couldn't read his face.

She didn't know what to think, and froze; all those sobering thoughts washed over her. She began to feel her shoulders clenching up to her neck, ready to take a blow.

Gresham turned to look at her again, but to her surprise, while the frown was still there it lay above eyes with the steady professionalism back in them again, and a small-relaxed smile began to grow across his face.

He spoke again, but this time with the utmost sincerity. "As a result of exemplary bravery and conduct in repelling the attack on Constantinople, your probationary period has been wavered and your . . . promotion, was confirmed in today's dispatches."

She glared at him, a wash of emotions poured out from inside her. She started to smile, baffled and overwhelmed with what he was saying. She kept her eyes on his as he walked back to her. He held out his hand and said resolutely, "rich runaway," he shook his head, "no, congratulations, Lieutenant Dane."

She took a firm handshake from both of them, and

stared at them dumbfounded.

She kept trying to say something to Gresham, but she kept hesitating. Gresham stared at her in expectation.

"You bastard," she eventually blurted out and slapped him on the arm, "so what was the pompous aggravation all about!"

She slapped him on his injured arm and he touched it as a twinge of pain shot up his side.

"Oh sorry," Mary said genuinely and reached out to touch it kindly.

Walker belly laughed at them both.

"Well I'll know now never to do it again," Gresham said calmingly, "do take a seat Lieutenant."

Gresham walked to the steamer trunk by the chesterfields; he unlocked it and opened up the two halves, to reveal a drinks cabinet inside. They were each poured a glass of juicy ruby port and they sat down in the comfortable armchairs. Before they raised their glasses in a toast Walker made to her career, Mary had one last question. "Sir, is it customary in this job to try and frighten the wits out of someone before you promote them?"

Mary gave Gresham a mock look of thunder. He understood and couldn't help smiling dryly at her, much to her quiet relief.

For half an hour they talked. Mary sat there trying to keep a level-headed appearance, but inside she was brimming with satisfaction and now feeling like she truly belonged where she was.

It turned out the three weeks in England were to be spent testing some new equipment for the Resurgence as well as repairs. Gresham informed Mary the prototype of a brand new aircraft was being loaned to them. It was supposed to be faster and more manoeuvrable and she was responsible for putting it through its paces.

She would also be given the task of training all the other pilots in the silent dive manoeuvre, so that the Resurgence could launch all its aircraft while still airborne.

Walker was called to the bridge, and they all stood up. He took his leave and left the room; Gresham and Mary stood alone, a little awkward all of a sudden.

For a moment neither of them seemed to know what to say. He looked to the door and picked up his hat from the table.

"Thank you," Mary suddenly said.

"What for?"

"For giving me a life."

He laughed a little, looked at the floor, and then began to walk back to his desk as he spoke. "You did that, you grabbed it with both hands and got it for yourself. And I think that process started a long time ago, not just a few days ago. You should be very proud of yourself." He suddenly looked a little vacant, as if thinking of something else all of a sudden. "I know I'd be," he said quietly.

He looked at the floor a moment, and then back at her. "Thank you for saving my life."

"As long as you're glad I did."

He didn't respond, he half nodded a couple of times and looked away.

"Did anyone survive the crash? Mary went on.

"No, we don't think so."

"Did you see . . . Arabella?"

Moving quickly, but trying to hide his hurry, he suddenly turned away and stood with his back to her, hands behind his back and faced the window.

"Yes," he replied flatly.

"How did she . . . if you don't mind me asking?"

"Mary, she . . . had had enough and - wanted some peace, badly. You know how that feels, don't you?"

Mary looked hesitant a moment. She smiled, almost a little embarrassed at herself.

"No." Her reply was definite in tone, but Gresham didn't seem to feel the force behind the word was directed at him.

"No?" he said inquisitively.

"No . . . there was a time I might have said I claimed to, but after meeting her . . . no, I'd be ashamed now if I said I knew why she wanted to die. I can't imagine what it did to her inside - to go through what she did."

There was a silence, he just stood there, with his back to her.

"We each of us have our own private hell Mary," he suddenly began, with a trace of reassurance in him, "It's humbling to experience someone else's . . . "

He stopped short of finishing what he was saying, almost like he couldn't quite put it in a way that would satisfy him.

Sensing the time had come to leave, she slowly turned to move to the door but stopped as he suddenly spoke up.

"Well," he went on, "whatever yours was - are you glad you came out of the other side of it?"

"Yes, yes I am . . . very much," she replied slowly, and pensively.

He nodded gently. "Good. In that case . . . I want you to have something, on top of the bookcase by the door."

She turned to see a small wooden box.

She picked it up with a look of gratifying curiosity. Gripping the lid of the box with one hand, she opened it.

Encased within was a gleaming new compass. It was set in a pristine gold casing attached to a chain, and had a gold lid that fastened over the face.

She picked it out of the box; it was cold, smooth and solid. It had the perfect mix of beauty and practicality she found most admirable in a possession.

"It's wonderful," she beamed. "Thank you . . . why did you - "

"Now," he interrupted, still without looking at her, "get back to your room and rest those limbs. Your breakfast will be getting cold as well."

She looked at her new possession for a moment, gratified, but a little confused and wanted to ask if he was alright, but she had the feeling he'd rather she didn't.

After everything that had happened, she didn't quite know how she felt about him anymore. She thought Arabella had summed up their feelings for each other perfectly but she now realised Gresham's words to her on the train had been a well-intentioned warning about what kind of person he was. Could she still see something else behind the man that had casually taken those lives? She thought about it, then looked at him, silent and only showing her his back, 'alright', she thought calmly, 'if that's what you want, then that's that'.

Reconciling herself to that thought, she turned to leave and walked through the door, but just before her last leg crossed the threshold, something made her stop.

She looked back at him one more time, still standing at the window, his hands behind his back, his head perfectly still and with more loneliness ebbing from him than Mary had ever felt in anyone. She breathed out slowly, as something made great concern well up inside her. She wanted to say something, she wanted to reach out and comfort him for some reason, but she couldn't fathom why, it was just something she felt.

She pulled herself away, and walked down the corridor, 'come on,' she said to herself, 'he obviously doesn't want anybody, let it go.'

She returned to her room to devour her scrambled eggs. She also found a little black box, similar to something you would keep jewellery in, sitting on the tray with her breakfast. Opening it, she found two brand new brass pips for her shoulders, to signify her new rank. She couldn't help letting her breakfast get colder by attaching them to her uniform and standing in front of the mirror straight away.

The rolled up newspaper that came with her breakfast was the latest edition of the London Times - god knows how it got aboard. On page four there was an article entitled, 'Fierce Lightening Storm Causes Blackout Over Turkish capitol.'

Later that afternoon, a couple of hours or so before she was due for her date with Ginny, she took an aircraft maintenance manual she had found in her room, and walked to what she had decided was her favourite window towards the stern. She also took a blanket to sit on and her watch, just like she used to do in her parents' garden. It was mid afternoon and everyone else was working, so it was quiet.

She gazed out at the sky for a while, and was surprised to find her mind was already calm enough to relax without having to lay with her eyes closed for hours to lose her worries.

Breathing out with a satisfied smile, she opened the book and thumbed a few pages. It was something she would have relished owning back when she was first learning to fly; she would have hidden it in her bedroom and read it cover to cover. To anyone else it would have been a drudge of a thing to learn but to Mary - back at her parents' house - if it gave her access to a world that was forbidden to her, it would have been a thriller that she couldn't have put down, until she got to the very last page.

Looking up, out of the window at the incredible view of the cloud tips, she could see the ship was moving slowly.

She decided this would be an excellent time to test her gift. Pulling the compass out from her inside pocket, she opened the gold lid to reveal the dial face. The ship was heading directly north, but this little snippet of information suddenly went out of her head. As she held the compass up to the daylight, she was surprised to see some engraved words on the inside of the casing.

She hadn't noticed them before; the daylight was picking them out.

Surprised and curious, she read them.

Then she froze; she was breathless.

She suddenly looked up and down the corridor as if she needed someone to reassure her that she wasn't seeing things.

She didn't know what to think. She kept reading them over and over to make sure she wasn't imagining it.

Mary
You die if you worry, you die if you don't.
Thomas Gresham

www.ingramcontent.com/pod-product-compliance
Lightning Source LLC
Chambersburg PA
CBHW051421170626
46809CB00006B/2261